THE ROYAL TRIALS

IMPOSTER

INTERNATIONAL BESTSELLING AUTHOR

TATE JAMES

The Royal Trials: Imposter
The Royal Trials Book I
Copyright © 2018 Katrina Fischer
Cover design © 2018 Amanda Carroll
Book design by Inkstain Design Studio

This book is a work of fiction. Names, characters, businesses, places, events and incidents are either the products of the author's imagination or used in a fictitious manner. Any resemblance to actual persons, living or dead, or actual events is purely coincidental.

Stay In Touch with Tate James

Facebook: www.facebook.com/tatejamesfans
Facebook group: www.facebook.com/groups/tatejames.thefoxhole
Website: www.tatejamesauthor.com
Newsletter: https://mailchi.mp/cd2e798d3bbf/subscribe

To Me.

CHAPTER 1

"That one," I whispered to the grubby-faced boy beside me. "You see? The one with the beer gut? He's half asleep, an easy mark."

We stared across the crowd to the cluster of guards following the smartly dressed royal steward as he went door to door through the richest part of Lakehaven—capital city of Teich—delivering invitations to the most eligible women in the kingdom.

"Are you sure *now* is the best time to be doing this?" my companion asked with a tremor in his voice. "Surely with the Trials about to start, everyone will be on high alert?"

I rolled my eyes and turned to glare at him. "That's *exactly* why now is the best time. Look at them all, acting like it's Frogs' Feast or something. Trust me, Flick, they aren't focusing on two unassuming kids who have wandered too far from the Pond."

My charge, Flick, screwed up his dirty nose as he inspected me. "You're not exactly a kid, Rybet. If those guards caught you, you'd be tried as an adult now that you're eighteen."

I gave him a bitter smile and chuckled. "So would you, kid. The royals don't give a shit about us dwellers. We've seen loads of Pond kids hung for bullshit crimes, and at well younger than eighteen, too." He blanched white under his freckles, and I cuffed him around the head. "So, don't get caught, okay? Master Bloodeye and I have invested far too much time and money into you to see you hang now."

If anything, this only made him look *more* like he was going to vomit, and I sighed heavily.

"Look," I offered. "Do you want me to go first and show you how easy it is?"

He nodded frantically, his dirty-blond hair flopping in his eyes and making him need to push it away again so he could see me. "What will you take from him?"

Turning my attention back to the guards following the steward, I considered what they were carrying that might make a target both easy enough to take without being caught and hard enough that Flick could prove he was ready to go out alone.

Our boss, Master Bloodeye, was no amateur. He took in orphans of The Pond, gave us a roof over their heads, clothes on their backs, and food in their bellies. In exchange, we stole for him and contributed to making him the unofficial ruler of The Pond.

Once upon a time—though really not all that long ago—the area we lived in had been the richest part of Lakehaven, with marble streets, sprawling mansions and *technology* for the Teichian nobles. That was before our deities had tried to kill us all with the Age of Darkness. Before the years of droughts that took away our water and then storms that plunged us into four years of darkness and rain.

Before the plague that followed.

I shuddered at the memory of bloated corpses lining the streets. Corpses I'd robbed at Master Bloodeye's orders.

Now, that once-wealthy area of the city was a relic, a painful reminder to us all not to piss off our gods.

Streets that had once been walked by women dripping in gold and jewels, escorted by their wealthy husbands and fathers, now lay under a foot of murky water. Technological advancements that the nobles had been first to access were now doorstops and washing lines. Technically, that area of town was supposed to be off limits. The buildings were too damaged to be safe, and the water seemed impossible to drain.

Technicalities never mattered much when you had nothing and no one.

It had taken no time at all for those abandoned mansions to become the new homes for those of us without one of our own... and so The Pond came to be. Our very own waterlogged slum bordering the palace grounds.

"That," I announced, spotting my target. We'd been trailing along the street some distance back from the royal emissaries but keeping them within sight. As they approached each house, one of the guards would withdraw a tightly rolled invitation from his jacket and hand it to the steward, who would then present it to the household.

It was a huge to-do. The girls would come rushing out to receive their invitations and gush and cry as though they had *no* idea they'd be getting one. All within view of the street, of course. What good would it do to be *chosen* by the palace and not rub their neighbors' faces in it? It took ages too; in the time we had observed them, only three invitations had been successfully delivered. No wonder Tubby looked half asleep.

"The invitations?" Flick squeaked in surprise.

"Yup," I nodded. "See how they all keep them in their left, inside breast pocket? Tubby over there at the back hasn't taken any out, but you can see he has some from the way his coat sticks out a little on that side. He's also only bothered to fasten two buttons, so it should be a cinch to slip a little hand like yours in there and snag one."

Flick chewed at his lip in nervous anticipation. He was usually pretty confident every other time I had taken him out, so his anxiousness was out of character.

"Hey, I'm going first remember? I'll show you *exactly* how to do it. Follow me and repeat what I do; you can't go wrong. Okay?" I bopped him on the head and tucked a stray piece of my own straw-blonde hair behind my ear.

"Okay," he nodded. "Let's do this."

"Remember, watch me *closely*. I will meet you at the Pig and Ferret when you're done, yes?" I eyed him sternly to make sure he understood. It was protocol to split up once you'd made a snatch-and-run, that way if you got caught you weren't dragging your partner down with you.

Not that I did this sort of work much anymore. Pickpocketing was for the children, like Flick. He was barely eleven but old enough to earn his keep and pay back his debt to Master Bloodeye.

He gave me a nod of encouragement, and I melted into the crowd. It took me less than two minutes to reach my mark, divest him of one scroll, and then slip back into the excited spectators. Then again, I was one of the best. At age eighteen, I'd already gained quite the reputation for myself in Teich. I was the notorious Rybet, protégé and suspected favorite of Master Bloodeye.

It was no mistake my name sounded like the noise a frog made. Technically, it wasn't my name, it was a nickname given to me at age five when Master Bloodeye saw how easily I could slip in and out of buildings and crowds unnoticed... slippery like a frog. I had no idea what my real name was, since he'd found me as a four-year-old, wandering the streets during the Darkness with no memory of my name or my parents. It wasn't uncommon, though. Years of drought, followed by such severe storms, had an impact on lots of people's mental health.

The guardsman had barely even blinked when my hand slipped inside his coat, lifted the rolled-up piece of parchment out, and slipped it up my own sleeve. That was the benefit to having so many people around, for sure.

When I had made it farther down the street, I glanced over my shoulder to ensure Flick was doing as instructed, repeating exactly what I'd just done.

Our meeting point, the Pig and Ferret, was only a few hundred yards away, but I needed to keep an eye on him to make sure he wasn't cocking it all up. I tracked him with my gaze as he made his way through the crowd and approached the same tubby guardsman, who was yawning heavily.

Flick's back blocked his hand from sight, but I knew he'd be making the transfer from the guard's pocket to his own sleeve, and then... I released the nervous breath I had been holding as Flick moved away. The guard was none the wiser.

Good boy!

Letting the tension drop from my shoulders, I turned my back on him to hurry my ass along to the Pig and Ferret, so he wouldn't know I'd stayed to watch. I wanted the kid to think I trusted him to do it all on his own.

Just as I laid my hand on the heavy wooden door of the inn, a commotion broke out in the street behind me. Dread pooled in my belly, and I turned to see what was causing such a fuss.

"Aana's tits," I cursed, ignoring the gasp of shock from a passerby as I rushed back into the crowd. As if I was the only one to curse using the names of our deities.

I still needed to get closer to see what was going on, but when I did, my heart lurched.

Flick... his wrist was held firm by that same overweight palace guard and the stolen invitation brandished in his panic-stricken face. *Shit!* How?

It didn't matter how, though. I needed to get him free of those guards or he stood no chance. The palace didn't care if he was only a kid. He was a Pond dweller, and they saw it as their civic duty to cull our numbers any way they could.

"Flick!" I yelled, pushing forward faster, only to be grabbed from behind by an arm like steel and dragged into a dark alleyway between two ostentatious mansions.

The fight-or-flight instinct was a powerful thing, and I had both. Thrashing hard, I threw elbows and heels into my captor to try and release his hold on me, but he didn't for a moment waiver. His arms held me firm against a strong body, and a large hand clamped down over my mouth before I could scream.

"Stop it!" he hissed in my ear. "Stop fighting, boy! Does your life mean so little to you that you'd throw it away to save a Pond orphan?"

Of course not, you idiot!

I wanted to scream the words at him, but it would be too hard to explain that I had no intention of being caught... simply of giving Flick time to get away. He'd called me boy, though, which was good.

"You caught a live one," another man chuckled, as if I wasn't already far outweighed by the first one. I didn't stand a chance against *two* grown men in hand-to-hand combat. The last thing I needed was to fight off a rape at a time like this.

There weren't many girls in my line of work. When you grew up in the slums, there was really only one career choice for a pretty girl. Whoring. That had never sat well with me, and thankfully Bloodeye had seen talents beyond the income I might earn on my back with my legs in the air.

I pretty much lived in "boys" clothes—a loose shirt and leather breeches with an oversized tunic to hide my womanly curves. It had clearly been too much to ask of Aana, our Goddess of Fortune, to bless me with a boyish frame. Thankfully, this guy seemed too distracted to notice as he restrained me.

"It's too late for him," the man snapped in my ear, and I got the distinct feeling he thought he was *saving* me. "They've caught him red-handed. There's nothing you can do now."

Sure enough, the palace guardsmen were already binding Flick's wrists and throwing him over the front of a horse to be taken to the royal dungeons. It was a crime to steal in Lakehaven. Hell, it was a crime to steal *anywhere* in the Kingdom of Teich, but it was a whole other thing to steal from the royals themselves.

As the smug guard rode away with my little friend, the man's grip loosened on my face, but not from around my waist.

"You can thank me now, kid," he muttered sarcastically. "I just saved your life."

"You can let me go now, *letch*," I sneered back at him, pitching my voice a little lower than a girl's and peering down at the hand still clamped firm across my abdomen. Any higher and he would have felt the evidence that I was most assuredly *not* a boy.

A gold ring on his pinky finger gave me pause, and I leaned a little closer to make out the crest. Then gasped in horror.

"Your Highness," I breathed with dread and revulsion. I'd just tried to kick one of the royal princes in the balls with my heel...

"Shit," the man—*prince*—holding me cursed, and the other man groaned.

"Seriously? You forgot to take off your ring? I'm never letting you sneak out with me again, big brother." The second man sounded exasperated, but also a touch amused.

I just wanted to get the hell away from them. *Big brother* meant that this was another of the crown princes!

"Please, Your Highness," I whispered, "Let me go; I swear I won't tell a soul that you're here in the city."

The one holding me released his grip abruptly, and I stumbled forward a few steps, letting my hood fall further over my face to hide my features.

"Go, then," he snapped. "But we were *never here.*"

Nodding as frantically as I could without displacing my hood, I kept my gaze firmly on the ground to avoid any *further* insult as I sketched a shaking bow and backed out of the alleyway. As I reached the crowd, I couldn't help myself... I glanced back into the shadows to get a look at the princes.

Could anyone blame me? No commoner had ever laid eyes on our princes in over ten years. Not since they'd ended the plague by summoning hundreds of *drachen*—a magical creature that was a small variety of dragon but looked a lot like a frog. The *drachen* had swept through the land, devouring the insects that carried and spread the plague, and within a year, it was extinct. The princes had barely been teenagers at the time but had just come into their magic and found a way to help the people where their parents had failed.

Typical of my luck, though, all I could see in the shadows were three sets of men's boots, and a ripple of fear ran through me. Three. All three princes were just within breathing distance of me... and I'd walked away with my life.

The notorious Rybet Waise didn't rise to such heights of crime in such a short time on luck alone, though. No, I had a natural instinct toward danger. Premonition, Bloodeye liked to call it, but I preferred "instinct." After all, none but the royals had possessed any magic since the last queen was murdered.

My instincts, the ones I'd trusted all my life to keep me alive, told me that this wouldn't be the last time I'd encounter the three mysterious princes of Teich.

CHAPTER 2

The heels of my companion's shoes clicked loudly on the street pavers as we hurried through the upper town towards the palace, and I ground my teeth in frustration.

"Seriously, Juliana? Have you still not learned how to walk a little quieter?" I scolded her in a quiet voice, keeping my presence in this part of the city as unobtrusive as possible. Half the success in surviving as a girl criminal in Teich was remaining totally undetected.

Juliana, my tagalong and the closest thing I had to a friend, had no need for such skills. Quite the opposite, as a courtesan, her business was won by *being* noticed.

"I *am* walking quietly," she grumbled even as the sound of her high heels echoed off the silent buildings around us. "But it wouldn't be the worst thing if we got stopped. This is easily your most insane plan to date."

"It's not insane, Jules," I snapped, feeling my already thin patience wearing even thinner. "You didn't have to come, you know. I know what I'm doing—and what's at stake—but I can't just leave Flick to be executed. He was under my watch, so it's my responsibility to get him out."

"Yeah, but babe—" she started to protest, and I whirled on her in anger.

"He's just a kid, Jules. What if that had been one of us?" I tightened my lips and glared at her, demanding an honest answer. She knew there was no other option. No one looked out for kids like Flick, no one cared. No one except other Pond kids.

Juliana gusted a long sigh and tugged at a perfect ringlet of hair, looking pained. "I know," she groaned. "But this is madness! Breaking into the palace to free a prisoner? You know what they'll do to you if you get caught."

"No worse than they plan to do to Flick," I retorted, arching a brow at her and hurrying farther up the street. We were almost at the north gate, and the sounds of partying was trickling out into the street. The celebration inside was the reason why this area was so quiet. It marked the start of the Trials, the three weeks of challenges and tests that would determine a bride for each of the Princes.

Once upon a time, our country had been matriarchal—the crown passed from mother to daughter when she became of age, along with the magic that sustained the balance of nature. All that had changed when our last queen was murdered, and her baby girl stolen.

That was the beginning of the Darkness, and Teich had never been the same since.

So here we were, about to enter the Trials with three royals looking for their soulmate, instead of just one. City officials swore the magic of the tests would remain unchanged, but I found that seriously hard to believe. Especially given the magic had all but disappeared from Teich entirely.

"They won't execute him on day one of the Trials," Jules continued, not willing to give up on changing my mind just yet. "Maybe just give it another night or two to think it over? Maybe Bloodeye can be talked into lending some extra muscle."

I snorted a bitter laugh. "I'm his favorite, not his daughter. No, he told me quite clearly, I was on my own with this one. Besides, what better time to break in? The *lucky contestants* get announced at dawn, so until then it's all drinking, dancing, and revelry."

"So, you're, what? Just hoping the guards will have been indulging?" Jules screwed her face up at me like I was insane, but I just shrugged.

"Pretty much," I admitted, tucking my dark cloak around me tighter. "This is where I leave you, Jules. If I'm not back by midmorning..." I sighed and shrugged. "Well, it's probably safe to assume I'm dead."

"Don't joke, Ry. It's not even close to funny." Juliana's voice quivered as she spoke, and I could tell she was on the verge of tears. Not what I needed right before the most foolhardy mission of my short lady-criminal career. So it probably wasn't going to help for me to admit I wasn't joking.

"I'll be fine, babe," I assured her, giving a confident smile. "I'm slippery, remember? They won't even know what hit them until it's too late. Besides, you still owe me that bag of silver from cards last week."

"Yeah, yeah," she grumbled, pouting about her loss. "I'll wait here as long as I can. Who knows, maybe I'll find someone to pay that bag of silver I owe you."

I laughed and gave her a quick hug. "That's the spirit! Work it, girl." Slapping her playfully on the ass, I took the opportunity to make a speedy exit.

As much as Juliana was just trying to keep me safe, her fears were only serving to make me nervous. It wouldn't stop me from breaking into the palace to save Flick, but when I wasn't totally focused, it could lead to stupid mistakes.

Leaving my glamourous friend behind, I slipped into the shadows below the towering wall I'd need to scale to get into the palace. It might have seemed like the most hairbrained idea in the world, but if I was totally honest, I had been eyeing up the royal palace for *years*, plotting what the best way in and out might be.

Of course, back then I'd been thinking more along the lines

of getting into the treasury, not the dungeons. But the same access points should work. Theoretically, anyway. It wasn't like anyone had blueprints of the palace layout, so I'd have been guessing where the treasury was, just as I'd be guessing where the dungeon was.

Sucking in a deep breath, I checked all around me for anyone who might be watching. When I found no one, it was time to begin. I wiped my palms dry on my dark gray breeches and set my fingers into the grooves of the worn stones.

One of my major advantages over men in this profession was that I was small and light. There was no way a fully-grown man could do what I was doing; their fingers simply wouldn't fit the cracks. But for me, they were perfect.

I didn't fuck around getting up and over the wall, then lying flat on the top for a moment to check that the gardens were clear before dropping down silently. Some of the partying nobles were spilling out onto the grass, but the beautifully manicured greenery should be more than enough to hide me if I was quick and quiet.

"Good to see the royals using their magic for the good of the kingdom," I murmured under my breath as I passed fragrant roses and heavily laden fruit trees. Meanwhile, the rest of Teich was struggling to get their crops to grow.

Several times on my dash across the gardens I needed to pause and wait for guards to pass me by, but they had all clearly been indulging, just as I'd suspected. In hardly any time at all, I was below a darkened window—which I seriously hoped indicated an empty room. Or at least a sleeping occupant.

Pushing off hard, I jumped and caught the worn sandstone frame before pulling myself up and into the room with barely a whisper of noise. So far, so good.

As soon as my feet and hands touched down on the plush carpet, I froze on the spot, willing myself to blend with the shadows so I could check that the room was clear—it was—before straightening and rushing to the interior door.

Cracking it just an inch, I peered out into the brightly lit corridor where several sharply dressed gentlemen stood chatting and laughing with cups of drink tucked securely in their fists. I could only hope they would move along soon because from a cursory glance around the room I was in, there was no other exit.

It was little more than a sitting room, probably used for guests to wait in until they were called by whoever they were visiting, but it offered me no other option but to stand there and wait until the men moved along.

Unfortunately for me, I'd already used up a good portion of my luck for the night, and they were in no hurry to get back to the main party. At one stage, one gentleman even leaned on the wall right beside my cracked door, making himself comfortable.

I groaned internally when this happened and slid down the wall to sit. There was no sense in wasting energy, and my legs were already burning from standing there so long.

Fishing around in my pants pocket, I pulled out an old, ladies' pocket watch that had been with me since I was a baby. Time was ticking by, and my chance of retrieving Flick from the dungeon was slipping further and further away...

But I'd come this far. Surely I couldn't fail now, when I was so damn close.

Just as despair was beginning to set in, my ears pricked up at the sound of the men bidding one another farewell, and I scrambled to my feet once more. Sure enough, when I peeked through the crack in the door, the three of them were departing my corridor—leaving it empty.

"Finally," I sighed, waiting only a moment more before slipping out of the room and darting in the direction *away* from the party sounds.

Dungeons would be down, it was only logical, so I set about looking for a staircase that would lead me to a lower level and hopefully away from the brightness of the magically powered lights in the corridor.

The sound of a woman's laughter trickled toward me, so I picked up the pace and, thankfully, darted into the entrance to a narrow flight of stairs mere seconds before I would have been seen.

"That was close," I breathed to myself in a whisper before eyeing the staircase. It went down, which was what I'd been looking for, so I shrugged and padded down it cautiously. My heart was still racing from the near miss in the corridor, so I was on high alert for running into anyone else who might sound the alarm to palace guards.

To my relief, the stairs led me through to a servants' area where—while bustling with people—no one even batted an eyelid at what they would have assumed to be a young boy in a cloak. Slipping into the mannerisms of a servant myself, I hurried through the other servants with confidence, and no one so much as stopped me. It was almost *too* easy, and I laughed to myself as I slipped out the other side of the room unobstructed.

"Alright, Rybet," I murmured under my breath. "Servants area, below ground level... dungeons can't be too far from here." To help with my disguise, I grabbed a sack of flour that had been propped against the wall and slung it over my shoulder.

Yep, nothing to see here. Just a servant boy carrying some flour to the kitchens.

Okay, so as far as disguises went, it was definitely not my best work, but everyone was so busy with the celebrations upstairs that no one really had time to look twice at me—exactly what I had been hoping for.

It took me longer than I'd hoped to locate the dungeons, so the relief was almost staggering when I found the dank stairwell leading down *further* and two bored-looking palace guards sitting on stools at the bottom playing cards.

"Here, boy, what are you doing down here, then?" one of them asked me, barely glancing up from his losing hand of cards.

"I came to..." I trailed off, searching for a plausible excuse for why a servant would be carrying flour into a dungeon. Finding none at the front of my mind, I shrugged and hoisted the flour off my shoulder. "Fuck it," I muttered, then swung the heavy bag hard, hitting the first guard clean in the face and knocking his head against the stone wall with a sickening crunch that made me cringe.

The second man—on whom I could smell the alcohol from where I stood—barely got a chance to open his mouth before I hit him in the temple with the butt of my knife.

The whole altercation had taken less than a minute, but I was left panting from adrenaline and nerves. It wasn't often I needed to kill anyone, but I'd be lying if I tried to say it hadn't happened in the past. Still, I had no idea whether these men deserved it and I was vehemently against senseless killing, so it was with shaking fingers that I checked their pulses to assure myself that they were still alive.

Feeling the steady thumps, I breathed a sigh of relief before dragging their unconscious forms into an empty cell and closing the barred door.

A heavy ring of keys hung from a peg near their card table, so I grabbed it and locked the door to the cell I'd deposited them in, hoping that if anyone came down, they'd think the guards were just two sleeping prisoners.

"Flick?" I called out in a loud whisper, praying for a response. The dungeons looked like they went for damn miles though, and

I got all sorts of leers and smartass remarks back from various prisoners, none who sounded anything like the little sandy-blond kid I was there to save.

Conscious of the ticking time, I grabbed a light orb from the guard area and started making my way down the long line of cells. Using the light, I peered into each one and called out for Flick but had no luck. They were all grubby men, some of whom I vaguely recognized from the Pond, but none was the gawky twelve-year-old I was seeking.

Shit.

A hand seized my wrist just as I was about to start down the next line of cells, and I stifled a small scream of fright.

"Well, well, what have we here? A dirty little thief breaking in to save his friend, eh?" The man holding my wrist in a death grip sneered at me, and I swallowed down a shiver of terror. I knew that voice. Everyone who had even remotely walked the line with the law knew that voice.

"Lord Taipanus," I gasped out, almost forgetting to lower my voice. Almost.

"Ah, I see my reputation precedes me," the king's spymaster boasted with a cruel grin curving across his scarred face. "Then you'll know how much trouble you're in right now, boy." He punctuated this with a rough shake, and my teeth rattled in my head.

I saw no easy way out of this situation. I was fucked. Well and truly fucked. There was no point in trying to fight Lord Taipanus; he was the spymaster for a damn good reason. He was utterly lethal and totally unbeaten in combat.

Still, I felt like I owed it to myself to at least try.

Just as I coiled my muscles to launch an attack on the Snake of Teich, an odd sound halted me. Was that... a woman's heels?

"Oh, Lord Taipanus," a woman gasped from behind me, "oh thank the stars, you found her. I was so worried."

"Her?" the deadly man repeated, frowning at me in confusion, then flicking his gaze back to the woman who had spoken. "You're mistaken, Mistress Mallard. This is a boy I caught trying to break someone out of the palace cells."

For my part, I said nothing. Let them figure it out between them; my night couldn't possibly get worse.

There was a rustling of skirts as the mysterious Mistress Mallard came closer. She clicked her tongue and chuckled. "Don't be silly; this is one of the young ladies chosen for the Princes' Trials. Her handmaiden was just telling me how they were set upon by bandits, so only the two of them made it in time. See?" The woman reached up and whipped the cloak hood from my face, knocking a pin out of my hair in the process and causing my moonlight blonde curls to cascade down my back. "Now, either that is the prettiest boy I've ever seen or it's the missing lady I'm looking for."

Lord Taipanus scowled at me for a long moment, his eyes

running over my delicate and clearly feminine features. "But why is she in the dungeons? And dressed like a boy?" He cast a disgusted look down at my shirt and breeches, then narrowed his eyes at me once more.

When the woman didn't respond for me, I licked my lips nervously and cleared my throat. "I, ah... I needed to ride, and I find trousers much more dignified to do so in. Besides, plenty of women wear pants; there are no laws against it. As for why I'm in the dungeons... well... I..." I really was an awful actress—surely another reason why I'd have made a hopeless courtesan.

"She has a terrible sense of direction and took a nasty blow to the head, didn't you dear?" Mistress Mallard covered for me, placing a firm hand on my forearm almost like she was reminding Lord Taipanus to let go of my wrist.

With a skeptical glare at me, he slowly peeled his fingers from my sleeve and settled his hand on the sword at his belt. "How do you know this is the girl? She could just as easily be a thief or criminal."

He wasn't stupid, this one. Then again, I didn't imagine it was the type of job one was awarded for being stupid.

"Oh, how silly of me," I tittered in my very best Juliana impersonation. "Here." I reached into an inner pocket of my cloak and produced the invitation to the Trials which I had stolen earlier that day. I had no idea why I'd tucked it into my pocket at the last second, but I'd learned to trust my own instincts and left it there.

Taipanus unrolled the invitation and scanned it quickly, his eyes darting up at me and back to the paper several times before he was satisfied.

"I trust that answers your question?" Mistress Mallard prompted him, holding out a hand to take the small scroll from him. "If you don't mind, I really do need to get Lady Callaluna changed and looking presentable. The announcement ceremony is in less than an hour, you know."

Lord Taipanus squinted at me for another long moment, then forced his lips up in a cold smile. "Of course, my mistake. It must have been someone *else* that was spotted scaling the north wall earlier."

Plastering on my most vacant smile, I batted my lashes up at the spymaster. "Goodness, then it definitely couldn't have been me. I barely have the strength to hold my head up let alone scale a wall that high!"

Mistress Mallard tugged on my arm to draw me away, and we made polite goodbyes before hurrying back out of the dungeons.

"You were laying that on a bit thick, dear," the older woman murmured to me as we rushed back up the stairs that would lead us back to the main palace area. "You're going to need some acting lessons if you're to make it through this alive, I think."

"Excuse me?" I choked out, still a bit in shock at my brush with death himself. "Who are you, anyway?"

She pursed her lips at me, giving me a small shake of the head as she kept up our quick pace through countless twists and turns of the inner palace. "I'm Mistress Mallard, dear. Head of Household for Her Majesty Queen Filamina." She paused to let that shocking news sink in, and I gaped at her. "More importantly, I'm an old acquaintance of Bloodeye. He asked me to keep an eye out for you tonight, just in case things went wrong. Good thing, too, hmm?"

"Bloodeye set up a safety net for me?" I exclaimed, thoroughly shaken. I hadn't realized the old criminal cared so much. "Well, thank you. Truly, you saved my ass in a big way. I promise I'll get the hell out of here and you won't see me again."

Well... after I get Flick out, that is.

The older woman barked a laugh and shook her head at me. "Oh no, dear. You misunderstand. You're not going anywhere until you're eliminated from the Trials."

Pulling up short, my jaw dropped open so far it could have hit the floor. "What?"

"You heard me, *Lady Callaluna.*" She arched a brow at me, and I saw the steel that Bloodeye would have seen in her. "I just vouched for you to the King's Snake himself. If you don't appear at the announcement ceremony in"—she checked her delicate wrist watch— "under half an hour, then it's *my* life on the line. Sorry, but I'm not taking that risk. I have grandbabies to think of, and Bloodeye's favors with me do not extend any further."

Stunned at what I was hearing, I followed silently behind her as she continued leading me through corridors, while desperately trying to make sense of my jumbled thoughts.

"Wait, this is insanity. I can't impersonate a *lady*!" I exclaimed as we arrived in front of a closed door and Mallard knocked sharply.

"Not right now, you can't. That much is clear," she muttered in a dry tone, and my cheeks heated. "So just smile, do what you're told, and generally *don't speak*. If you make it through the first pick, then we can work on those acting skills."

Flushed at her implication that my speech was unrefined, I scowled. "I meant if anyone finds out I'm a fraud, then I will face the executioner."

Mistress Mallard knocked on the door again, louder this time. "Is that any worse of a position than where I just found you?" This point rendered me speechless. "Exactly. Now, shut that pretty mouth of yours and try not to get us both killed before daybreak, yes?" When I said nothing, from lack of anything *to* say, she gave me a sharp nod like it was all sorted.

Whatever else I might have said—had I found the words—was cut off with the door slamming open and a wizened old man peering up at us from his frail-looking four-foot-something height.

"Master Schneider, this is the Lady Callaluna, our last lucky participant in the trials. She was set upon by bandits and, sadly, lost all her luggage on her way here. Can you see she is properly dressed and looking presentable in time for the opening ceremony?" She gave the old man a warm smile, but there was an edge to it that was clear she wasn't asking a question—rather, giving an order.

The old man scowled his feelings on the matter, but stood aside to usher me into the room. When Mistress Mallard didn't follow, I turned to her in panic.

"You'll be fine here, dear, just remember what I said." She gave me a pointed look and tapped her lips. "I'm off to find you a maidservant."

"Oh!" I exclaimed, an idea popping into my head. "I have one; she's waiting just outside the north gate. Red hair, blue dress. You can't miss her."

Mistress Mallard raised her brows at me but nodded and bustled away in a swish of skirts and click of heels, leaving me alone with Master Schneider.

"Why," the old man croaked, "is your maid out there and not in here with you, hmm?" When my jaw flapped and no sound came out, he waved his hand in dismissal. "Ah, save it. I don't care. We have work to do if you're to be ready for the ceremony. Now, strip out of those clothes and let me see what I'm working with."

CHAPTER 3

Half an hour later—I had no damn idea how he managed it, but somehow—I was stepping out onto a freaking stage with twenty-seven other glittering, primped, floral-smelling girls.

The audience section was crowded with aristocrats and general onlookers. All of them were looking somewhat worse for wear at the end of a long night's celebration, but for the most part it was well disguised by the elaborate masks they wore.

Wearing masks to court events was a longstanding tradition in Teich. Since it was forbidden for commoners to look upon royalty, it had just become easier over the years to incorporate masks into court attire. That way the royals could be free within their homes without fear of being seen and having to put that person to death.

From what I'd observed, on less formal occasions the masks were more of a suggestion with some ladies merely painting the mask shape on with glittery products, but for events—such as this—the best mask makers in the land were called upon for their finest work.

A herald began reciting his welcome speech, which he'd clearly been working on for a long-ass time, judging by the swell of pride in his chest and the flamboyant way he commanded the stage. But the core message was clear.

"What the hell?" the girl beside me muttered under her breath, much like a lot of the girls were doing. "No one said anything about people going home today; we were *invited*."

I stifled an eyeroll and bit my tongue to keep from responding. But seriously, just because they'd been sent an invitation did not mean they were guaranteed anything more than exactly this. A chance.

"So, what?" another girl murmured from somewhere down the line. "We have to be interviewed by the princes, and they will send seven girls home right now?"

"Not interviewed," someone corrected her. "He said *inspected*."

"So, we can't speak to them?" the other girl blurted out, sounding outraged, and the herald spun around to glare at her.

"No," he hissed. "Of course you can't speak to them. They are the future of this kingdom; you are nothing but eye candy until one of you becomes the future queen."

"*One* of us?" the outspoken girl squeaked. "But there are three princes; won't three girls be chosen?" I didn't blame her for this assumption; it was what the city officials had implied when they'd announced the Trials.

"Three cannot rule when King Titus relinquishes the throne, only one can. Therefore, one woman will win this whole affair and one prince will become the next king. Now shut your pretty mouths and let me continue." The herald's face was hard, and he was not looking for any disagreements or arguments. He was far too good to speak with *women*... or that was the impression I gathered from the snooty way he turned his back on us once more.

"One by one, these beautiful contestants will be blindfolded, then taken into a private room for Their Royal Highnesses to conduct their inspections. When all are done, seven will go home and twenty-one will stay." He paused for dramatic effect, and as he'd probably been hoping, the crowd tittered with whispers and speculations. Aana's tits, there was even money changing hands as nobles placed bets on who would stay or go.

Growing up in the Pond as I had, I'd never had need of a mask, but standing up there on the stage and being stared at by so many incognito faces, I almost felt naked with my face exposed.

"Once the seven losers have been sent home, the first Trial will begin," the herald continued, and a gasp rippled through the room. The first trial wasn't supposed to happen for a week. Tradition dictated the first week be spent training the prospective brides in the ways of the court and enjoying evening meals with the royals. It was a chance to make a good impression, I guessed, or perhaps it allowed the royals a chance to see what sort of people were competing to win the kingdom.

I tuned out on the rest of what he was saying, instead choosing to eye up the ladies and their jewelry. Would it be pushing my luck too far to snatch a piece or two before making my escape?

"Let's begin." The arrogant herald clapped his hands dramatically, perfectly timed with someone ringing a bell, which made the whole thing just painfully scripted.

Whatever, it really didn't matter. This early elimination was exactly what I needed to get the hell out of this place with my skin intact. All I needed to do was leave an *awful* first impression, ensuring there was simply no way the princes would select me.

Simple.

Infuriating people in positions of power happened to be a specialty of mine, too.

One by one, girls were blindfolded with a strip of midnight-black silk, then led from the stage and through a small door, which must be where the princes waited.

The girls waiting with me were a jumble of nerves, whispering to each other about how they *hoped the princes would like them*, or how one of them had heard Prince Alexander's favorite color was blue, so she had an advantage since she'd worn blue. Another was sighing her love for Prince Louis, a man she had *literally* never set eyes on before. The whole thing was laughable, but I bit my lip to hold it in.

I wanted to tease them that I'd not only spoken with the three royals, I'd almost kicked one in the nuts. But that would have been suicide, so I kept my trap shut.

As my turn drew closer, the skin across my bare shoulders prickled with the unmistakable feeling of being stared at. Scanning the room, it wasn't hard to locate the interested party, and my stomach flipped with fear.

Lord Taipanus, the King's Snake, glared down at me from a viewing balcony. His dark eyes were glued on me and burning with malice. But for what? Had he already worked out that I was an imposter? He'd been sitting there the whole time we'd been onstage, yet his glare had only just turned menacing when I'd turned to look at one of the girls gossiping.

Curious.

The birthmark on my shoulder blade tingled, and I sighed. The odd, silvery mark, which looked more like three matching scars than a proper birthmark, was somehow linked to my intuition. It sometimes tingled when danger was near, but I didn't need any warnings this time. I knew beyond a shadow of doubt that Lord Taipanus was the most dangerous thing in this whole damn city.

And I had caught his attention.

I groaned under my breath and chewed the inside of my lip. The sooner I could insult some royals and get the hell out of the damn palace, the better.

Shaking off the creepy feeling of Taipanus's glare, I stepped forward when the herald called my assumed name and forced myself to stand perfectly still as he tied the heavy silk across my eyes. At least the blindfold would afford me a small amount of anonymity, just in case—Aana forbid—my path ever crossed with the royals in the future.

"This way, Lady Callaluna," a meek-sounding woman said, taking my hand in hers and leading me across the stage to where I'd seen the other girls exit. None of them had returned, so I could only assume they'd been taken elsewhere after it was all over. Hopefully, the ones who were rejected would just be free to leave on the spot; I was badly in need of some sleep.

"Just here, m'lady," the woman whispered, stopping me and dropping my hand. The blindfold was secure, and the only sign I had of her departure was a whisper of fabric against stone flooring.

For a long time—too damn long, in my opinion—the room was silent, and I stood there with my fists buried in the full skirt of my dove-gray gown. Finally, I lost my patience.

"Is this it then?" I demanded of the silence, knowing full well I wasn't alone. "This is how you choose who is worthy of your Trials? See who can stay silent the longest?" I snorted a seriously un-ladylike laugh and shook my head. "Well, if it was, then I guess I lost. What a shame."

A small sound broke the silence, sounding *almost* like someone smothering a laugh with a cough, and the scrape of boots on stone alerted me to someone approaching me.

For all my bravado and bluster, my insides were twisted up in all kinds of knots as the man stepped into my personal space, so close I could practically feel his body warmth. These were the freaking *princes*! I needed to hold my tongue before I found myself facing the executioner next to Flick.

"Did Harry not explain the rules of the game to you, My Lady?" The man in front of me spoke, his voice a deep rumble that sent a physical shiver through me from head to toe. I recognized that voice from the alleyway; he was the one who had grabbed me when I'd tried to save Flick.

"Game?" I sneered, unable to help myself. "That's all this is to you, huh? A game. No regard for the fact that your *winner* will be the next queen of Teich, so long as it's fun for you three along the way?"

Oh, holy Aana's nipples, Rybet shut the ever-loving fuck up!

My heart just about leapt from my chest when the prince placed a finger under my chin to raise my face, almost like he wanted to look into my eyes—had they not been covered by silk. His touch was electric, his skin almost uncomfortably hot against mine, and I needed to bite the inside of my cheek to keep from gasping aloud.

"A lady of Teich with fire in her belly," he murmured with an edge of amusement. "Not from Lakehaven, certainly. We would have seen you before at court functions."

"Lady Callaluna," another man responded for me, as though reading "my" information off a paper, "from Riverdell. Apparently her retinue was set upon by bandits on their way here, and only herself and her maid survived." He clicked his tongue, and I heard the sound of papers being tapped on a table. "That fire served her well, it would seem."

"So it would," the prince holding my chin captive repeated.

As close as he stood, with his warm breath feathering over my cheekbones, I needed to mentally steel myself to speak without my voice shaking.

"I am standing right here," I snapped, when I felt confident enough. "I would have thought the royal princes of Teich had better manners than this."

There was a long pause—within which I possibly pictured at least seventeen different ways they could have me killed before sundown—and then one of the princes burst out in peels of laughter.

As much as I hated to admit it, he had a sexy laugh too, all dark and velvety, and against my better judgement, I could feel a flutter of attraction in my belly. Damn it.

"How very right you are, Lady Callaluna," this third voice said, his words still rounded by amusement as he approached where I stood with his brother. "I must apologize on behalf of my brothers.

We do not socialize with ladies of your standing often, so we do forget our manners. Hopefully, you'll be able to remind us of them in the coming weeks." This prince circled around behind me as he spoke, and even though none of them touched me more than the fingertip under my chin, I got the distinct impression I was now sandwiched dangerously close between at least two of them.

Still, those words caused me to practically choke on shock and outrage as I sputtered my response. "Excuse me?" I coughed out, jerking my chin out of the first prince's hold and turning in the vague direction of where the third stood. "You mean to *keep* me here? After I have been so rude to you all?"

"But of course," number three purred in that velvet-smooth voice, his fingers brushing my long, pale blond braid over my shoulder, then tracing the lines of my birthmark. "Don't you *want* to stay, Lady Callaluna? After all, isn't it every girl's dream to become a princess?"

"I, ah..." This time my voice did quiver, and I needed to lick my lips before trying again. Damn them, damn *me!* Was I really so sex-deprived that just the princes' physical nearness was turning me into a simpering idiot? "Of course," I lied, not wanting to push things any further than I already had. "It's all I have ever wanted."

"Excellent," number three murmured in approval, brushing his fingers across my bare shoulder blades once more before stepping away—hopefully not noticing the way my body involuntarily leaned toward his touch.

"Wise choice, My Lady," number one rumbled, his warm thumb stroking lightly across my lower lip before he, too, stepped away.

"Welcome to the Trials, Lady Callaluna," the second one, the one who'd read out "my" name and origin, called out to me from wherever he sat. "This all suddenly became more interesting, I think."

At a loss for words and reeling from what had just happened, I didn't even bother attempting a curtsey before taking the same maidservant's hand as she reappeared to lead me from the room. It was for the best, both as a sign of disrespect and, more importantly, as it saved me from falling flat on my face. That was one thing I'd never really learned how to do—curtsey like a lady.

How in Aana's fortune had that gone so wrong? Instead of getting myself kicked out, I'd just... what? Painted a big old target on my chest?

I groaned to myself as the woman removed my blindfold, and I blinked into the morning sunlight. She'd led me outside to a beautiful courtyard where other ladies sat sipping tea.

"Please make yourself comfortable," the woman encouraged me. "Lord Taipanus and Lady Savannah will be out shortly to bind everyone to the Royal Trials."

"Bind us?" I repeated, frowning at her in confusion.

She gave me a smile and a look that said this was information I should surely already know. "Yes, m'lady. Once selected, the hopefuls must swear an oath to the magic of the Trials that they will see them through to the fullest of their abilities and not leave unless given the express permission by the king or queen themselves. It's tradition, ma'am."

"Oh," I murmured, giving her a vague nod. "Yes, how could I have forgotten. The... binding oath." She smiled again, then left me to get to know my new competition.

Binding oath. Well, shit.

CHAPTER 4

The oath was just that, and more. There was mention of magical backlash should any lady attempt to break their word, either through leaving without permission or by not giving the Trials their full effort. There would be no half-assing these tests to deliberately get eliminated; everyone was now here to win.

"The first trial begins now and concludes at the end of the week with a final test," Lady Savannah, an older woman with impeccably styled gray hair and a deep green velvet gown, informed us. She'd pushed her jewel-studded mask up onto her hair, and the age lines around her eyes were clear to see.

A small part of my mind wandered as she spoke, pondering on whether she'd been a part of the last queen's household or if Filamina had brought her on when she ascended the throne.

Technically, King Titus and Queen Filamina were royals in their own right; however, their kingdom had been a much, much smaller land mass than Teich was. When the last queen had been murdered and her daughter disappeared, they'd stepped in to fill the void and had done the best they could to maintain the balance of nature with royal magic.

"This first week focuses on training. Certain skills are required of a royal, so each day, beginning today, you will be given a brief introduction to a new skill and then tested on your mastery of it come sundown. In the evenings, you'll dine with the royals themselves, and that shall be your chance to get to know your prospective husband, lord, and king." Lady Savannah sounded like she barely even remembered the days when our queen had ruled overall and never took a king. Times sure had changed.

"Ma'am?" One of the girls—a mousy sort of girl who smelled vaguely like ink and parchment—raised her hand tentatively, and Lady Savannah nodded to her. "How will girls be getting eliminated? There are still twenty-one of us here, so I am guessing there is about seven each week who will go?"

"Very observant, Lady..." Savannah trailed off, raising her eyebrows in question.

"Agatha, ma'am. Lady Agatha of Rockford." The mousy girl announced her title with a hint of pride that made me smile. She clearly loved her home and wasn't ashamed to proclaim it.

Lady Savannah nodded. "Lady Agatha is indeed correct; each night the lady with the lowest competency in that day's training subject will be eliminated. At the end of the week, there will be a final trial that sums up everything you have learned. The lowest score on that will also go home, but the highest... well, the highest scoring lady will spend the night with one of the princes."

Girlish giggles broke out among my companions, but I tasted bile. Were they serious? The *lucky winner* of the first trial got the *privilege* of spending a night in a prince's bed like a common whore? What the hell kind of game was this?

"Now, now," Lady Savannah chuckled, holding her palms up to silence the chatter. "Nothing unseemly, of course. Just a chance for one-on-one time to... talk. Get to know each other without the outside distractions of tests and eliminations."

I couldn't stop a huge eyeroll at this line. Nothing unseemly? Who was she kidding? Had she never *met* those three smooth-talking, walking hard-ons?

"Let's get you going now to the first training which will be in"— she paused to consult her notes— "in botany. Quickly now, ladies, straight over to the greenhouse with you."

A stunning girl with raven-black hair made an outraged sound, propping her hands on her hips. "We don't get to change first? You can't possibly expect me to do *gardening* like some commoner while dressed like this. This dress is silk. Do you know what happens when you get mud on silk?" The arrogant sneer to her lip said she was seriously not used to taking orders from anyone. This... could be entertaining.

"I do, Lady Gracelin," the older woman responded with a withering smile. "I also know what happens when you defy the royals. Now, move." Her command snapped out like a whip, and the dark-haired beauty—Lady Gracelin—looked like she'd been slapped.

The bitchy part of me wanted to smirk at her being told off, but I had better sense of self-preservation than that. These ladies were technically my competition, yes. But I didn't want to win this ridiculous game, and they were my best chance of making sure that didn't happen.

Not that I considered myself even remotely in the running to win this damn thing, but with the binding oath forcing us to try our hardest and my out-of-the-ordinary intuition working on my side, I needed to do everything I could to help someone else win. Just in case.

"What sort of queen requires botany?" one girl, a pretty blonde with delicate features, pondered aloud as we all walked across the palace grounds in the weak morning sunlight. "Unless maybe it's floral arranging? I could see that as a valid skill, and it's already something I'm quite accomplished at."

"I highly doubt it's flower arranging," the mousy girl that had spoken earlier commented. "That doesn't really seem important enough to include in the Trials."

The blonde bristled and planted her hands on her hips. "I'll have you know, *Lady* Agatha, that floral arrangement is an art form and one that should never be underestimated. You can't just trust your house staff to slap a bunch of flowers in a vase and be done with it."

The mousy girl, Agatha, rolled her eyes, and I hid a smile. She had more spunk than I'd originally given her credit for.

"I'm sure we will soon find out," a pretty redhead interrupted before things could turn nasty between Agatha and the blonde. Actually, each of the twenty other ladies still currently competing for the crown—and a prince's hand in marriage—were stunningly beautiful, which made sense, given the blindfolded inspection we'd all just been subjected to.

Considering we had been expected *not* to speak, and I didn't see any other likely rulebreakers in this group, that inspection could've only had to do with physical appearance.

There really wasn't much more time to debate or ponder anyway as we approached the impressive glass structure that was the palace greenhouse. The double doors stood open, and several men in palace uniforms pottered around, doing whatever they did to tend the plants. All twenty of us entered and made our way down the rows of plants until we reached the end where a bunch of cushions were placed on upturned crates. A quick glance around told me I wasn't the only one curious about today's lesson.

"You have got to be kidding me," the haughty Lady Gracelin from earlier scoffed as she eyed up the seating that had been laid out. "I am not sitting on that dirty cushion. Is this a joke or something? We are aristocrats, for Reichan's sake."

Agatha rolled her eyes again, brushing past Gracelin and choosing a seat. I smothered my own smile over her swearing to Reichan, god of wealth. *Figures.*

"Either you sit on that *dirty cushion* or you stand for the next six hours, Lady Gracelin," a man responded, joining our group with his arms loaded full of leather-bound notebooks. Several women just gawked at him, but some took his suggestion and snagged themselves the more comfortable looking seats before they disappeared.

For my part, I squinted at the man curiously. There was something about his voice that sounded almost... familiar. I couldn't quite place my finger on it though. Perhaps we'd crossed paths in the Pond? But what a palace gardener would be doing in the slums of Lakehaven, I had no idea.

While I scrutinized him, I saw the moment his shoe clipped a plant pot and the stack of notebooks began to topple from his pile. Lunging forward, I managed to catch a few while he regained his balance, then placed them back on the top of his pile with a small smile.

"Thank you, er, Lady Callaluna, isn't it?" He gave me a lopsided smile that did indescribable things to my insides as I made the mistake of meeting his eyes. They were a vibrant, clear blue—the color of a summer sky—and seemed to hold me locked in place for far longer than what would be deemed acceptable for an *actual* lady.

Breaking his gaze and desperately trying not to blush, I nodded. "Yes, sir. Lady Callaluna of..." I hesitated. Where the hell was Lady Callaluna from, again?

"Of Riverdell," he finished for me, his lips still holding that slightly secretive smile. "Of course. Please, take a seat; we have a lot to cover this morning."

Riverdell. Yes! Must remember that... Come to think of it, I really needed a hell of a lot more information on my new identity in general. Hopefully Mistress Mallard was going to follow through on her promise to train me up for this role.

Pursing my lips together to keep from betraying myself as a Pond dweller through speech alone, I sat my expensively dressed butt down on a cushion beside Agatha and tried really damn hard not to check out the young gardener's ass when he bent over to pick up the one notebook I'd missed.

"Welcome, ladies," he greeted us all after he'd stacked his notebooks on an empty crate. "I will be your tutor for botany and alchemy. You can call me Lee." He scanned all twenty-one of us with his stunning blue eyes, and I could swear he hesitated a little longer on me. But maybe that was wishful thinking on my part.

Damn, I really was sex starved.

It had never really been something I'd thought that much about before, never been something I craved, like Juliana claimed she did. Sure, I'd done it a couple of times before, but I couldn't say I'd really *enjoyed* it… But this morning, first with the princes and now here with Lee the gardener, I was starting to wonder if I had been doing things all wrong.

"This morning, until we break for lunch, you'll be learning all about plants that can be utilized for both healing and harming. This is a subject that is very dear to one of the prince's hearts, so you'd do well to pay attention and learn. You never know when the knowledge you gain here today will save your life." Lee continued addressing us all with a certain air of confidence that told me all I needed to know about his position as a tutor in these trials. He clearly knew what he was talking about.

Lee began handing out the notebooks to each of us, and I took the opportunity to check him out a little more. He was taller than me, but that wasn't hard. I was average height for a lady, and he had at least a head on me. His frame was lean but strong, his tanned forearms visible from under his rolled-up shirtsleeves showed firm muscles, which had doubtlessly been built up over time in the gardens here. I wasn't foolish enough to think that the gardeners had an easy job, especially considering how well-maintained everything was.

"I'll be presenting each species to you as we discuss them. I recommend you make thorough notes or, perhaps, sketch what they look like." His eyes caught on mine as he said this, and I got the feeling that was a loaded suggestion. Less *if you like* and more *this is what you need to do to succeed*.

His sunshine-streaked, honey-blond hair flopped over his forehead, and he broke eye contact to brush it away while I ducked my head to my notebook. It was a shame I sucked at drawing, but maybe this would be a good lesson for me to fail. Smiling to myself, I closed the notebook again, intending to take no notes.

As soon as the thought about deliberately failing this botany class entered my head, a sharp stabbing sensation lanced through my body, and I screamed in pain, falling to the dirt floor in a heap.

"What in Zryn's balls was that?" I groaned, then clamped a hand over my mouth. Certainly a *lady* wouldn't be swearing to the god of wrath's testicles. Or maybe one would, had she felt what I'd just experienced.

"That, Lady Callaluna," Lee murmured quietly as he knelt to help me up out of the dirt, "is what happens when you consider breaking the binding oath. Stings, huh?"

"You know what it feels like?" I frowned up at him while half-heartedly brushing dirt from my dress.

Lee shrugged. "You'd be amazed how often those binding oaths are used around the palace. That was just a warning shock; it'll be worse next time."

"You were thinking about leaving?" Gracelin exclaimed, folding her arms over her impressive chest and staring at me like I was clinically insane. She was perched on the very edge of a crate like she was afraid it would bite her. "What idiot would give up their chance at being queen because of a stupid plant class?"

Feeling my cheeks warm and cursing my pale complexion, I ground my teeth together and tried not to verbally flay this arrogant airhead. "I wasn't," I gritted out. "It must have been a mistake."

Lee watched me with narrowed eyes a moment longer, and I ducked my head back down to my notebook, flipping it back open once more. So much for that idea.

Thankfully, he began his lecture moments later, and the stares and whispers moved off me as everyone gave the handsome gardener their full attention.

For the next six hours, he instructed us in countless flowers, herbs, roots, and seeds. Some held impressive, almost unbelievable healing qualities, while others could kill a man, or woman, dead in seconds.

As it was turning out, this class was proving to be more interesting than I had really anticipated. Several of the deadly plants I was already familiar with from the Pond, although I'd had no idea they could be used as a poison. That was definitely information I stored for a later date.

"Ladies," Lee addressed us, standing from his own crate, where he'd sat cross-legged all morning to lecture. "That concludes the first half of the day. You are now invited to lunch with Her Majesty Queen Filamina. After that, your test of today's class will commence."

He paused, and his lush lips tightened a fraction. "I'm sure I don't need to impress upon you the importance of doing well in these tests. Losing... does not bear a desirable outcome."

His eyes were burning into the top of my head as he said this, but I kept my gaze securely locked on my notebook in my lap. I'd given enough away already, and it was only day one, for Aana's sake.

Now, I just needed to make it through lunch with the queen without betraying myself as an imposter.

CHAPTER 5

Lunch with the queen was surprisingly painless. After we were handed out simple satin masks to wear, we were escorted to assigned seating, and I was relieved to find myself at the other end of the long banquet table. Admittedly, the ladies I was seated with probably thought I was one hell of a rude bitch for refusing to interact with anyone, but so be it.

After the meal, the queen left us, and we were told we had a half hour of spare time to freshen up before the afternoon test would commence. Most ladies rushed to change, but as I literally had nothing but the clothes on my back, I dawdled.

"What are you *doing*, Lady Callaluna?" a woman hissed, coming up behind me and smacking me on the rump hard enough to make me yelp. "You need to get freshened up! Allow me to you show you to *our rooms*." Juliana grinned broadly at me, and I snorted a laugh.

"Don't get too comfortable; I didn't exactly take the most detailed drawings this morning, so we could well be heading home." It was wishful thinking. Despite my subpar sketching skills, I knew I'd retained a huge amount of the information simply by listening to Lee's soothing voice all morning. Thanks to that oh-so-handy binding oath, there would be no deliberate fails this afternoon, and I suspected I'd be staying at least one more day.

"Uh-huh, whatever you say, *mistress*," she replied, laying the sarcasm on thick. "That old broad, Mallard, has got us set up in the guest quarters, but I doubt they've managed to get any fresh clothes delivered yet. Probably the best you can do is tidy your hair up a bit and wash that massive smudge of dirt off your face. How'd you even manage that?"

My hand flew to my face. "What?" I exclaimed. "Where?"

"Right here." Jules ran a finger down pretty much the full length of my left cheek, and I groaned. It had to have happened when I fell to the ground after being zapped by the binding magic. That was *hours* ago. Why had no one pointed it out?

"Great," I muttered under my breath, feeling irrationally sour. Having dirt on my face was not something that would have ever bothered me before, but the idea that I'd been sitting there in front of Lee with a big old smear on my cheek made me cringe.

Juliana shrugged as she held open a door for me. "Don't stress, babe. It's not like any of the princes saw you, and you wore a mask to lunch with the queen, right?"

I muttered my agreement but was still embarrassed as all hell. I would have actually preferred one of the arrogant, self-centered princes see me rather than someone who might possibly be my first real crush in years.

"Stop looking so sullen, Ry," Jules laughed. "Anyway, I'm supposed to tell you that if you survive today's test, then Mistress Mallard will meet us in our rooms after the evening meal to commence *aristocrat training*."

I arched a brow at her. "Really? Is that what she called it?"

"Not in those words, but it's what she meant. I for one think this whole damn thing is pretty hilarious. Imagine if you actually won!" She was full on laughing at this prospect now and pushed open the doors to a mind-blowing suite, which must be where we would be staying.

"Never going to happen, Jules. I hardly think the kingdom would appreciate an imposter for a queen, and there is no way I can borrow this woman's identity for that long. We're lucky the real Callaluna hasn't shown up here already." I sank down onto the edge of the huge bed, then groaned at how damn soft it was. Maybe I could take a little nap instead of washing? I hadn't slept in far too long already, and it was starting to make me cranky.

"Bloodeye has it handled," Juliana informed me, hauling me

back up by the hand and attacking my face with a washcloth. "The real Callaluna won't be an issue."

Grabbing her wrist, I gave her a sharp look. "Please tell me he didn't have her killed, and more to the point, why is he getting involved? I thought I was on my own if I wanted to be stupid enough to infiltrate the vipers' nest." That wasn't me being dramatic, those were the words he'd used when I'd told him I was going after Flick.

"That was before you managed to find a way into the Royal Trials and then score me a free pass as your maidservant. Let's just say Bloodeye is seeing a lot of potential for keeping you here." She gave me a meaningful look, and I nodded.

"Makes sense. He's never really had a full agent on the inside before. Do you know if he is doing anything to help Flick?" I hadn't forgotten about my whole reason for being there. Not by a long shot.

Jules shook her head, and my heart sank. "Not that I know of, but I did some asking around this morning and discovered they won't be conducting any executions until after the Trials are finished. So, you still have time to get him out."

This gave me a small amount of hope again, and I breathed a sigh of relief. "Okay, good. That's good. So, we have three weeks at least."

Jules nodded and made quick work of re-braiding my hair. "Alright, that's the best I can do. Hopefully there will be new clothes here by the time this test is over because otherwise you'll seriously draw attention to yourself if you don't change."

I sighed and rubbed at my face. This was all the sort of stuff I needed to get used to if I was to maintain my cover as Lady Callaluna. Thank Aana that Jules was here with me for it all.

"Ladies," Lee greeted us all as we returned to the greenhouse. "You all look lovely. Is everyone prepared for this afternoon's test in competency?" He ran his gaze over the group of girls, all of whom had changed into more garden appropriate gowns, except me. When his gaze reached me, he paused, and I could swear there was a small smile pulling at his lips.

Ugh, whatever. It surely wasn't any worse than spending all morning with dirt on my face.

"This test will be a practical one. This morning I showed you six plants that can be useful for healing, as well as six poisonous ones. You may have noted that the six poisonous ones looked very similar to the healing plants. Hopefully you all noted down the subtle differences between them all, as your test is to locate the six *healing* plants from within the palace grounds. When you have them all, you will bring them back here and brew a tea from each one. To determine if you are correct or not, you'll then drink each tea." Lee's brow furrowed at this, and I could tell he didn't approve of that part. "You need not worry about permanent damage or death if you choose wrong, as I'll have antidotes on hand for all of the six poisons, but it will result in lower marks."

Whispers ran through the group of ladies as everyone soaked in the information that we might possibly be poisoning ourselves this afternoon. What fun.

"You have until sundown, and you may venture anywhere within the grounds. All twelve plants are growing here, so please choose wisely." He pursed his lips and looked stern. "One of you will be eliminated tonight, so take your notes with you, and for the love of Barmzig… try your hardest." This last warning, and his mention of our goddess of mercy, was delivered with his bright blue eyes locked hard on me. Apparently, my thoughts about deliberately failing hadn't gone unnoticed after all.

The ladies scattered, grabbing their notebooks from their seats, where we'd all left them before leaving the greenhouse for lunch. Breaking Lee's knowing look, I waited for the immaculately dressed ladies to move out of the way before heading to where I'd been sitting all morning… only to find my notebook gone.

"Is everything okay, Lady Callaluna?" Our instructor's smooth voice sounded a whole lot closer all of a sudden, and I tensed.

Ducking down to check behind my crate, I mumbled my answer. "Uh-huh, yep, all good. Just… can't find my notebook."

Damn it all to hell, it was nowhere to be seen.

"You definitely left it here?" Lee asked, and I could hear the frown in his voice before I even turned to look at him.

I gave him a tight smile and nodded. "Yeah, same as everyone else. I guess someone might have picked it up by accident?"

We both glanced around at all the other vacant seats, and Lee would have seen the same thing I'd seen—no extra notebooks. Somehow, I didn't believe this was an accident at all.

Oh well, maybe I'd be going home tonight after all?

"You're at a serious disadvantage not having any notes from this morning's class, Lady Callaluna," the young gardener murmured, scowling now like he, too, suspected this was a deliberate act. "Perhaps I will walk with you for a bit, if that would be acceptable? I need to be out checking on things anyway."

Fighting a blush that was just so completely unlike me it was ridiculous, I nodded my agreement and fetched one of the small baskets from the stack near the greenhouse door. There was no sense in shoving dirty plants into the pockets of my dress, even if it was already stained.

Lee held the door open for me, and as I passed by him, his hand brushed the small of my back. Such a small movement, seemingly so innocent, yet my body lit up like Lakehaven's sky on Frogs' Feast. It was all I could do not to melt back into his touch and demand more, which was sheer insanity.

This was a man who I had barely known half a day, and I was ready to swoon like... well, like a lady. The sooner I dropped the act, the better. It was seriously starting to compromise my own strength and sanity.

Thankfully, Lee didn't seem to notice as he walked beside me through the gardens at a polite distance, so there was no risk of any more body parts brushing, much to my disappointment.

"I won't influence your test in any way," he informed me after we'd walked for a few minutes in silence. "But I just find you somewhat less painful than some of the other ladies. If you wouldn't mind me keeping you company?"

I snorted an unladylike laugh at this and grinned up at him. "Less painful? Careful with those compliments you're throwing around, Lee. You might accidentally flatter someone."

His eyes widened as he realized what he'd just said, and he started to backtrack. "That's not... I didn't mean to say any of you were painful... I mean..."

"It's fine, Lee. I know what you meant." I laughed at his awkwardness. "You don't really get much time to speak with women one-on-one, huh?" It was just a hunch, but the faint blush in his cheeks confirmed it.

"Large groups I'm fine with," he admitted, "But no, you're right. I don't often get to speak like this..." He waved his hand to indicate the fact that we were alone. "Aside from the current circumstances, ladies don't have much reason to speak with a lowly gardener, now do they?"

I shrugged. What would I know? "Maybe not here, but things are different where I'm from. You're an attractive man; why shouldn't a lady seek you out for... *conversation*, regardless of her rank?"

He paused, his eyes narrowing on me for a moment, and I quickly remembered the role I was supposed to be playing. That was way out of character for a prospective queen.

"Things are so different in Riverdell?" he asked, and I nodded hesitantly.

"Uh-huh," I responded, ducking his intense gaze once more. "As you can see, ladies in Riverdell are more outspoken than in Lakehaven."

He seemed to accept my weak explanation easily as a smile curved over his lips. "I'll have to visit there sometime, in that case. I find this outspoken nature of yours rather refreshing."

I smiled back but said nothing as we continued along the path leading into the more secluded section of gardens, much further away from the palace buildings. Just off the path, something caught my eye, and I paused.

"Score," I whispered under my breath, bending to pluck a few leaves of nettlefish, an herb that was meant to cure toothache. Just as my fingers brushed the fuzzy leaves, I froze. Something... didn't feel right. I knew that its deceptively similar counterpart, monksfoot, could cause severe vomiting and the only perceptible difference between them was the width of the leaf.

Pulling my hand back a fraction, I frowned, searching my mind for which one this was.

Monksfoot. I was almost sure of it.

But just a foot to the left…

"Nettlefish," I announced with confidence as I plucked several slimmer leaves from a plant growing so close it almost seemed to be from the same root. Sneaky.

"Good work, Lady Callaluna," Lee murmured in admiration. "You had me worried a moment there. What reminded you?"

Giving him a smug smile, I ignored the question. "Lady Callaluna," I repeated. "Sounds so formal."

Lee shrugged but arched a brow at me. "Such is etiquette between a gardener and a lady, is it not?"

Ugh, probably. I should get better at not voicing my every thought aloud.

"Like I mentioned, *Lee*, things are more relaxed in Riverdell." *And thank the stars you've never been there, or my disguise would be totally shot by now.*

He said nothing for a bit as we walked, but I could feel his attention on me from the corner of his eyes.

"So, how about Calla?" he suggested after a long time. "But only in private, of course. I wouldn't like to be reprimanded for my lack of courtly manners by Lady Savannah." Something about this amused him to no end but didn't bother me. It was still a stolen name, shortened or not. Still, "Calla" made me feel like somewhat less of an imposter than "Lady Callaluna of Riverdell."

"Sounds perfect," I replied with a smile. "But does that mean you intend to see me in private more often?"

Another plant caught my eye, and I bent to grab the flowers. This time I was confident I had grabbed the right one, as my intuition didn't spike, and the yellow bloom was exactly as I had attempted to draw it.

"Would you like that, Calla?" Lee asked me in a heated voice when I straightened. "I thought you were here to marry a prince and live out a happily-ever-after in the palace."

I snorted a laugh, unable to peel my eyes from his handsome, somewhat nervous-seeming face. "Princes be damned. I never wanted to be a part of this ridiculous *game* in the first place. If it weren't for that binding oath, I would have grabbed the monksfoot back there on purpose."

His brows shot up in surprise, but a small smile tugged at his lips. "I take it you were pressured into accepting the invitation, then?"

I grimaced, thinking of the guilt trip Mistress Mallard had laid on me. "You could say that."

"So you're here now. What makes the princes of Teich so unappealing? The twenty other girls here would probably slit each other's throats to win." Lee sounded genuinely curious, but not outraged. Thank Aana for small mercies. It had occurred to me after the words were out that he could be a mole, reporting everything we said back to the royals. Then again… did I care? Citizens of

Teich had freedom of speech, and I couldn't be punished for my opinions... could I?

Pursing my lips, I tried to find the most diplomatic phrasing for my answer. "Look around you, Lee. Look at how lush and green everything is here."

He did as I asked, looking somewhat proud as he took in the gardens. Rightly so, I guess, when he was one if the gardeners working to maintain the grounds.

"What do the gardens have to do with the princes, Calla?" The way he said my new nickname gave me belly flutters, and I struggled to stay focused.

"Everything. Have you been into Lakehaven lately? Or farther abroad? Have you seen the damage that the Darkness caused to the lands? The suffering that people endure every day, while what little magic remains is used to maintain a pretty garden for the queen?" I paused, glaring up at him. "Dare I ask, have you ever ventured into the Pond? Seen how almost a third of Lakehaven's population is living?" I could tell by the guilty look on his face that his answer was a resounding *no*. "How could I ever love a royal who allowed his people to suffer just so he might experience beauty on his own doorstep? No, I am certainly not here for the princes of Teich, and I will happily walk away if I'm eliminated."

Something I'd said had offended him, I could tell by the tight set to his jaw and the way he avoided my gaze all of a sudden. It didn't make a difference though; everything I'd said was true.

"It won't be that easy, Calla," he said finally, his voice sounding disappointed, almost... regretful?

"I know." I shrugged, giving him a reassuring smile. "I'm not stupid; that zap the magic gave me earlier was not fun. I know I will need permission from the royals to leave, but hopefully they'll be happy to be rid of me when they see I'm not interested in becoming queen."

Lee shook his head and sighed heavily, leading me back down the path. "That's not what I meant. I think once the princes meet you, they won't be able to let you go." He looked down at me, meeting my eyes with his heart-stopping gaze. "I know I wouldn't."

His admission made my breath catch, and thousands of butterflies erupted inside me. The way he stared at me made me feel totally naked, and I was liking it way more than I had any right to.

"Yet another serious character flaw for the princes, then. People cannot be owned, no matter whose throne you sit on." With a monumental effort, I broke his gaze and continued hunting for herbs. It was considerably easier than feeling like my soul was being examined by a blue-eyed gardener.

"You intrigue me, Calla," Lee admitted some time later, when I'd gathered five of the six correct plants for the test. "It's not proper for a palace employee to speak so openly with a lady competing in the trials, and yet... I can't seem to make myself walk away."

Hiding a self-satisfied smile, I reached out to pick a beautiful white flower that had caught my attention. It was growing almost from within a tree trunk, and the delicate shape was a cross between a tulip and a rose.

Bringing it to my nose, I inhaled the sweet scent of it and sighed. "This is gorgeous," I commented, turning back to Lee. "What sort of flower is it?"

Frowning, he took the bloom from my hand, his fingers brushing against mine in a way that made me feel naked all over again. "It's an ophelia bloom," he murmured, looking confused. "These supposedly died out when Queen Ophelia was killed. I've never seen one here before..." Glancing past me, he stared at the tree I'd plucked it from, like he was committing its location to memory. Looking back to me, he tucked the flower into my braid, weaving the stem in before smiling. "It suits you, Calla."

This time there was no hiding the stupid grin on my face and my cheeks heated with awkwardness. How sad that at the age of eighteen this was the most flirting I'd ever engaged in. I'd need to talk with Jules about how to do it without embarrassing myself.

"We should start heading back; what do you have left to find?" He indicated to my basket, and I peered down at what I'd collected so far.

"Just... teichian violets," I announced. "Then I'm good."

He nodded, following my lead as I started walking once more. "I'm impressed by how well you've done without any notes. You must have a good memory."

"Something like that," I agreed, not willing to discuss my intuition with someone who really was a stranger to me, no matter how badly I wanted to taste his lips. "You can head back if you need to prepare the test, though. I won't be too much longer."

He hesitated, but the way he glanced back toward the way we'd come said it all.

"Go," I urged him. "I'm sure it would be better for your reputation if we weren't returning together anyway."

His lush lips curved into a smile that gave me a crazy urge to kiss him. "It's not *my* reputation I'd be worried about, Calla. But I would hate for anyone to think you've cheated on this test."

Biting the inside of my cheek and carefully averting my gaze from his handsome face, I shrugged. "So, go. This last one will be easy to find; I might even beat you back if you dawdle."

He huffed a short laugh and ran a hand through his honey-blond hair. "Yeah, okay. I'll see you back there, then. Just..." He trailed off, scuffing his shoe in the dirt. "Just don't take too long. I have a horrible feeling I might be worried if you did."

A broad smile spread across my face, and my stomach did a weird flippy thing. Oh geez, I had it bad for my teacher. Surely there were rules against that? Actually, there probably were. I just wouldn't know because I'd never in a million years have thought I'd end up competing in the Royal Trials.

Lee gave me an awkward sort of wave, like he had reached out to touch me and then changed his mind, before hurrying back toward the greenhouse. Despite the fact that I was fairly certain he was just flirting, I still found myself hurrying to locate and pick the teichian violets and rushing back to the greenhouse for the test.

As I entered, I found I was the last one to return, and all twenty other girls turned to stare at me. Ignoring them, I made my way back to my crate seat, which had been set with a mortar and pestle as well as six steaming mugs of water on a tray.

"I see everyone is back," Lee commented. "That's a good start. Let's get on with this test then, shall we? You're to grind each plant you've gathered and steep it in the hot water. After the teas are brewed, you must drink each one to prove your confidence in what you've learned." His lips tightened, like he disagreed with this test but had no say in the matter. It made sense that someone else was pulling the strings on tests. Somehow I found it hard to imagine a person as kind as Lee creating a test that would poison women.

I was confident in my herb choices, so I held no nervousness at the prospect of ingesting poison. Looking around me, I noticed several girls were pale and sweating already, their hands shaking as they began grinding plants.

"Ready?" Lee asked the girl closest to him, standing over her completed tray of teas when she placed them on the ground in front of her. "I have antidotes to all of the poisons, so you have nothing to fear *here*." She looked relieved, but I frowned at the odd emphasis he'd placed on that last word. Was he implying there was something to fear outside of this test?

All of us watched in silence, holding our breath as she took the first cup in a shaking hand and screwed her eyes shut tight.

"Okay," I heard her whisper under her breath. "I can do this. I *can* do this."

Without another moment to psych herself out, she took a large mouthful of the tea and swallowed quickly, gasping when she was done. For a long moment, no one spoke and all eyes were on the girl who'd gone first.

"Congratulations, Lady Bella, you got the first one correct." Lee's smile held the same relief the rest of us seemed to be sagging with. "Please continue."

Emboldened by her success, she drank the next five with more confidence. Luckily, the next four were all correct, too. Unluckily, the last one was not.

"Here." Lee produced a bucket at lightning speed, just in time to catch the vomit that hurtled out of her mouth like a freight train from before the Darkness. "Drink this," he told her, holding out a small vial when the first round of vomiting ended, and she gasped for breath. "Quickly, before it starts again. Then you're dismissed; you can go clean up and have a rest before dinner."

Lady Bella gratefully threw the antidote back and wiped her

mouth off on a delicate handkerchief from her pocket. "Thank you, Lee," she whispered, still as pale as a sheet.

As she scurried out of the greenhouse, sniffling with unshed tears, Lee moved on to the next girl to begin again.

This continued over and over, with most girls getting at least one of their herbs wrong and needing to drink an antidote. Some were easy, like Lady Bella's vomiting. Others were more serious, like the woman who ingested shadowbloom and went into cardiac arrest. That one required both an antidote *and* a round of chest compressions before she was dismissed from the test. Five girls, myself included, got all six plants correct. I knew this because for some reason Lee left my test until very last, so I got to sit there and watch my peers drink poisons.

"Why did you make me go last?" I asked the handsome gardener as I helped him pack up the crate seats and used teacups.

He sighed, not looking at me as he rinsed the mugs under water in the small sink. It was a luxury that the palace still had things like running water, but I guessed if anyone had it, it would be the royals.

"Because now you know who your competition is, Calla," he confessed. "Scores from each test don't just dictate who gets eliminated each night, but they count toward an advantage in the final test come the end of the week." He turned the tap off, drying his hands on a rag, then turning to face me. "Call me crazy, but I find myself wanting to help you win this thing... within the confines of my own binding oaths, that is."

"Why?" I frowned at him. "I kind of got the impression you liked me." My cheeks heated with embarrassment as I said this, but I pushed forward anyway. "Shouldn't you be hoping I get eliminated?"

A dark shadow passed over his features, and he shook his head, dropping eye contact and folding his muscled arms over his chest. "No one would wish for that, Calla." His words felt heavy, loaded with knowledge of something bigger. Something he wasn't permitted to share with me. "You should go," he reminded me. "You have dinner with the royal family soon, don't forget."

I laughed, trying to ease the sudden tension between us. "How could I possibly forget? This is my big chance to snag myself a prince!" I pursed my lips, looking down at my dirt-covered gown that I'd been wearing since dawn. "Maybe I'll just go as I am?"

Lee snorted a laugh and shook his head in disbelief. "I almost believe you would too. Just be careful, okay? And... if you ever need to talk about anything, you can leave me a note under here and I'll come find you, okay?" He tapped a pot containing a scary-looking plant with teeth. "Just don't get your fingers too close to this part or you'll lose one." He indicated to the bulbous part of the plant—the part with teeth—and gave me a serious look.

A bit confused at his offer, I nodded slowly. "Sure thing. Thanks, Lee."

Giving him a small wave, I left the greenhouse and made my

way back to my room, where Jules would be waiting. A certain sense of uneasiness came with me, though, and I pondered over the information I'd just gained.

Why did Lee think I might need to talk with him about dinner? Or did he just mean in general? I hadn't gotten the feeling he'd made that offer in a flirtatious way, so I doubted he'd just meant if I was feeling stupid horny and wanted to ease off the pressure a bit. It was more *sinister* than that.

Shaking off the cloud of intrigue, I pushed open the door to my room and groaned at all the dresses laid out around Jules. Whatever dinner had in store for us, at least I'd look the part.

CHAPTER 6

Dinner was an elaborate affair, complete with evening gowns, gloves, and intricate masks, as per tradition. The royal family would be in attendance, so we were all required to cover our faces, just as they themselves would.

A steward showed us into the banquet hall and ushered us to our assigned seats. Next to mine there was an empty space with no place card. Cold dread pooled in my stomach as my eyes darted around the table. Two more empty spaces were directly opposite, and the only other places at the table were the throne-like chairs on either end— clearly where the king and queen would be sat. Which meant...

"Oh, for the love of Zryn's hairy balls," I cursed under my breath, then froze when a heavy hand planted on my shoulder.

"Such colorful language for a Lady of Teich," a man with a deep, rumbling voice commented, his breath brushing the exposed skin on the back of my neck and making me shiver. "I do hope that wasn't your reaction to the seating assignments." Across the table, the other two princes in their dark masks stood behind their own seats—waiting, like the rest of us, for the king and queen to be seated. I glanced down at the fingers on my shoulder. He wore the same ring I'd seen in the alleyway that first time I'd run into them, and I bit my lip to rein in the snappy retorts that came to mind. I wanted to leave with my head preferably *intact*.

"Your Highness," I murmured, "not at all. I must have... gotten a papercut." I fingered the place card with my fake name on it as I lied. Thankfully, the remaining royals arrived then, stirring everyone into motion taking their seats, and I was spared the need to lie any further about my imagined papercut.

"Lady Callaluna," the prince beside me murmured, picking up my place card as I arranged my slippery satin skirts on the chair. Having grown up in pants and shirts, I'd had no idea how cumbersome it was to have just *so much fabric* to deal with. "Such a pretty name."

Pursing my lips, I swallowed past the guilt at what might have happened to the *real* Callaluna. "Do I get to know *which* Highness I'm speaking to? Or is that all part of the 'game' too?"

The huge man seated beside me—because now that I was seeing him properly for the first time, I realized he really was an intimidating size—just threw his head back and laughed. Pompous ass.

"Stop it, Thibault," one of the masked royals opposite us chastised him. "Just because the lovely Lady Callaluna has a sharp tongue, doesn't mean you need to bait her."

Narrowing my eyes at the one who'd spoken, I pursed my lips to refrain from taking *his* bait. I got the distinct feeling that they were enjoying my temper, so I'd need to make an effort to hold it back.

"His Highness Prince Thibault, then?" I turned to the man beside me and arched a brow. It wouldn't have been hard for them to see it either, as my mask consisted of loosely woven metal lace, which would have done a poor job of concealing my face if that had been the aim. "Charming to meet you without the blindfold."

A broad grin arched his full lips, the only part of his face truly visible other than his dark eyes. Extending a hand, he picked up mine and pressed a lingering kiss to my knuckles.

"A true pleasure, Lady Callaluna," he responded, his voice a dark, rough promise.

"So that makes you"—I tugged my hand from Prince Thibault's grip and turned to the man who'd just spoken— "His Highness Prince Alexander? And His Highness Prince Louis?" This last guess was aimed to the third man, who had yet to speak and seemed to be doing everything possible not to look at me. From memory, Alexander was the oldest, followed by Thibault, and Louis was the youngest. It had become pretty common practice for parents in

Lakehaven to name their sons after the princes, and in that same order, too; otherwise I wouldn't have remembered. After all, what use to me was knowledge of the royals?

Alexander gave a short nod, acknowledging my correct guesses, but someone tapping on a wine glass interrupted us before he could say anything further.

"Shit," one of the two across from me cursed under his breath, and I frowned. They all spoke with a similar, husky tone, so it made it hard to pick who was speaking unless I was watching his lips move.

"Are toasts a cause for concern around here?" I asked them with a nervous laugh because even Thibault beside me was practically vibrating with tension. Immaculate waiters moved around the table, placing a crystal flute of sparkling wine in front of each of us, and I placed my fingers lightly on the stem of mine.

"You'll see soon enough," Thibault murmured, all traces of joking gone from his rough voice. "It's at this stage of the night that someone gets eliminated."

I scrunched up my nose, not understanding all the drama. "So? Someone gets to go home to their family and escape the farce that is this 'game' you three set up. What's with all the tension? You're all strung tighter than a crossbow right now."

"For one," Thibault growled quietly so only I could hear, "we did *not* set this up. And for another..." He broke off with a sigh as his father stood at the head of the table, an indication that we all do the same. "Never mind. You'll see."

His reply had only served to confuse me further, so I watched him curiously from the corner of my eye as the king made some generic welcome toast to all the ladies competing to marry one of his sons.

Lifting my glass to my lips, I felt a disconcerting number of eyes on me, but I ignored them to enjoy the taste of my wine. It was of far better quality than anything I'd ever tasted in the Pond, including stuff we'd stolen from merchants.

Everyone sat back in their seats, and chatter started up around the table. The ladies on the other sides of all three princes had recovered from the shock of being seated next to royalty and began attempting to engage the three of them in lively conversation, leaving me to my thoughts.

It was only a few moments later when someone screamed in horror that I realized what they'd been so tense about. Further down the table, one of the ladies competing in the trials collapsed forward onto the table and was convulsing. Foam seeped from her mouth, and her eyes were rolled so far into her head that only the whites were visible.

"Someone help her!" The girl who'd been sitting beside her screeched, tears flowing down her face. "She's dying!"

Even as ladies screamed and wept, one thing became painfully clear to me. No one would be helping this lady, who I recognized as the one who'd taken Shadowbloom in the test that afternoon.

"This is how you *eliminate* ladies?" I hissed, whirling on Prince Thibault but not sparing the other two from a venomous glare as I turned. "You can't just send them home? You need to *kill them*?" I was so horrified and disgusted that my whole body was shaking.

When none of the princes responded, not even to meet my accusing gaze, my stomach rolled like I might vomit. This was *not* what I'd signed up for. Not even close. In fury, I made to shove my chair back from the table and leave, but a strong hand clamped down on my knee under the table, pinning me in place.

"Don't." Thibault ordered, his voice broken and rough. "Don't draw attention to yourself, Lady Callaluna. Not now."

Horrified, I shook my head, staring around the table. Many of the ladies wept openly, but they'd noticed—just as I had—that none of the royals seemed surprised by this turn of events. Even when two of the smartly suited waiters approached the dying woman, then proceeded to drag away one of the kingdom's elite sweethearts... still none of them seemed concerned.

"Ladies," the king of Teich addressed us when the body had been cleared, "as you've just seen, the price of failure in these Royal Trials is high. Your guardians were all made aware of this prior to giving permission for you to enter, so don't think you can go crying to them." Our monarch's voice was cold and cruel, and I fought back bile in my throat. "You all took a binding oath that *only* I can free you from, but let me get one step ahead of you. *No one* leaves these trials unless it's on a funeral wagon or as a bride. Is that perfectly clear?"

A stunned silence filled the room, and Thibault's hand tightened on my knee, like he was warning me not to do anything stupid. Not that I needed any warning. Halfway through the king's merciless speech, I'd spotted the person undoubtedly behind the violent turn of events.

Lord Taipanus.

The King's Snake stood in the shadows near the back of the room, a twisted grin on his face. He hadn't even bothered to wear a mask in the presence of the royals, and the look on his face gave me chills.

I'd killed before, sure. But I'd never enjoyed it. Not the way this evil man was clearly enjoying this sick display.

"Every night of this week of tests, you'll be presented a toast. You *will* accept the toast; to decline will be considered treason." The king's ice-cold eyes flashed with danger from behind his mask. "Every night, the lowest scoring lady will be eliminated from the competition. Now, let's all enjoy our meal, shall we?"

As if someone had just cut our strings, all the ladies at the table sagged in disbelief. Only one of us was making it out of this palace alive, and suddenly the tests had taken on a whole different purpose.

We no longer fought for marriage and a crown. We fought for our *lives.*

Prying Thibault's hand from my knee, I shoved it away from me and scooted my chair away from him. "Don't ever touch me again," I hissed at him when he opened his mouth to say something. "What kind of monsters allow *this* to happen? I hope whoever your bride is, you forever see her bathed in the blood of twenty ladies." I included Alexander and Louis in this accusation as well, glaring daggers at them across the table. "I should have guessed that our royal princes were nothing but spineless cowards. After all, not one of you has lifted a finger to help the people of Teich since curing the plagues." The ladies within hearing distance around us gasped at my words, but they were all too cowed to speak up.

"Lady Calla—" Prince Louis spoke for the first time since arriving at the table, but I was in no mood for their aristocratic bullshit.

"Save it," I spat in disgust. "You all make me sick."

Thankfully, none of them pushed the topic any further, and I was left alone with my trembling emotions for the remainder of the somber meal. The second our king and queen left the table and we were free to depart, I was gone without a backward glance at any of them.

Rushing down the corridor away from the dining hall, I spotted Juliana waiting for me near the hallway leading to the guest quarters.

"Jules," I barked at her, and she jumped in fright, turning away from the other maid she'd been speaking to. "Take the night off or something," I instructed her. "I'm going for a walk to clear my head."

"But Ry—uh, Callaluna—what about that thing we were supposed to do tonight? With Mistress Mallard?" She was trying to give me subtle hints about our lesson in how to be a convincing *lady,* but I hadn't forgotten. I just didn't care.

"Screw it. Just... go check on things back home. I'll see you later, okay?" I didn't wait for her response before turning my back and hurrying out to the gardens. There was only one person I wanted to speak to, and I suspected he already knew what had been waiting at dinner.

"Lee?" I called into the darkened greenhouse as I pushed the glass doors open. "Are you here?"

Silence was my only response, but that was to be expected. Picking up my satin dress skirts to prevent them from trailing in mud, I made my way over to the carnivorous plant and found a notebook and pencil resting on the rim of the pot.

Pressing the tip of the pencil to the paper, I paused. What the hell did I even say? This was a man I'd known a day. Was I really ready to accuse him of being in on this revolting "game"? The idea that he'd even known about it, let alone had anything to *do* with it, made me almost physically ill. But it couldn't have been a coincidence that our first class was about poisons...

Eventually, I just scrawled one word. *Why?*

Cursing my own stupidity, I tucked the note under the pot and stormed back out of the greenhouse. I badly wanted to say more in my note, like "Why didn't you warn me?" or even "How could you let this happen?" but most of all, the message I'd wanted to leave was "I need you. Find me?"

I wasn't even a full day into my imposter life, and I was becoming a different person. It scared the hell out of me, and I needed to get a grip before I entered into a full-on identity crisis. I was Rybet Waise, dammit. Not Lady Callaluna of Riverdell.

I was stronger than this. I didn't cower or shake in the face of bullies like Taipanus. They'd locked us into this revolting game and given us death as the only way out. Well, fuck taking lessons to act like a lady. I'd be damned if I died by my own hand, so I'd win this game... and then I'd make them pay for all the unnecessary lives lost.

Taipanus had no idea who he was messing with. But he'd soon find out.

CHAPTER 7

Almost as though my furious thoughts held some magical power of summoning, a cold hand grabbed my bare upper arm as I stormed back into the palace and slammed my back into the stone wall of the hallway.

"*Lady Callaluna*," Lord Taipanus sneered at me, his rancid breath filling my nostrils and making me choke. I pursed my lips and said nothing. "I found two of my guards somewhat out of place this morning—locked in a cell not one hundred feet from where I found *you*. I don't suppose you would know what happened to them, would you, lady?"

"What?" I exclaimed, trying not to inhale too deeply. "That's awful. Those poor men."

"Save it, girl," Taipanus snapped. "I know you had something

THE ROYAL TRIALS: IMPOSTER

to do with it. You must have others working with you because no scrawny girl could have bested two grown men alone." This was insulting, to say the least, and I bit down hard on my tongue not to correct him. "I'll figure out your purpose here soon enough, and when I do"—He leered a cruel smile at me— "you'll *wish* you'd drunk poison at dinner."

"Lord Taipanus," a man called out, drawing the Snake's attention from me, "is everything all right here?"

The spymaster hesitated, glaring back at me a moment before releasing his grip on my arm and moving away a step. "All okay, *Gardener* Lee," he replied with an oily smile. "I was just warning Lady Callaluna here about the dangers of being alone at night. Nowhere is safe, these days. Not even the palace." This was delivered as a warning to me, there was no doubt about it.

"That's a wise warning, Lord Taipanus," Lee replied, coming to stand in front of us with his hands stuffed in his pockets. "I'd be happy to escort you to your room if you'd like, Lady Callaluna?"

Jumping at the chance to get away from the spymaster, I nodded and slid out from the wall where Taipanus had previously held me pinned. "Thanks, Lee," I murmured. "You never can be too careful. I appreciate the offer."

"Pleasant dreams, lady," Taipanus called after me as I hurried down the hall with Lee. "Don't forget our little chat."

I shuddered but didn't bother replying. Bloodeye had warned me once about the stupidity of poking a snake with a stick, and I wasn't dumb enough to do that now. If I was to survive this nightmare, I'd need to stay well off the Snake's radar.

"Want to tell me what that was all about?" Lee asked me in a quiet, husky voice when we got a safer distance away. "Lord Taipanus is the last person you want to be on the bad side of."

"I'm well aware," I snapped, then frowned at him. "Why does your voice sound weird?"

"Oh, ah." He coughed into his hand, "I was experimenting with potions." He slipped a vial from his pocket and drank a small sip, then cleared his throat again. "So, Taipanus?"

Rolling my eyes, I kept walking and didn't bother answering. As badly as my body was coursing with tingles that he'd come to find me, I was still horrified at the events of dinner.

"Perhaps you have something to tell me?" I challenged him, reaching my room and placing a hand on the doorknob. "I knew something was up when you were all cagey about dinner. You knew what was going to happen, didn't you?"

Lee glanced around us, like he was checking if anyone might overhear. We were totally alone, though.

"We can't talk out here," he implored. "You never know who is watching or listening."

Arching a brow at him, I twisted my doorknob and swung the door open in invitation.

"Seriously?" he exclaimed, eyes widening as he stared through the open doorway. "That's probably pushing the bounds of propriety pretty far, Calla."

I snorted a laugh at this and grinned. The concept of him trying to *protect my reputation* was a bit hilarious, given I'd grown up around whores, thieves, and murderers. "My, er, maid is out for the night, so no one will even see you. Besides, I'm sure you'll be the perfect gentleman."

He hesitated only a second longer before stepping inside my room and allowing me to close the door behind us. "I wouldn't be so sure," he muttered, almost too quietly for me to hear, and I stifled a grin. Was it bad that I was *hoping* he wouldn't be a gentleman?

"So, start talking," I ordered, flopping down on the overstuffed chaise lounge. "You knew someone would die tonight?"

"You don't seem terribly shaken," he observed, dodging my question. "I noticed you weren't all that affected watching the girls who drank poison during the test as well. Have you seen a lot of people die, Calla?"

"Don't evade my question, Lee; it's not as cute as you think." Okay, it was probably cuter than he thought, and I'd just evaded *his* question, so I guessed we were even.

Giving me a small smile, he sighed and sat on the opposite end of the lounge from me. With several other armchairs available, maybe I wasn't the only one feeling this insane, magnetic attraction.

"Yes," he confessed after a long silence, "I knew what was

coming. There was no way to warn you, though. And I knew you wouldn't be at risk..."

I scowled at him. "So it was okay to let that poor girl, Lady... uh..." Crap, I had no idea what her name was.

"Lady Janaira," Lee informed me. "And no, of course it wasn't *okay* to let her go to her death tonight. You seem unaware that you're not the only one being held by binding oaths. I had just as much choice in how tonight played out as you did, Calla."

I huffed a sigh but knew in my heart he was right. He wasn't evil, not like Taipanus. If he could have stopped it, I'm sure he would have. "We're totally screwed, aren't we?" I asked him, sagging further into the couch, which somehow managed to move me closer to Lee.

It wasn't a huge lounge to begin with, so we were already within touching distance. Something Lee proved by running a fingertip over my bare upper arm.

"He bruised you," he murmured softly, his rough thumb stroking the tender skin where Taipanus had grabbed me. "That man acts so untouchable, so indestructible. I look forward to the day he gets stripped of his position."

I laughed, turning on the couch slightly to face him. "As if that would ever happen."

"I'm a servant, Calla. I hear a great many things, one of which is that there's no love lost between Taipanus and the princes. King Titus's reign is ending, and I would put money on it that whoever ascends to the throne will take out the trash." His fingers continued stroking down my bare arm, making my skin tingle as he reached my hand.

"You have a lot of faith in those arrogant pricks," I commented, biting my lip as he turned my hand over and began tracing patterns on my palm. "You didn't see them at dinner, Lee. They just sat there, totally uncaring as a girl died at the table. And for what? For accepting their *invitation* to compete in the Trials? She didn't deserve to die. None of us do."

Lee's fingers on my palm paused, and there was a tense silence before he spoke again, leaving me wondering if I'd overstepped. Who knew how long he'd worked in the palace; maybe he had a different opinion of the asswads who called themselves princes.

"I think," he finally said in a careful voice, "not everything is what it seems around here, and you should consider giving them the benefit of the doubt. After all, you don't really know any of them, do you?" There was a faint note of hope in his voice as he finished with that question, and I smiled at him.

"No, and I don't really intend to," I replied, feeling sure of my feelings. The princes held no romantic interest for me. None whatsoever. That crazy sexual tension I'd felt with Thibault was just... hormones or something. Carryover feelings from my day with Lee. "Believe me, I wasn't lying about not wanting to jump headfirst into bed with those Neanderthals. Can you even believe their idea of a prize is the *opportunity* to spend the night with one of them?" I made a gagging noise, and Lee burst out into laughter.

"I'm serious." I frowned at him as he shook with amusement. "It's not actually funny, you oddball. Anyway, the king made an announcement—or rather more of a threat—that he's not granting anyone permission to leave the trials."

Sobering up and shifting somewhat closer to me on the couch, Lee peered at me with his intense blue eyes. "So what will you do?"

Meeting his gaze unflinchingly, I ignored the charged shocks of attraction racing through me and answered honestly. "Win."

His brows shot up in surprise, and his long lashes blinked a couple of times. "Win? You mean..."

"Become the next queen and marry one of those conceited pricks? Not a chance in hell. But there's no way anyone will make me poison myself for their own amusement. I'll win this stupid game, and then they'll live to regret all this bloodshed." There was an edge of steel to my tone that surprised even me. Before just now, I'd still been considering tucking tail and running in the hopes that the binding oath wouldn't kill me. But hearing my own conviction as I spoke that declaration aloud... that changed things.

Lee held my gaze for a long moment, his face an unreadable mix of emotions. Just when I was about to tell him it was okay to leave, he wouldn't hurt my feelings, he reached forward. Slipping his long fingers into my hair, he cradled the back of my head and pulled me closer until our lips were a scant breath apart.

"I shouldn't be doing this," he whispered, sounding conflicted. "This could really fuck things up for them..."

By *them* I assumed he meant the princes. Not that it was any contest in my mind—Lee was ten times the man any of those royal toads were.

"Do you really care?" I challenged him, my lips brushing against his ever so lightly as I spoke. He gave a pained groan and answered me in the only way I needed him to—closing the short gap between us and claiming my mouth with his own.

The butterflies that had set up a nest inside me the moment Lee and I had met all took flight at once, filling me with the most giddy, intense, girlish feeling I'd ever experienced. It was a sensation that I never wanted to end, and it only increased as his lips moved confidently against mine.

Stunned, ecstatic, and a little out of my depth, I had no idea what I should be doing with my hands. Should they be on his shoulders? His face? Why was I so damn ill-prepared for a situation like this?

In the past, kissing had been a rushed affair. A box to tick on the way to sex. Certainly nothing like the languid, erotic way Lee's mouth met mine. Gently, he coaxed my lips apart, and our tongues met in an explosion of sparks.

Overcome with desire and arousal, I was no longer worrying about where my hands should be. They practically had a life of their own as I explored the hard planes of Lee's chest. I wasn't the only one getting carried away, either, as Lee's grip shifted from my hair and down my back to rest on my waist.

The warmth of his palms through the thin satin of my dress had me moaning and arching my spine, desperate for more. Thank Aana and all her fortunes, Lee was on the same page as me, pressing me backward onto the couch even as his hands reached up to cup my breasts through my dress.

Murmuring an incoherent sound of approval, I snaked a leg around his waist, pulling him closer until I could feel his hardened length pressing against my core.

"Calla," he groaned, grinding against me and sliding one palm down the exposed length of my thigh. "This isn't right, we shouldn't be doing this. Not like *this*."

Parting my lips to argue, I barely had gotten a sound out when the unmistakable click of a door closing shocked me from my lust-induced stupor.

"Well *this* was unexpected," my best friend exclaimed, meeting my eyes over Lee's broad shoulder as she glared down at me. "When you said to take the night off, it didn't occur to me you would be *entertaining*."

"Jules," I panted, wide-eyed as Lee hurried to sit up and then gallantly offer me a hand up. "This is, ah, Lee. He—"

"Was just leaving," Lee finished for me, standing and trying to subtly adjust his pants before striding to the door. "I'll be seeing you, Calla."

The brief flash of panic that had struck me when he'd started his hasty exit was soothed by the heated, desperate look of desire on his face as he looked back at me.

"Uh-huh," I agreed, still numb and buzzing from our sexy make-out.

No more words were necessary, though, as he was gone before I could even blink twice.

"Ahem," Jules fake coughed, dragging my attention from the door where I'd just been *staring* after Lee like a lovesick girl.

"What?" I asked her, cocking a brow and feigning innocence. "Don't give me that look; it's nothing you wouldn't do."

She pursed her lips and scowled. "Exactly. But it's *not* what Rybet Waise would do. What's gotten into you, girl? Did they brainwash you or something?"

Shaking my head, I dodged her accusing eyes. "It doesn't change anything. Now, sit down and shut up; I need to tell you what happened at dinner."

CHAPTER 8

The mood when I entered the training arena the next morning was somber to say the least. Gone were the nervous, girlish giggles and whispers, and not a single smile was in sight. The king's display of cruelty at dinner the night before had thoroughly shaken everyone, and looking around at the girls, I found plenty of pale, drawn faces.

"Welcome to your first combat class," a man greeted us, entering from the doors I'd just come through. "I trust you're all here?" He passed by me, his arm brushing mine, and I yelped at the static shock that zapped me.

Our tutor for the day paused, peering down at me with sage green eyes framed in dark lashes. "Everything okay, Lady Callaluna?"

Sucking in a deep breath, I stared back up at his handsome face with wide eyes and nodded. "Uh-huh. Just a shock."

A sly sort of smile pulled at his lips, but he said nothing more as he continued through the gathered girls to the table where various practice weapons were laid out.

"Look around you," he instructed us, any trace of his smile gone and a frown firmly in place. "You'll find that not only is Lady Janaira gone, but so too is Lady Hyacinth. She decided to ignore all of the palace's warnings regarding the binding oath you all took and attempted to abandon the Trials." Our tutor looked grim at this news, and his jaw ticked like he was clenching his teeth way too hard. "Perhaps some of the rest of you tried as well but were smart enough to abort the attempt before suffering any permanent damage." His green gaze swept across the gathered ladies, and several of them shifted uncomfortably. "Hopefully, you're all intelligent enough not to try again. Now, let's move on. I'm your combat tutor, Ty. This morning you'll be learning some basic self-defense skills that could save your life one day."

"Excuse me, Ty?" A pretty blonde girl, who I vaguely remembered as Lady Rosealee, put her hand up. "Why would we need to know how to fight? Doesn't a princess or queen have her own guards?"

"She does," Ty agreed with a nod, "but what happens if those guards are not around for whatever reason? What happens if she is caught alone or her guards are killed? What then? She just swoons and lets herself be killed or worse?" Lady Rosalee flushed with embarrassment, but Ty wasn't done. "I understand you've yet to take a history and politics class with Zan, but I would have thought most well-bred ladies knew of our country's history and how our current royals came to rule."

Agatha cleared her throat. "Yes, sir. Queen Ophelia and her baby were attacked by unknown invaders. Her guards were all killed, but she was an accomplished swordswoman and managed to kill several of her attackers before they ran her through and stole the Princess Zarina."

"Can't have been too accomplished then," I muttered under my breath and instantly felt the burning gaze of our tutor on me.

"Something to add, Lady Callaluna?" he prompted me, and I bit my lip to keep quiet.

Shaking my head, I plastered on my most innocent face. "Not at all. Just speculating what must have happened to Princess Zarina."

Ty narrowed his eyes at me but accepted the cover up. "It's widely accepted that she was either killed or sold into slavery. Certainly, no other kingdoms have asked ransom for her, so we must assume the worst. But Lady Agatha is correct. It is because of what happened to Queen Ophelia that our royals *must* know how to fight and defend themselves, not simply rely on others."

I bit back the smart remark resting on my tongue that it *still* hadn't saved Ophelia or her baby. Drawing more attention to myself just really wasn't necessary.

"Please step forward and receive a practice weapon from my assistant Gerald, and then we can begin." Ty nodded to the middle-aged man standing silently beside the weapons table and then stepped aside, clearly expecting everyone to do as he instructed.

After a moment's hesitation, the ladies began to move as instructed, and I stole an opportunity to inspect our newest tutor.

He was handsome, which I was beginning to think might be a requirement to work at the palace. Taller than me, probably taller than Lee too, Ty was broad-shouldered, and his arms, which he folded over his chest, were thickly corded with muscles. He was clearly no stranger to combat himself, which was likely why he'd been picked to tutor us. It seemed odd, then, that he wasn't wearing a soldier's uniform. Instead he was just dressed in a loose cream shirt and soft black pants, much like the rest of us.

It was somewhat heartening to see that most of the other ladies had used their common sense when getting dressed this morning and opted for pants over skirts. It wasn't like women weren't *allowed* to wear pants, but in the years since the Darkness, our once progressive country had really regressed back into old ways and older traditions.

Making my way over to Gerald to receive my practice weapon, I discovered it harder than anticipated to pull my attention from Ty. There had to be something in the air within palace grounds because acting like a hormonal hussy wasn't like me *at all*. First Lee and that explosive kiss we'd shared, and now I found myself inspecting Ty—

picturing what he might look like without his shirt. I'd put money on it that his chest and shoulders were just as muscled as his arms...

"Ahem," someone fake-coughed, ripping my focus back to what was in front of me. "Your sword, m'lady," Gerald, a nondescript man in the palace guard uniform, said in a bored voice. In his hand he held out a wooden sword, and I took it from him with a grimace.

It'd been *years* since I'd needed to train with a wooden sword. Bloodeye had started me on edged blades when I was barely seven years old, so it was going to take all of my creativity not to stand out during this lesson.

"Form two lines, facing one another," Ty instructed us, and the ladies all shuffled around to oblige. "Because of Lady Hyacinth's early departure, we have an uneven number of people, so I'll be filling in the gap. We will rotate partners every so often to keep you on your toes."

He summoned Gerald up to demonstrate with him what we were learning, and I had to bite my cheek not to laugh—not that the two of them were bad swordsmen by any means, but just at how painfully simple the moves were.

Sighing internally, I turned to my partner and gave her a small smile of encouragement. At least I knew this was one class I wouldn't be failing. The damn binding oath wouldn't let me.

"You ready?" I asked her, and she shrugged.

"I guess," she responded, waving her practice sword in front of her like some sort of magical wand. "My father always told me it wasn't a lady's place to handle weapons, though."

Frowning, I inspected her. She was roughly the same height as me but with a slimmer build and autumn-colored hair. Poor girl wouldn't last two minutes in the Pond.

"Well, I guess he was wrong if this is what the royals have instructed them to teach us." It was the politest way I could phrase it, but the scowl creasing her brow suggested she'd taken offense at me calling her father wrong. "Whatever," I quickly added before she could get all uppity at me. "Let's get on with this."

Hefting my wooden sword, I tested its weight before *slowly* starting the three-step sequence Ty had just demonstrated to us. Each time before my "blade" reached hers, I needed to coach my partner on how to block the strike, so when Ty called for us to switch partners, I let out a sigh of relief.

My next handful of partners were only moderately better than the first, and I found myself spending a huge part of the morning just instructing them on how not to get whacked with a wooden sword. It only got worse as Ty changed the sequences to progressively harder combinations, and by the time it was my turn to pair with our tutor, my arm ached.

"Feeling fatigued, Lady Callaluna?" he teased me, swinging his wooden sword like it weighed nothing at all.

Grumbling under my breath, I rubbed my aching arm and took

the second's break to stretch out my tight lower back. "Maybe if you were a better tutor, I wouldn't have needed to spend the entire morning correcting everyone's form."

His dark brows shot up, and a small smile ticked at his lips. "Oh, really? You think you have these forms down?" I glared a challenge at him, too tired to rein it in, and he understood exactly what my face was saying. *You're damn right I have them down, you assface.*

Okay, maybe he didn't receive the message in those exact words, but his narrowed eyes said he was going to test me. Damn it all to Zryn, why couldn't I just keep my mouth *shut* for once?

"Well then, let's make this more interesting for you, *m'lady*," he murmured in a dangerous sort of voice that made me shiver and my nipples tighten. Shit, something really was wrong with me. "Ladies, mix things up a bit. You're free to use any of the techniques learned today. Think of it as a mock fight and do whatever your instincts tell you to do."

Turning back to me, he threw down a challenge of his own in the way he smirked at me. "Ready?"

Hefting my practice sword—that felt like it was made of lead—I grinned back at him. "Born ready, Ty."

Without another second of banter, Ty launched his attack. For such a big guy, he moved with the speed and grace of a striking cobra, and I was embarrassed to admit to myself how much effort it took to parry his strikes.

I did, though, and it was clear to see how surprised he was by how well I held my own.

"You're holding back," he grunted when I ignored the fourth or fifth opportunity to strike at him with a more advanced move—one that he *hadn't* taught us.

Cocking a brow at him, I flicked my tongue across my dry lower lip to moisten it. "If I were, the oath would have zapped me by now."

Ty scowled, and I could tell he was trying to work out how I'd sidestepped the magic that required I put in maximum effort during the trials.

"Huh," he muttered, countering my attack with one of his own. "Sneaky. All right, ladies!" He raised his voice to be heard, even as he continued "fighting" me. "Feel free to deviate from the skills I have taught you today. Use whatever you can to disarm your opponent."

I huffed and gritted my teeth. It'd obviously clicked that his instructions had been to use any of the techniques *he'd* taught. A second later, when he left me another wide opening and I ignored it out of stubbornness, a sharp spike of warning shot through my brain, and I hissed.

"Bastard," I growled, but his only response was a wide, self-satisfied grin on his sexy fucking face. Ugh, why did that shadow of stubble need to enhance his strong jaw so much?

Unrestricted by specific phrasing, my objective was clear. Disarm my opponent.

"Curse you, Ty," I muttered only just loud enough for our tutor to hear. "You stupid fool. This is on you, now."

His head tilted in confusion, but it was soon pretty clear what I meant. Our mock battle picked up intensity in sheer seconds as I gave just as good as I got from the well-accomplished combat instructor.

Before long, we were both sweating and breathing heavily, and all the ladies had abandoned their own mock battles to stare at us with open mouths. Damn it all to Zryn, talk about painting a damn target on my back.

Eventually though, the fatigue in my arm from swinging the training sword for hours, combined with the relentless assault from Ty's considerably stronger strikes, caused me to falter, and I watched as my wooden blade flew from my fingers and skittered across the sawdust-covered ground.

"That was an interesting fight, Lady Callaluna," Ty murmured when neither of us had moved for a long moment. We'd just stood there, our chests heaving as we stared at my wooden blade on the ground. "I take it this is not your first fight."

"No," I replied, not caring to elaborate. "It's not."

He gave a short nod, then glanced over at all the ladies who had been spectating our fight. "Breaking for lunch early. The queen is unwell today, so you're at your leisure until this afternoon's test."

Everyone scrambled to return their weapons to Gerald. I staggered over to my own to pick it up, but Ty got there first.

"Huh." He frowned, holding my wooden sword in his huge fist and turning it over.

"Problem?" I snapped, holding my hand out and feeling more than a bit peevish. Staying under the radar as an imposter in Lady Callaluna's life was imperative and displays like the one we'd just put on did *nothing* to help.

"Yes," he replied, holding out his own practice sword for me to take instead.

The *problem* was instantly obvious. His weapon weighed a mere fraction of mine.

"Huh," I echoed his noise of surprise and glanced up just in time to catch his death glare shot at Gerald across the arena. "It's not a big deal; probably just shoddy workmanship."

"No such thing around here," he replied in a growly rumble that both frightened me and—dare I say—turned me on a bit. Without a doubt, he was going to make a big fuss about it.

"Well, I'm not bothered by it, so if you could please let it go, Ty?" I laid a hand on his forearm to try and refocus his attention away from Gerald and onto me. It worked, but I really wasn't prepared for the intensity of his gaze when he looked down at me.

"I can't do that, little one. Someone is trying to sabotage you, and that goes against the rules. I need to report this to Lord Taipanus." His brow was furrowed and his eyes fierce, but the hand he laid over mine was gentle and caring. The mention of the King's Snake caused me to suck in a deep breath of fear though.

I shook my head firmly. "Don't," I snapped. "The last thing I need is more attention. Besides, that surely wouldn't end well for *you* as combat instructor. If I hadn't been disadvantaged by a weighted weapon, I very well could have beaten you. Me, a lady aristocrat." I almost choked over that last part, but I needed to maintain my disguise.

He still scowled, but his heavy sigh told me he agreed with me. I used the opportunity to withdraw my hand from under his. Not because I really wanted to, but there were still a couple of ladies in the arena and it probably wasn't a good look to have me touching our tutor in such a way.

"Fine," he grudgingly agreed. "But I'm rearranging the fights for the test this afternoon. You'll be even more disadvantaged by the time your test comes around because the muscles of your arm will have hardened. I'll need to give you an easier opponent."

"No," I argued. "You can't do that. I won't knowingly send someone to the bottom of the scorecards and then watch them poison themselves at dinner tonight. Even fatigued as I am, these girls barely stand a chance. Give me Lady Gracelin; at least it'll be a slightly fairer fight with her." The brunette beauty had shown at least some degree of competency with her sword during our sparring session, and she had that gleam in her eye that said she'd do anything to win.

Ty rubbed the back of his neck, watching the last of the girls leave the arena while he thought over what I'd said. Finally, when we were alone, he nodded.

"Very well, if that's what you want. But in exchange, I want something from you."

I was unprepared for this to be a negotiation, so I squeaked a noise of shock when his huge hand took the wooden sword from mine and he strode across to the table to dump both of them.

"Come on," he prompted, taking my hand as he neared me again and tugging me along behind him. "We only have just over an hour, and you'll need to eat as well."

CHAPTER 9

"Wait, where are we going?" I demanded, hurrying to keep up with his long strides as we navigated hallways of the maze-like palace. I sounded outraged, but I was quietly burning with curiosity.

He glanced over his shoulder at me and grinned. "Why? Worried your reputation might be sullied by being seen with a soldier?"

"Should I?" I asked back, thinking about all the time I'd spent with Lee—a gardener—the day before. "I guess that is something ladies would worry about, isn't it?" This last part was mostly under my breath, but the bark of laughter from Ty made me acutely aware he'd heard me.

"Riverdell really must be a different sort of city than Lakehaven," he chuckled. "I'm taking you to get some of this amazing muscle rub that my friend makes. It'll help to keep your arms and legs from seizing up with acid. Don't worry. I use it all the time, so I can vouch for how well it works."

It actually sounded like a great offer, so I quit arguing and let him lead me around the palace to an old stone structure covered in creeping ivy.

"After you, m'lady," Ty instructed me as he held the heavy wooden door open, and I stepped through into the shadowy gloom. "It's brighter up at the other end," he told me as the door swung shut behind us. His hand rested in the small of my back, and I made no attempt to move away from his touch as we wandered past furniture covered with dusty old sheets.

"What is this place?" I asked in a hushed whisper, not wanting to disturb the peace of the building. It clearly hadn't been used in a *long* time, if the layers of dust and creeping plants along the insides of the walls were any hint.

Ty gave a soft laugh, his thumb swirling circles beside my spine as he indicated I should go through the next doorway. "It used to be Queen Ophelia's garden retreat," he informed me. "After she died, no one wanted to step foot in here. They all said it was haunted by her ghost."

"But not you?" I questioned, still looking around at the dust-covered paintings and lamps. I could see the area he was steering us toward at the end of the room, where the walls and ceiling gave way to murky glass and sunlight streamed in.

"No, my friends and I found it to be kind of soothing in here, so it turned into a bit of a hang-out spot when we didn't want to be found by our, uh, superiors." Ty gave me a small smile when I glanced up at him, then nodded to the glassed-in section. "I have a pot of the muscle cream on the table down there."

We made our way past the dusty lounges until we reached the table in question, and I nearly jumped out of my skin when someone popped out from behind it.

"What in the name of Zryn's hairy old balls? Lee?" I screeched, seeing who it was that had just scared several years off my life.

"Calla!" he exclaimed, looking just as shocked as I was. "What, ah..." His wide-eyed gaze flickered to Ty and then back to me. "What are you doing here? With *him*?"

Rolling my eyes, I placed a hand over my thundering heart. "I take it this is your friend who made the muscle cream?" I asked Ty, and he shrugged with a smirk. Judging by his lack of surprise, I gathered he'd already known Lee would be here.

"That's right, you two have already met." He grinned at both Lee and me, but it wasn't a malicious one. "Lee, I needed to grab some of that muscle relaxant cream you made for me. *Calla* here needs some."

"Don't call her that," Lee muttered, ruffling a hand through his blonde hair. "That's my thing."

Smothering a laugh, I tried not to roll my eyes at their banter.

"Whatever," Ty snorted. "Sit your butt down, little one. We need to get this cream on fast before you stiffen up."

Grumbling under my breath about his choice of nickname for me, I perched on the edge of a motheaten velvet armchair.

"Here." Ty handed me a soft, woolen sweater that smelled like Lee. "Hold this over your chest if you're modest, but I need your shirt off to get at your biceps."

Modest, I was not. But Lady Callaluna surely was.

"Can't you just give me the cream, and I can do it myself?" I protested, tugging at the end of my long braid. "This doesn't seem like a very ladylike thing to do."

Lee smirked at me when I said this, and I felt my cheeks heat slightly. "So, even in Riverdell this is pushing the lines of decency? Damn, I was hoping that it might be the last city left unchanged by this old-fashioned crap."

"Already planning a move there, huh?" Ty joked, and Lee shrugged. "Come on, Lo, we promise to be utter gentlemen and not ogle your goodies." He waggled his eyebrows. "But time is ticking, and we need to get this cream on. It's got to be massaged into the muscle, and unless you're also crazy flexible, I don't see how you'll manage that yourself."

"Lo?" I repeated, giving him a *what the hell* look as I wiggled out of my shirt and held Lee's sweater to my chest. It wasn't like I was naked underneath—and I could already feel the stiffness starting to set into my upper arm—so there was no sense in arguing further. In fact, I didn't even really need Lee's sweater, given I was wearing both a bra and a white tank top under my shirt, but it seemed like the ladylike thing to do.

"Yeah, Lo." Ty dragged over a footstool and sat in front of me. "Little One. LO. Seeing as Lee says I can't call you Calla, and this sort of seems like we've passed the point of *Lady Callaluna*, don't you think?" He balanced the small pot of herbal-scented cream on the arm of the chair I was in and scooped out some onto his fingertips. "Arm," he ordered, and I obliged, extending my right arm, which had taken the worst of the strain.

"I think," I replied, then paused to groan as his strong fingers massaged the cream into my muscles. "I think that if anyone found out I was making friends with my tutors while I'm supposed to be winning myself a husband, I'd be the next one drinking poison at dinner."

"Well, best that no one finds out then," Lee murmured, perching on the edge of the table and watching us with his intense blue gaze.

"No one finds out what?" a new voice asked, and I tensed.

"Relax, Lo," Ty murmured in a quiet rumble. "That's just Zan. Hey Zan! We have company."

"What? Who? And why are you—" The new addition abruptly cut off what he was saying as he entered my line of sight, and I gave a small finger wave. "Oh. Company."

"Hello," I greeted him with a small smile. It was taking all my effort to maintain an even voice and not start shaking at the combination of these three men in such close confines with me. Not because I was scared—I could handle myself in that situation—but because they were all so *damn* attractive. "Zan, right? Ty said you're teaching tomorrow's class?"

His gaze glued to me, the new guy just nodded silently, then turned his scowl to Lee. "Care to explain?"

Lee shrugged and grinned. "Nothing to do with me; Ty brought her here."

"Ty?" Zan prompted, but the big man was focused on massaging my arm with strong soothing strokes, so he didn't bother to respond for a long time. Longer than what could be considered polite or comfortable, given they were speaking *about* me and not *to* me.

"Other arm, Lo," Ty rumbled and started rubbing the cream into my left arm despite it not having taken anywhere near the strain as my right. "I'll fill you in later, Zan. For now, use your manners and say hello to Lady Callaluna."

Wiping the scowl from his face, he turned to look at me once more. "I do apologize, Lady Callaluna; that was rude of me. I just wasn't expecting to find anyone in our sanctuary, let alone one of the ladies competing in the Royal Trials."

Flushing, I realized what he was saying. I'd invaded their *secret* space, and it was more than inappropriate for me to be there.

"You're absolutely right," I agreed, swatting Ty's hand off my skin so I could shrug my shirt back on. "I shouldn't be here. I wouldn't want any of you to get in trouble for showing favoritism or anything. Thank you for the cream, Ty, Lee, but I'll be going now." Rushing now in my embarrassment, I didn't even bother re-buttoning my shirt as I scrambled out of the chair and hurried through the room. "Thanks again, bye!"

Whatever they said in response was muffled when I closed the door firmly behind me, then rushed through to the main entrance. One thing was for damn sure—I needed to get my head in this stupid game and quit fawning over the sexy tutors.

There was so much more at stake than just a marriage proposal. This was my *life*, and I didn't intend to make any stupid slipups thanks to silly-little-girl crushes on my teachers.

CHAPTER 10

U pon returning to the combat arena, I did everything I could to avoid Ty's gaze. If I was going to make it through three weeks of trials alive, I needed to keep my wits about me. That meant shoving all memory of his strong fingers rubbing my sore arms firmly out of my mind. It *definitely* meant not eyeing him up and wondering what it'd be like to have all of that hard, manly body pressed up against me without the hinderance of clothing between us.

Would he be a skilled kisser like Lee?

Snap out of it, Rybet! I mentally chastised myself and shook my head to clear the all too realistic images from my mind.

Our test for the afternoon was a series of one-on-one fights to display what we had learned in the morning session. Ty, along with an older man in a Royal Army uniform, would judge, scoring each match to rank everyone's skills. And choose tonight's poisoning victim, I guessed.

"You'll be battling with metal weapons this time," the older man, who'd introduced himself as Commander Hansel, announced to us. "Don't worry; they're all blunted so you need not fear for your lovely skin. They just pack a little more weight behind your blows to emulate a real fight."

He and Ty began handing out short swords to each lady, and when Ty reached me, he made a point of checking my blade all over—even running his thumb down the blunted edge—before handing it to me.

I took my blade and moved to sit in the bleachers with the rest of the girls, giving it a few test swings on my way. It was lighter than my wooden practice sword, which was probably a good thing, despite how much Lee's cream had helped my aching arms.

"Ladies, let's keep this clean and civil," Commander Hansel instructed us. "Tutor Ty and I will score you on blows landed, with an automatic win if you disarm. If neither of you can disarm your opponent, we will stop the fight when the first lady reaches five touches. Clear?"

Everyone nodded and murmured their understanding, so the commander unrolled his parchment to announce the first pairing.

I watched each match with focused intensity, if for no other reason than I was avoiding looking over at Ty, who spent just as much time staring at me as watching the combatants. The ladies had improved since we'd started our training in the morning—not by much, but at least they mostly held onto their weapons.

Gracelin and I were announced around the halfway mark, and I pushed up from my seat, noticing how loose and pain free my arms were. I'd need to beg a pot of that cream from Lee before I went back to my real life.

We each took our places in the arena in front of Ty and Commander Hansel, with the other girls watching from the bleachers. Our fight started out smoothly enough; I simply concentrated on defending her blows using the techniques we were supposed to have learned in the morning session. Whenever there was an easy opening, I scored a strike against her.

When I reached four strikes, Gracelin was visibly fuming. Sweat beaded on her forehead, and the looks she gave me could have been enough to kill just on their own.

"You know, it's a bad look if you win this match," she hissed at me between erratic swings of her sword, "considering the preferential treatment you've been getting from Ty all day. Mostly during the lunch break."

Her accusation made me falter, and she landed her first blow. It was a harder-than-necessary smack to the thigh, and I winced at what felt like a sharp tip stinging my skin. It had to have been my imagination, though, as I'd seen Ty run his thumb down the edge to prove it was blunt. But he hadn't handed Gracelin hers, the commander had.

"I don't know what you're talking about," I responded to her, circling out of the way to regain my balanced fighting stance.

"Oh no?" she snarled back, quietly enough that no one else could have heard her. "I'm pretty sure that Ty would be executed if the royals found out he's seduced one of us. We're supposed to be off limits, you know? Untouched. Maybe they'd execute you both right there at the dinner table." Her eyes sparkled with malice, and I instinctively glanced over at Ty.

Just that second of hesitation must have been all she needed, as she rushed at me with her blade extended. It was only by my own intuition that I dodged at the last second, causing her *definitely* sharpened tip to sink through my shoulder rather than my heart.

What happened next was all a bit of a blur.

Gritting my teeth, I wrenched myself off Gracelin's blade. She made a wild, animal sound of anger, but barely had time to lift her sword again before I'd smacked her wrist hard with the flat of my own weapon and forced her to drop it.

"What in the name of Gewalt is going on here?" Commander Hansel roared, snatching up Gracelin's blade and inspecting the bright red of my blood staining the tip. "These were all supposed to be blunt weapons!"

"Lady Gracelin," Ty snapped in a voice like ice. "Explain yourself immediately."

The pretty brunette gaped at our tutor in outrage. "Explain myself? I have nothing to explain! I had no way of knowing my sword was sharpened! You handed them all out," she accused Commander Hansel. "If anyone is to blame, it's you!"

Ty and the commander shared a long, loaded glance while I stood there clutching my shoulder and feeling blood stream down my shirt.

"I'm taking Lady Callaluna to the medical wing," Ty said eventually in a voice that brokered no arguments. "I trust you can score these remaining tests without me?" Hansel gave a short nod, and Ty turned to me. "Are you okay to walk, or shall I carry you?"

"It's my shoulder, not my feet, Ty," I snapped, the pain making me angry. "Just point the way."

His eyes narrowed at my waspishness, but a small smile played at his lips as he ushered me to the arena exit. "Gewalt save me," he breathed, invoking our god of war as we made our way back to the main palace. "You'll cause me a heart attack before these trials are over, Lo. I can already tell."

I snorted a laugh, finding the whole situation suddenly ridiculous. "At least your last days will be exciting," I offered, chuckling and then groaning as pain radiated through my shoulder once more.

Ty sighed and gripped me around the waist while we walked, looking like he was supporting me, but it felt a whole lot more like he just wanted to touch me. "Lee's going to kill me for getting you hurt. Prepare yourself for some fussing."

CHAPTER 11

The mention of Lee had my stomach all in knots of nervous excitement the whole way to the medical bay, but I was disappointed to find just a stern-faced old woman attending.

Ty was shooed away almost as soon as we got there, too, so I had to endure a full hour of stitches and potent-smelling ointments alone before I was permitted to leave, myself.

The nurse had warned me while I was undergoing her care that the herbs used on my wound would likely make me drowsy, but I really didn't understand the full effect of her warning until I was leaving dinner that night.

Just like the night before, we'd each been handed a flute of sparkling wine before the meal began. Even though this time we knew what to expect, it didn't make it any easier to see one of the kingdom's sweethearts writhing and foaming at the mouth as she died a painful death by poison.

Thankfully, I was spared the added stress of being seated with the princes this time, as they'd been given seats amongst the other ladies. Presumably the idea was that they'd "get to know" different girls each night, even if it did feel like at least one of them was staring at me for the entire meal.

I barely ate my food that night, which was unheard of for a kid from the Pond, but every bite I took made me feel physically ill. The girl who'd died had been my first sparring partner of the day, so I couldn't help but feel I'd let her down. I *could* have taught her so much more, but I was more concerned with keeping my own secrets.

It was a rough shove in my injured shoulder as all of us left the dining hall after the royals that jolted me from my depressive thoughts and caused me to cry out.

"Next time I won't miss," Gracelin hissed in my ear as she shoved me again into the wall. "You don't belong here, *Callaluna*. Everyone knows it too."

With that unimaginative threat, the curvy aristocrat stalked away with her nose in the air, leaving me shaking my head and wondering how in the name of Aana I'd ended up in this situation. It took all my willpower not to follow after her, grab her by the hair, and smack her perfect face into the stone wall... but that wouldn't be ladylike. Would it?

"You look lost in thought," Ty murmured, seeming to pop out of thin air and almost startling me. Almost. "How's your shoulder?"

"Fine," I replied, yawning a little and waving a hand to dismiss his concerns. "I've had worse."

Ty made a low sound in his throat and narrowed his green eyes at me. "You have?"

"Huh?" I blinked up at him, my head suddenly swimming with fatigue. "I meant..." *Crap, dammit Rybet. Focus!* "I meant it *could* have been worse. If she'd been stronger or better with a blade."

The combat tutor nodded slowly, and I could tell he wasn't totally convinced by my cover-up. Zryn's balls, what did I care? I got the feeling that Ty, or even Lee for that matter, wouldn't go running to have my head cut off even if they did find out I was an imposter.

Not that I should be taking unnecessary risks, nonetheless.

"I'm just crazy sleepy all of a sudden," I admitted to him, feeling every bit the delicate lady I was playing.

He frowned, his eyes scanning my face before he nodded sharply. "I'd better see you to your room then. I've already caught enough bitching from Lee about letting you get hurt during combat today. Gods save me if he found out I left you alone in this state."

I snickered at the idea of lovely, sensitive Lee yelling at musclebound Ty. "That's sweet of you, thank you."

He grunted at that, clearly not accustomed to being called *sweet*. "Yeah well, it's not totally selfless. I sort of have a little bit of a crush on you, Lo."

"Oh?" I teased, feeling all kinds of girlish excitement at this confession. "I thought this morning you wanted to kick my ass."

He barked a loud laugh as we came within sight of my door. "I *still* want to kick your ass, Lo. But your fighting skills only made me want to get to know you more."

We'd reached my room, and I paused with my back resting against the door as I peered up at the big soldier, unwilling to end this moment of honesty so soon. But guilt nibbled at my gut, souring the fizzy tingles he caused with his words.

"Ty," I started, chewing my lip. "I know you and Lee are friends..."

"We are," he agreed. "He, Zan, and myself have been friends for a very long time."

I nodded. "Right, so I just wanted to be upfront and tell you that he kissed me last night. So whatever is happening here..." I indicated between the two of us and shrugged.

Ty's brows shot up in surprise, and I instantly regretted saying anything. I'd just kind of assumed Lee had told him already, since they were such great friends.

"Lee kissed you?" he repeated, and I nodded. "Interesting. That's against the rules."

I bit my lip, trying to squash the panic rising inside me. Had what Gracelin said been true? Would these gorgeous tutors be executed if the princes found out? Surely Ty wouldn't say anything;

Lee was his friend.

Sucking in a breath, I braced myself for what he might say next. "Ty, you won't—"

The rest of my question was cut off abruptly by the crush of his lips against mine. Stunned, for a moment I was motionless. Then my wits caught up to me, and I threw caution to the wind. If Ty wasn't concerned with these "rules," then who was I to judge?

Reaching up with my good hand, I grabbed onto the back of his strong neck, pulling him down closer to me as my mouth opened to allow him entry. He needed no further coaxing as his tongue met mine in a frenzy of motion, engaging with me in the same passionate way that we'd fought one another in the practice arena. It was hurried and heated and every molecule of my being seemed to warm with his touch.

I was like a woman possessed as I pulled Ty closer, feeling the heat of his body through my thick, layered evening gown. Once again, I cursed the Darkness for regressing women's fashion so badly that I was almost entirely covered from neck to ankle in fabric. Sleeves, it had seemed, had been necessary to cover my bandages for dinner.

"I should go," Ty finally said, panting as he pried his lips from my own, "before the bedroom behind this door becomes too tempting to resist."

Drowsy from the pain medication and filled to overflowing with lust, I opened my mouth to invite him in. But one thing stopped me.

Lee.

"Don't worry about Lee," Ty ordered me, like he could read my mind. Or maybe just my guilty face. "I'll have a chat with him and let him know that he's not the only one who knows how to break rules."

"Ty, that's not—" I protested, but a quick, bruising kiss made me forget the rest of that sentence.

"I'll see you around, Lo," Ty promised me, throwing me a sexy wink as he hurried back down the corridor, and then he disappeared from sight.

For a long time, I stood there, sagged against the door with my fingertips pressed to my lips. One thing was for damn sure, I was the *furtherest* thing from queen material right now. Even if my orphaned upbringing could have been ignored.

Snorting a laugh to myself, I turned the door handle and let myself into the ornate guest rooms.

"Hey." Jules came rushing out of the bedroom the second I had closed and latched the front door. "How was it tonight? Did they…" She trailed off, pulling a face that I assumed was meant to represent death by poisoning.

"Uh-huh." I nodded, flopping down on the overstuffed couch, then groaning at the spike of pain through my shoulder. "I never thought much of our monarchs... but I never expected this."

Jules sighed heavily and sat beside me, taking my wrist in her hands and starting to work on the multitude of satin-covered buttons running up the inside of the sleeve. "I think a lot of people would be shocked if they knew what was going on here. It's probably a good thing one of the princes will be ascending soon." She paused, her lips pursed. "But do you think they'll be any better?"

"Based on what I've seen of them so far?" I wrinkled my nose and grimaced. "I honestly don't know. I hope so, for the good of Teich. But I doubt they'll change if a raging bitch like Gracelin becomes queen."

Jules snorted. "Never going to happen, babe. It'll be you or no one."

"Me who? Rybet Waise, Pond orphan? Or Lady Callaluna, imposter?" I rolled my eyes and grinned. "Yeah, that'll be the day. I just need to make it out alive and then disappear."

"Something else is bothering me," Jules pondered aloud as she helped me maneuver my injured shoulder from the dress. "Why now? Why are the king and queen suddenly willing to abdicate for one of their sons and a girl chosen through a series of ridiculous tests? They're not old or ill..."

"I wondered the same thing," I admitted. "I have a theory about it, but it's just a feeling more than anything."

Jules sat back and gave me a stern look. "I'm not stupid enough to ignore your *feelings*, Ry. Spill it."

I hesitated a moment, considering how crazy this would make me sound. But this was Juliana. She already knew I was walking the thin line of abnormal.

"Okay, so I think it's to do with the balance of magic. Our royals are supposed to have more than just magic of their own. They're supposed to hold the balance for the entire kingdom, right?" I paused to check that she was still with me. I loved her to pieces, but she really wasn't the brightest star in the sky. "Well, that's not exactly what *these* royals are doing for us, is it?"

Jules shook her head, frowning slightly but seeming to follow. "No, they have their own magic, but the rest of the people lost theirs. Not to mention the Darkness. But they saved us from the plague in the end."

"Barely." I snorted. "And that was the young princes, not the king and queen."

My friend's eyes widened, and her brows rose. "You think they don't have enough magic to keep the land alive? So they're... passing the job to one of their sons before anyone sees them fail?"

I shrugged. "Maybe? Haven't you heard about what's been happening in the Wilds?"

"Yeah, the fact that it's turned from wild jungle to barren wasteland overnight? It's being talked about a lot in the Pond at the moment. You think that has to do with the land's magic?"

"Don't you?" I arched a brow at her. "Anyway, that's as far as

I've gotten on my theory, not that it really helps us at all. Hey, I was thinking I might try to get down to the dungeons and check on Flick." Jules seemed to freeze at my suggestion, and I rolled my eyes. "Don't worry, I won't be stupid and get caught. I just think I might know someone with access to the dungeons." My mind wandered to Ty and that explosive kiss we'd just shared.

"I don't think that's a good idea, babe," Juliana replied, shaking her head. "Whoever this person is, you can't trust them. You can't trust *anyone* here."

I frowned. "So, what? We just leave him down there for three weeks thinking he's going to be executed? Or that no one cared enough to try and save him? He's just a kid, Jules!"

"No, that's not what I meant," she rushed to disagree. "Look, just... leave it to me, okay? I'll get a message to him and make sure he's okay. They don't watch servants anywhere near as closely as they watch you *ladies*."

"I hope you're speaking figuratively," I murmured, thinking about my less than appropriate rendezvous with both Lee and Ty. Then again, did I really care? I faced possible death every night at dinner just for being a competitor in the Royal Trials. I may as well enjoy myself along the way.

Jules poked me in the good arm. "So we're agreed then? I'll handle Flick and make sure he's okay; you just stay alive long enough to find a way out of this mess."

"I suppose," I reluctantly agreed. "This week seems easy enough so far. At least I have combat nailed, and I can't imagine history, or whatever it is, is all that difficult."

Jules beamed. "That's the attitude! You'll be Queen Callaluna in no time! Or... Queen Rybet? Yeesh, you might need to pick a new name, girl. That was just a nickname Bloodeye gave you anyway, wasn't it?"

Scowling, I whacked her with the back of my hand and stood up to shed the heavy dress. "Come on, *servant*. Let's see if we can order some late-night snacks from the kitchen. I could barely eat at dinner." My jaw cracked with a heavy yawn. "And then bed. Yes?"

"You got it, Your Majesty," Jules teased, making her way to the door and throwing me a cheeky wink over her shoulder. Smartass.

CHAPTER 12

The looks I got from the other ladies as I entered the library were nothing short of horrified. Apparently tight leather pants and a tailored, sapphire-blue shirt were *not* considered acceptable attire for a lady in a library.

Whatever. I'd woken up aching and sore from the combat class the day before and was in no mood to navigate skirts. Just because I'd worn a couple of pretty dresses lately didn't suddenly make me a professional at skirtsmanship—this, I was aware, wasn't a word. But it should be.

"Politics, intrigue, and etiquette," announced our tutor for the day—Zan. It was the same guy who had walked in on Ty massaging my arm at lunch time in their sanctuary, and I flushed with embarrassment as his gaze swept over me. "That is what you'll be learning with me. You have two classes, as you do in all of this week's subjects, and today's will focus on both politics and etiquette."

My stomach sank to my feet as I noticed almost every lady in the room sitting up a bit straighter, like they were excited for this class. Not so much me.

Combat was a subject I'd known I'd excel in. It came as easily to me as walking or breathing. As for botany and alchemy, we all seemed to be on the same footing, and I could fairly much trust my instincts to make it through that class alive. But politics? *Etiquette*? I was so doomed.

"This morning, I will be presenting you with a series of portraits of some of the kingdom's most frequent guests. I'll show you what they look like and tell you their name, title, and country of residence. You must memorize these for your test this afternoon." His dark, serious gaze swept the room, and I gnawed at my lip with nervousness. His eyes were so dark they almost looked black from where I sat. It was more than a little unnerving.

"At the end of my session this morning, you'll be allowed some time to yourselves to conduct your own research here in the library. I expect you all to find at least one interesting fact that you could use as a conversation opener with each dignitary. Your test will comprise of a mock introduction wherein you curtsey, greet them by name, and begin a polite conversation to show you have done more than simply memorize their face." Zan tapped a small device against his palm, waiting for his words to sink in and be understood. Or that's what I assumed his dramatic pause was for, anyway.

"If you're all comfortable, we shall begin." He aimed his device at the ceiling, from which a large screen dropped down, and the first image of a rotund man in a velvet suit appeared. I marveled at the technology, which had to be a carryover from before the Darkness. much like how most of the city still operated running water and functional sewerage within their homes.

"Duke Gobardlian of Richtenstein," Zan began, pointing up at the more-than-life-sized image of the duke. Somehow, Zan's rich, warm voice made even this utterly dry subject seem engaging, and throughout the next sixteen images—two for each of the seven kingdoms, plus Teich—I didn't lose my focus once.

I did sort of wish we'd been given a pen and paper to take notes, but given that the whole point was an exercise in rapid memorization, it would have defeated the purpose somewhat.

"That's all of them," Zan announced some time later. "I hope you all paid very close attention because I will not go through them again. For your test, three dignitaries will be chosen at random for you to 'greet,' but I suggest you brush up on *all* of the ones I've introduced you to so far. You have two hours."

Around me, girls hurried into motion, rushing into the rows upon rows of books within the royal library. No doubt they were all heading for the section containing facts and information about all of the surrounding kingdoms—it was what I'd do if I didn't have more pressing matters on my mind. Memorizing just a handful of geographic facts was a hell of a lot smarter, and a better use of time, than something personal to each dignitary, like what their favorite dog was called.

"Not in a hurry, Lady Callaluna?" Zan asked in a somewhat mocking tone when I was the last one left seated. "Don't tell me you already know all of these faces? You can't possibly get top marks in both Lee's *and* Ty's classes and then also know *every* important person discussed today." Despite his almost condescending tone, his face looked intrigued. Like he hoped I *could* kick this class's butt.

Giving him a tight smile, I brushed my somewhat wild blonde hair over my shoulder and stood from my chair. "Not at all, Zan. Just taking a moment to collect my thoughts and consider the best way to attack the challenge. Is there an index section, by any chance? To save me from wandering aimlessly through the shelves."

A slow grin spread across his lips, and he gave me a small nod. "Very good start," he murmured, and I hadn't failed to notice not one other girl had paused to consider an index. Luckily for me, I'd spent a good deal of time in the Lakehaven public library when I was growing up—not just learning to read, but because it was the warmest place to be during winter when you truly had no home or warm clothing.

Zan showed me the low stack of small drawers that contained

index cards for every book in the royal library. The sheer number of drawers almost made my eyeballs burst from my head as, at a glance, there had to be ten times as many drawers as the public library. Still, this was the palace, and if there was one thing I was learning it was that the royals were selfish bastards.

"Thank you." I dismissed him with a tight smile, but waited for him to leave my line of sight before going to the drawer I had in mind. Unlike my competitors, I was unconcerned with learning fun facts about Maledonia or Carpresney. There was another aspect of the test that had my stomach knotted up and sweat dripping down my spine.

Quickly, I located the section I was looking for, then replaced the card into the drawer before setting out in that direction. There would be no explaining why I was in that section if I still held the index card in my hand.

Thankfully, I wound up in a hidden-away area of the mezzanine level, far away from geography, politics, and whatever other sections the other girls were buzzing around like a swarm of brightly dressed hornets.

Releasing a little bit of the breath I held, I ran my fingers over the spines of the books until I located one that sounded like what I was looking for.

Curtseying and Bowing: How to Survive Court Life.

"Thank Aana for that," I muttered to myself, pulling the book off the shelf and flipping it open to the contents. "Should just name it Curtseys for Dummies. That's what I need here, anyway."

I'd managed to survive this far because each time we'd come into close proximity to the royals, we had already been at the dinner table where only a small head dip had been needed. Or so I'd gathered by copying the other girls.

Here, though, we would be getting scored on the perfection of our curtsey, something I was doomed to fail at if I didn't learn what the hell to do—and learn *fast.* Just that first contents page already made me groan in fear. There was more than one type? And which one you used depended on what status the person you were greeting held?

"I'm screwed," I whispered, closing the book and smacking it lightly against my forehead.

"How so?" Zan's rich voice asked from close behind me, and I sucked in a breath of fright. How in the gods did people keep sneaking up on me? I was a thief! It should not be this easy to startle me!

Whirling to face him, I tucked the book behind me and gave a tight smile. "No reason. What are you doing up here?"

Zan's brows rose, and a small smile played at his lips. "What am *I* doing up here? This is the royal library, and I'm a scholar." He had a valid point, and I pursed my lips. "What book do you have there, Lady Callaluna?"

"Hmm?" I blinked up at him with my very best confused expression. "What book?"

His smile spread wider. "The one you're hiding behind your back. Show me." He held his open palm out to me, and I shook my head in refusal. "No?" He laughed, sounding surprised. "Lady Callaluna, surely you aren't so childish..."

My eyes narrowed at his insult, but before I could formulate a snappy retort, he'd stepped into my personal space. His strong, manly form boxed me against the shelves, and while I desperately scrambled to regain my scattered wits, the fucker reached behind me and plucked the book out of my weakened grip.

"Zan," I growled, "I understand you're one of our tutors but—"

"If you're going to give me a warning about propriety around a lady, you can probably save it... Calla. Or is it Lo? I can't keep up with all these affectionate nicknames." He arched a brow in challenge, then turned his gaze down to the book in his hand. "Well, that's not what I expected."

Cheeks flaming with heat, I ground my teeth together and tried to wrench the book from his grip. To my dismay, he held firm and even went so far as to hold it up out of my reach.

"Very mature, Zan," I hissed at him. "Give it back. It's not what I was looking for anyway."

"Oh no?" he challenged. "Well good, you won't mind me sitting here and reading it then." He stepped back from where he'd caged me against the shelves and sank into a large, leather armchair.

For a long moment, I stared at him. But when he gave me a smug smile and proceeded to flip the cover open, then *read aloud,* I lost my temper. Marching over to him, I held my palm out and glowered death.

"Zan. Please give the damn book back; I don't have that much time to—"

"To learn the appropriate forms of curtsey for all seven kingdoms that we share borders with?" He arched one of those chestnut brows at me and gave me a smug smile. "I have no doubt that *as a lady* you would have been learning these forms from infancy... especially now."

His mention of *especially now* had to do with politics. Teich had always been the ruling kingdom for all other kingdoms. When our magic imploded, so too had theirs. When our technologies failed, so had theirs. Because of this, tensions between each nation had been more than sensitive ever since, so whenever dignitaries visited, everyone walked on eggshells.

Or that's what I'd gathered from the snippets of conversation I'd picked up on previous visits when I'd lightened the purses of a few nobles here and there.

"Well, clearly it's not a high priority in Riverdell; otherwise I wouldn't be in this current predicament, now would I?" I needed that damn book, so I decided to switch from denial to snappish sarcasm.

Zan flipped over a few more pages, focusing his intense dark eyes on the book—thank Aana—rather than me. "This Riverdell sounds like a fascinating place, Lady Callaluna. I'll have to visit some time."

Grinding my teeth together in an effort not to punch my

etiquette tutor in the gorgeous face, I released a loud, vexed breath. "Zan," I asked as politely as I could with my teeth still clenched in anger, "may I please have the book back?"

"Huh," he murmured, slapping the book closed and looking up at me in curiosity. "And Ty said you had no manners."

I'd take that up with Ty later, but in reality, that was the extent of my attempt at manners. Abandoning all pretense of ladylike decorum, I darted forward as quick as a whip and snatched the book from Zan's grip. Unfortunately for me, he was no *lady* either and retaliated with equal speed as he grabbed me around the waist and pulled me clear off balance and into his lap.

"Luna, darling," he teased. "Falling for me so soon? What will my brothers think?"

"Brothers?" I frowned, struggling in his grip and getting nowhere. "Ty and Lee are your brothers?"

Zan made a noise in his throat, then shrugged. "As good as. We're all very close."

"Do you intend to let me go?" I asked in a sharp tone, desperately trying to ignore the fact that I was sprawled halfway across his lap with my palms pressed to his chest, our faces mere inches apart. "I hardly think this would be *appropriate* behavior. As an etiquette tutor, you would know that."

His grin spread, but he didn't make any move to release me. "I think you're a woman of many secrets, Luna... so I'll cut you a deal."

I snorted and rolled my eyes at what was undoubtedly about to be a terrible deal. They always were. "Go on then," I said in a dry voice.

"I'll help you learn these correct curtsey forms if you provide me with some entertainment." His dark eyes glittered with something dangerously close to mischief. "Tonight, instead of dinner, there will be a dance. It's meant to be a surprise—an additional etiquette test to see how you all handle yourselves dancing with noblemen."

"Fantastic," I muttered, rolling my eyes. "Another excuse for those arrogant pricks to objectify the women who are literally dying to become wife to one of them."

Zan barked a laugh. "Lee wasn't joking about your distain for the royal princes. Well, this is going to be fun. When one of the princes asks you to dance—because one of them will—you're to find a reason to kiss him."

My jaw dropped open, and I almost forgot the compromising position he held me in.

"Sorry, fucking what now?"

Zan smirked. "You heard me, little Luna. Do we have a deal?"

I narrowed my eyes at him in suspicion. "How will you know if I do it or not? Last I checked, tutors weren't invited to dinner."

"They needed more dance partners for all you lovely ladies, so some staff have been invited. In disguise of course."

"Of course," I murmured, thinking of the masks we were all required to wear. It'd be almost impossible to pick Zan out of a crowd if the masks were elaborate enough and especially if there were more than one brunette man... which was sort of a given. Shit. I was going to have to do this...

"And you'll teach me all seven curtsey forms before we have to return for the test?" I pursed my lips and squinted at him, searching for some additional loophole.

His lips twitched like he was holding back a smirk of triumph, and I seriously considered punching him in the balls and winging the damn test. But there was the small matter of getting poisoned if I was bottom of the class, not to mention the damn binding oath forcing me to try my hardest to win.

"I will," he agreed. "But you won't have much time left to find discussion topics. Some of these forms are really difficult."

It was my turn to look smug, and I gave him a sly wink. "I don't need any time. You already gave us all the information we needed."

Zan threw his head back and laughed at this, and I instinctively clapped a hand over his mouth to shut him the hell up. We *were* still in a library, and I desperately didn't need someone coming up to the mezzanine and finding me in his lap—willing or not.

He removed one hand from my waist to pry my fingers from his face. "Not just a pretty face and abrasive personality, huh, Luna?" He held that same palm out to me to shake. "Do we have a deal?"

Grumbling to myself, I scowled but took his offered hand. "Deal. But if I get beheaded for being inappropriate with a royal, I *will* come back and haunt your snarky ass."

He snickered another laugh but *finally* released me. "Well, let's get on with this then. Hopefully you're a fast learner."

CHAPTER 13

After my crash course in perfect-form curtseys from all seven kingdoms *and* our own, I was able to bluff my way through the afternoon test without anyone so much as suspecting I might not have had the gentile upbringing of a lady.

That night Jules must have been given the memo about it being a dance as well as dinner because she had the most absurdly elaborate gown waiting for me after my shower.

"Seriously?" I questioned her, eyeing the offensive garment. "No, you're joking. Aren't you?"

Juliana looked almost offended as she folded her arms over her chest and glared at me. "Are you questioning my fashion sense, Rybet Waise?"

"Wouldn't dream of it," I hastily replied, backing right the fuck down. Jules was as vicious as a street cat when she thought she was being insulted.

"Good. Now get dressed." Her stern scowl was enough to make me drop my towel and scramble into the scarlet, beaded creation.

It was no better on my body than I had expected.

Full length sleeves skimmed the backs of my hands and covered the sticky bandage on my shoulder wound. Beaded fabric cut severely across my throat, entirely covering my front, but the back more than made up for that small level of modesty. Just a thin strip of red glass beads held the sleeves together across the top of my back, leaving the rest of my flesh exposed all the way down to the crack of my ass. In the front, a dramatic split cut up the left leg, stopping barely short of the red lace thong Jules had provided me with.

"Babe, how the hell am I supposed to move in this without flashing my vagina to every man and his friend?" I pouted as I turned back to my best friend, but the look on her face said it all. I was wearing this dress whether I liked it or not.

"You're sneaky. You'll make it work." She waved off my concerns as she held out a pair of matching high-heeled shoes. "Come on, you'll be late if you keep fucking around."

I sighed heavily but didn't waste breath arguing. High heels weren't something I'd a lot of experience with, but given I could balance on a wire when required, they should really pose no serious challenge.

"If someone tries to cop a feel tonight, it's on you," I muttered at her as she quickly styled my hair into a simple updo. "I can't promise I won't break his hand."

Jules scoffed. "Uh-huh, unless it's Lee the gardener or *Ty* the soldier?"

My face flamed, but I shrugged. "I guess their hands might survive." If I were being totally honest, I hoped they *would* be in the invited guests for the night—and that they'd try to cop a feel. *That* I'd allow.

While Jules finished my hair and makeup, I let my mind wander onto that scenario. But for some gods-cursed reason, when I was picturing those hands on me... there was a third set. Zan's. Ugh!

"Done," Juliana announced, snapping me from my sordid thoughts. "Now go and impress. I have to pop into the city to take care of... business. But I should be back before you, so no more late night make-out sessions, okay?"

I rolled my eyes at her and smiled. "Yes, *mother*. Have fun with your 'business' tonight." I threw her a knowing wink and headed out of our rooms to make my way to dinner.

The walk from my room to the great hall actually worked well in my favor, giving me time to adjust my gait to the new shoes and heavy dress. Every damn inch of the thing was crusted with beads, including the train, which trailed on the ground behind me. Hopefully there would be some way to pick it up if I really did need to dance.

I paused just outside the great hall. Shit. Dancing. How could I have let that slip my mind? I didn't know court dances! I only knew bawdy tavern dances, which were usually danced to dirty, offensive songs like "The Bonnie Princes' Whore Woman" and similar catchy tunes.

Actually, that would have been a strangely appropriate choice of song during the Royal Trials.

"In or out, Callaluna," an annoyed-sounding girl prompted me. "Some of us have a royal husband to woo, you know."

Stepping aside, I allowed the pretty redhead to brush past me. I couldn't place her name, but recognized her as being close with Gracelin.

"They're all yours," I muttered, sneering at her back. "I wish you all the happiness."

The girl turned slightly to give me a baffled look, then sniffed, tugged her mask down, and tossed her hair as though dismissing me. I followed her because what other options were there? Refuse to play this sick game any longer and suffer who knows how painful of a death thanks to the binding oath magic?

Stupid me for not thinking that one through.

Inside the great hall, the long banquet table had been removed and a handful of well-dressed, masked gentlemen mingled with the ladies who'd already arrived. We were down to eighteen now and would be losing another one tonight.

"What do you think this is all about?" Agatha asked, coming up beside me and bouncing slightly on her toes with what I could only assume was excitement. Strange girl.

I shrugged, feigning ignorance. "Looks like they're mixing it up tonight with a dance." I nodded to the string quartet in the corner playing gentle background music. "Because poisoning an innocent girl at a dance is so much more acceptable than the dinner table."

Agatha's lips twisted into a grimace. "Maybe they've decided to skip it tonight, seeing as we're already one down from the first night?"

"No harm in wishing," I murmured with a sigh. "But I doubt it." The mousey girl said nothing in response, and I glanced down at her. "You'll be fine, though. I imagine your test went okay today?" We'd been tested in private, so no one could cheat by using someone else's knowledge, but Agatha just had that studious, bookish look about her.

She nodded. "Of course, Zan gave us all the info we needed during the class section. I spent the lunch break taking a nap."

Despite the fact that one of our peers was staring down death, I couldn't help snorting a laugh. I wondered how many of the other ladies had worked out that their lunchtime "assignment" had been a wild goose chase. When Zan had done the initial introductions of each dignitary, he'd given us a key piece of information pertaining to each person's country of origin. That was all that had been required to pass the test.

"Do you think the princes will ask us to dance tonight?" she asked me, her voice devoid of all emotion so I couldn't get a read on how she felt about that.

My teeth nipped at the inside of my lip in a nervous habit as I thought about Zan's confidence that one of the princes *would* ask me to dance. "I'd say so," I responded to Agatha's question. "The whole point is to get to know their prospective brides, isn't it?"

"Or make them feel better about killing us all off," she muttered under her breath, but it was enough to make me raise a brow under my mask. It was sort of comforting to know I wasn't the only one horrified by the brutal form of "elimination" that these trials required.

I sighed. "Something like that."

Any more conversation between us was interrupted by the arrival of two tall men in black fabric masks. They made some polite greeting that I paid little attention to and handed us each a glass of wine.

My attention was elsewhere. Despite my common sense telling me not to, I found myself scanning the room for our tutors. It was a pointless endeavor though. In the dim, candlelit room, it was impossible to identify them based on hair color, and several of the "gentlemen" even wore hooded cloaks. Damn them.

"Looking for someone in particular?" the gentleman who stood in front of me asked but sounded like he didn't really care about the answer. "The royals will be arriving soon, if that's what you're waiting on."

When I automatically wrinkled my nose and frowned, I was

thankful for the red, beaded mask I wore. At least no one could see my honest reactions to the pond-scum we had for a royal family. I'd never met the woman—she'd died when I was a baby—but I could safely say I wished Queen Ophelia were still alive. Everyone who'd lived during her reign spoke nothing but good of her, yet here we were—our own king poisoning ladies every night for his own entertainment.

"I wasn't," I replied without elaborating, then changed the subject. "Apologies, where are my manners? I'm Lady Callaluna, and you are?"

"Oh, er," the man stuttered, his eyes darting around the room as though looking for answers.

Shaking my head, I waved it off. "Secret identities tonight, got it. No need to come up with a weak lie."

"Right," he sighed, sounding relieved.

I sipped my drink and inspected his hands, clutching nervously at his own wine glass. They were calloused, and his nails were cut to the quick. Servant of some sort for sure. "Makes sense," I agreed. "Forces all the ladies to *assume* they're engaging with nobles, regardless of whether their companion lives in a mansion or"—I took another look at his hands and then his shoes— "or the stables."

He visibly startled at my guess, and I allowed myself a smug smile.

"How'd you know?" he demanded, his shoulders slumping slightly.

I shook my head again and took another sip of wine. "Don't worry;

it was a lucky guess. You have a piece of hay stuck to your boot."

His scramble to unstick the offending piece of hay was covered by a flurry of motion as the main doors flew open and the royals made their grand entrance. Looked like tonight, unlike the last two nights, we were all expected to show the correct level of respect as they made their way to the thrones at the end of the room.

Biting the inside of my cheek so hard it almost bled, I tucked my foot and sank into the customary Teich curtsey—deep enough to befit our monarchs' presence.

The five of them—King Titus, Queen Filamina, and their three sons—swept past me in a flutter of expensive silks and floral perfumes. My pose wobbled slightly, and for a second I saw a vision of myself faceplanting at the queen's feet.

Thankfully, that clear image was enough to scare me into freezing on the spot and successfully staying on my feet until we were permitted to stand once more.

Releasing a long breath, I almost forgot my "gentleman" companion until he spoke.

"Nerve-wracking, isn't it?" he murmured, and I glanced up to see his attention glued firmly on the royals. "Queen Filamina frequents the stables, and it never gets easier."

I gritted my teeth, thinking of their callous disregard for life in the Royal Trials. "They're certainly not what I expected."

"That's one way to put it," Agatha agreed, tapping me on the elbow to announce her presence. "Callaluna, there's a buffet over there if you want to eat anything before you lose your appetite."

I smiled at her and gave a polite nod to the stable hand before following Agatha to the food table. She had a damn good point. Once I saw someone foaming at the mouth and convulsing on the floor in a pool of sequins, beads, and silk, I really wouldn't feel like eating.

As we filled our pathetically small plates, a herald made an announcement to welcome everyone to this "splendid affair" of a dance and instructed us to all "enjoy ourselves." Like that was so possible under the circumstances.

Agatha was approached by another masked gentleman before she'd even started on her food, but she—unlike me—had been raised in an aristocratic household. She wouldn't have dreamed of turning him down to eat mini pastries and quiches with me.

"Lady Callaluna," a husky voice spoke from slightly behind me, and I turned ever so slightly to see who had recognized me. Not that it was a hard task. Ladies masks and dresses didn't afford us anywhere near the anonymity that the men gained.

A quick glance at the signet ring on his gloved hands had me gritting my teeth and turning to face Prince Thibault fully. "Your Highness. How lovely to see you again."

Praying to Aana that my fortune would hold, I sketched another quick curtsey and successfully returned to standing without any major incidents.

"How I wish I believed that." The prince smirked. "Such a shame it sounded like you were eating broken glass as you said it."

I sighed, giving up my attempt at cordial manners. "I can't imagine why," I drawled sarcastically, letting my gaze drift over the crowd once more in a clear act of disrespect. "It's not like you and your family are a pack of mentally disturbed, bloodthirsty murderers or anything."

Prince Thibault actually choked on the sip of wine he'd just taken, and I got the satisfaction of watching him cough and splutter for a moment before he replied.

"Lady——" He broke off, shaking his head and patting his mouth with a handkerchief. "You realize you could be executed for saying things like that?"

I shrugged and tossed another gulp of wine back like I really didn't give two shits. This was, in fact, news to me. I had been under the impression that our citizens' right to free speech included insulting the princes to their faces. Guess not.

"At least I'd be dying having spoken the truth," I told him, stubbornly defending my opinion, "as opposed to dying by my own hand with a glass of poison. And for what? Having a crappy day in combat class?" I was getting fired up again now and turned my death glare on the arrogant son of a bitch. Damn him for being so freaking huge, though. I was forced to look *up* at him, and that was a position I didn't appreciate in my current mood.

"From what I hear, that would never be a problem for you," Prince Thibault muttered with an edge of... curiosity? Hard to tell. I'd already had way more wine on an empty stomach than I really should have had. "I understand you were injured, though. How is that?" His gaze raked over me, and I squinted to try and make out what color his eyes were under his mask. Damn candlelight made everything so difficult.

"Just fine," I snapped. "Not that it makes a difference in the long run. Only one girl is surviving this *game* of yours, and I think it's a safe wager that it won't be me." Feeling depressed at the discussion *once again* about everyone dying, I gulped the last of my wine, then wiped my mouth off on the sleeve of my dress. Classy. Also, a dumb idea, as the beads scratched my lips.

Prince Thibault let out a long-suffering sigh and ran a hand through his dark hair. "We didn't ask for this, you know?" His voice had taken a somewhat bitter edge that made me do a double take. "Our family is not native to Teich, and the Royal Trials are. This was the only blend of customs that the high priests of Sal would allow."

I rolled my eyes and snorted. Sal was our god of destiny and also the ruler of the other gods. But magic had abandoned us a long time ago, along with the gods. "Sure, you let those magicless windbags dictate something as important as this." I gave him a sarcastic smile and hoped the effect wasn't lost thanks to my mask. "Whatever helps you sleep at night, Your Highness. Now, if you'll excuse me..."

"You have somewhere better to be?" he challenged me, sounding surprised. Arrogant prick.

"Yes," I responded in a haughty tone. "Anywhere but here."

Replacing my empty glass onto the table, I whirled around to make a dramatic exit with the train of my red dress flying. Thwarting what I'd pictured as a very impressive moment, I whirled—as imagined—then walked straight into a hard man-chest.

"Oomph." I groaned, rubbing at my forehead where I'd just collided into Prince Alexander's golden torque. Amazing. Another one to deal with. Could my night get any better?

"Lady Callaluna, how delightful," the prince greeted me, and I sighed.

"Prince Alexander—I mean, Your Highness," I replied through clenched teeth. "It must be my lucky night. To what do I owe the... *pleasure?*"

The oldest prince said nothing for a moment, and even under his mask I could tell he was scowling at me. The tight slant to his mouth said it all.

Looking past me, he asked his brother, "Why does it sound like *pleasure* means something totally different in Riverdell?"

Thibault barked a laugh and stepped forward to clap his brother on the shoulder. "It does. Good luck, brother." With that encouraging sentiment, Prince Thibault left me alone in the oldest prince's intense gaze.

"Was there something I could do for you, Your Highness?" I pursed my lips and looked for some way to escape. Where was that stable hand? Surely I could attach myself to him for the rest of the night?

The prince made a fake-sounding cough and gave me a tight smile. "I was just coming to ask how the food was, but now I find myself wanting to dance. Must be this song." His lips curved in a mocking smile, since the musicians were taking a break as they flicked through sheet music to find their next tune. "Would you do me the *pleasure*, Lady Callaluna?"

He held an open palm out, and I stared at it like he was presenting me a venomous *drachen*. Dancing with a freaking *prince* was sure to lead to disaster. "I—"

"I'm afraid I must insist, Lady Callaluna," he interrupted my weak protest. "You've already rejected my brother's advances. Do you really want to draw any further attention by rejecting me as well?"

I was sorely tempted to call his bluff and tell him that *yes*, I would be willing to take that risk to avoid touching his bloodstained hands. But across the room, Lord Taipanus stared straight at me with his cruel, snakelike gaze.

Despite how foolish, brave, and reckless I was in almost every other situation, I wasn't stupid enough to ignore my instincts when it came to the King's Snake.

"Sure," I snapped, reluctantly placing my hand on his. Of course, my reluctance to touch him was more symbolic than anything—

given that he, too, wore soft leather gloves. Frustratingly, they wore those gloves as religiously as their masks and signet rings. How was a common criminal supposed to learn anything about a man when he was so carefully concealed?

The musicians began a new tune, and Prince Alexander expertly led me into the cleared section of the room, which already had several other couples preparing to dance.

"Calm yourself, lady," he murmured, his lips dangerously close to my ear as he tugged me closer into a dance hold. "An accomplished gentleman can lead any dance, regardless of his partner's skill level. Just give up control for a few minutes and *follow*."

I snorted a laugh at this advice, but what other options were there? Fight him and demonstrate to the whole damn room how utterly *un*accomplished I was at court dances? Or maybe try and fake it and end up flat on my ass? Yeah... neither seemed like the most conducive route to maintaining my disguise.

So against my better judgement, I *let* him lead.

Our first few steps were a bit rocky, until Prince Alexander pointed out the little loop in my dress train which allowed it to be picked up out of tripping range. After that, well, it was strangely enjoyable.

Not my partner, obviously, but the simple glide and twirl across the floor, perfectly timed to the skilled instrumentals... it was soothing. For a short time, I let my mind wander away from my distasteful partner and pictured someone more desirable in his place.

What would it be like to dance with Lee? Or Ty? Somehow though, I knew it would be Zan who would be the best dance partner. It was all too easy to imagine the prince's strong grip on my body as Zan's. Even if he was a cocky, overconfident jerk himself.

When the song started to draw to a close, I found myself almost wishing it had gone longer.

"Not bad, Lady Callaluna," Prince Alexander murmured as he twirled me in close and pressed my back to his chest. "See how nice it is to relinquish control every now and then?"

A small smile arched my lips almost without permission, and I let him twirl me back out, then dip me low for the dying notes of the song.

Blame it on the wine or the fact that I'd just been picturing Zan in his place, but the memory of my deal with Zan skittered into my mind, and before I knew what the hell I was doing... my lips were against his. *His*. Prince freaking Alexander's!

"Shit," I breathed, breaking away almost as fast as our lips had engaged. "I'm so sorry; I don't—"

The rest of my spluttered apology was cut short as Prince Alexander shifted his grip on me, pulling me close once again and claiming my mouth in a bruising kiss. Suspended as I was in his embrace, off balance with my hair almost brushing the floor, I was as helpless as a kitten to fight him. Instead, I took his advice and *let him lead* one more time.

By the time he'd placed me back on my feet and released his grip, I was beyond dazed and confused. My lips tingled like they'd been stung by a hundred tiny bees, and my heart was racing fast enough to leap from my chest.

"Ah," I started. "That was—"

Before I could finish my lie, claiming that was inappropriate and unwanted, the smashing of glass and a woman's scream jolted my awareness back into my surroundings.

Not five feet from where the prince and I stood, a silk- and chiffon-clad lady had collapsed to the marble floor. Her body convulsed in the throes of death, just as we'd witnessed the two nights prior.

Those bastards hadn't even given us the respect of a toast so we had some warning. They'd just slipped it in when everyone's guard was down, when—gods forbid—some of the ladies might have been enjoying their evening.

My belly full of wine lurched painfully, and I pressed a hand to my mouth.

Prince Alexander said nothing, but his hand on my chin turned my gaze away from the dying woman. Like that made a difference.

"I can't do this," I gasped out, shoving his hands off me and dashing out of the great hall. Fuck the royals. Fuck their customs and traditions and *etiquette*. I couldn't bear to be in the same room as those murdering bastards a single second longer. And to think I had just *kissed* one of them! What the hell was wrong with me?

I kept running until I hit fresh air, then collapsed in a heap on the damp grass, sobbing.

CHAPTER 14

How long I lay crumpled like that in my expensive evening gown, I had no idea. But it was Lee's gentle touch on my spine that brought me back.

"Calla," he breathed, crouching down to gather me in his arms as I peeled myself off the grass. My arms wrapped around his neck like vines, and I clung on with a death grip as he lifted me from the ground. "You're shivering. We need to get you warmed up."

Words were too difficult to form as my teeth chattered violently, so I just pressed my face into the side of his warm neck and cuddled closer as he walked. My mask had pushed up and its beads tugged painfully at my hair, but I wasn't unlatching my grip on Lee for anything.

He didn't speak again as we crossed the grass, and I vaguely recognized that he was taking me to the sanctuary that he shared with Ty and Zan. Logically, it seemed like a terrible idea. Running out of the great hall without being dismissed, then engaging in a late night rendezvous with royal servants? It wouldn't do me any favors if we were caught, but on the other hand... did I really care?

"Wait here," Lee murmured in a soft voice, placing me down gently on a velvet-covered couch and detaching my arms from his neck. "I'm going to grab you some blankets and a heating appliance."

I gave him a vague nod and pulled my knees up to my chest when he stepped away. It really wasn't even a cold night, but I'd been in this state often enough to recognize shock when it hit me.

"Lee?" a man's voice called through the darkness. "Are you here?"

Lee's response was a hushed whisper that I couldn't make out, but a double set of footfalls followed, and when Lee reappeared, carrying blankets, he was accompanied by Ty.

"Lo," the big man said with almost a sigh of relief. "You're here, thank Aana."

Ty sat on the couch beside me and tucked one of Lee's blankets around my shoulders, hugging me in tight to his side with a huge, muscled arm.

"You were looking for me?" I murmured through numb lips. "Why?"

Ty snorted. "Why? Don't be dense, Lo. We all saw you take off out of the great hall. It just took a while to find where you'd gone."

"Oh," I replied, noticing for the first time that they were dressed in fine suit pants and crisp, white shirts. Of course they'd been there, posing as gentlemen for this newest installment in the Royal Trials. Although Death Trials would have been a more appropriate name for them. "Won't you get in trouble for leaving?" I paused, frowning. "Will I?"

It had been the furthest thing from my mind at the time, but now a shiver of fear coursed through me thinking what sort of punishment these sick royals might cook up for my show of disrespect.

Both Lee and Ty paused before responding, which did nothing for my anxiety. "I think you'll be okay," Lee finally answered. "Zan has a, ah, special relationship with the royals. He stayed behind to smooth things over."

I laughed a bitter sound. "Of course that arrogant ass would actually be friends with the princes. I don't want him sticking his neck out for me, though. If they feel the need to punish me, then I can take it." Because it couldn't be any worse than dying of poisoning. Unless it was torture... that'd suck.

Ty shook with a laugh of his own and pulled me into his lap. "That's better," he commented, wrapping his arms around me tightly. "Lee, weren't you getting a heating appliance?"

Lee nodded and disappeared back into the darkness.

"You have heating appliances here?" I asked, tucking my head into the crook of Ty's neck to get comfortable. "I didn't think they worked anymore."

"They don't, most places. The palace grounds seem to have been spared a lot of the damage the Darkness brought, so a few little things still work, like heating appliances and artificial lighting in a lot of the palace." Ty shifted under me, then reached up and tugged my mask from where it was tangled in my hair. "You looked stunning tonight, Lo. You have no idea how badly I wanted to steal you away."

"Why didn't you?" I prodded. "I would have much rather danced with you than that... *prince*."

Ty chuckled, his broad hand stroking down my bare back under the blankets. "I should have. That asshole could have done with getting his ego bruised a bit." He paused for a moment, tracing circles down my spine. "But I saw you kiss him."

My whole body tensed, and a wave of revulsion ran through me. Not at the kiss... but at the fact that I'd enjoyed it. I'd *enjoyed* kissing that sadistic, murdering bastard, and then a girl had died.

"I don't want to talk about it," I snapped, my brow pulling down in a deep frown. "It was a stupid deal I made with Zan for his help during etiquette class today."

"Ah, I see." Ty nodded slightly. "I should have known it was something like that. Fucking Zan."

"Hey, watch it," Zan himself barked out, appearing from the shadows and flopping down on the couch beside us. "'Fucking Zan' just fixed things up with *you-know-who* and saved lovely Luna from a public whipping." I gasped, staring at him with wide eyes. "I accept thanks in the form of sexual favors." He said it with a playful wink, so I knew he was joking. Or at least half joking. Arrogant ass.

"Looks like you already have that part taken care of," I replied with a smirk, noticing the faint smear of red lipstick on his mouth. Zan frowned at me, and Ty reached out and smacked him lightly on the forehead.

"You've got lipstick on, idiot," Ty rumbled with something that sounded like anger, and I smiled. He had been such an angry, intimidating brute when I'd met him, but now he was proving to be quite the protective teddy bear.

Zan scowled and muttered a curse under his breath as he wiped his mouth off on the sleeve of his dark shirt. "It's freezing in here," he commented, changing the subject. "Where's Lee?"

"Gone to pull out a heating appliance," Ty responded. "But that's why we have blankets."

Zan's eyes narrowed, and he inspected the heavy blanket draped over Ty and me. "You're probably going to need to share. Those heaters take forever to kick in." Without asking permission, he scooted closer and tugged a bit of blanket over himself. Frowning, he lifted the blanket and inspected my feet, where they were tucked on the couch between him and Ty.

"Lovely Luna, why are you still wearing those uncomfortable looking shoes?" He arched a brow at me, and I shrugged.

"I don't know," I admitted. "I think I'm in shock and still a bit drunk."

"That explains why you're still trembling," Ty commented. "And why you went through with Zan's insane dare."

I wanted to laugh, but a wave of shivers skittered through me, and I cuddled tighter into Ty's warmth. Zan just sighed and removed my shoes for me. He then tugged my feet into his lap, where he wrapped his own warm hands around them and rubbed little circles into my frozen toes.

Lee returned then, carrying two small, metal boxes, which he set up on the table facing us before pushing a series of buttons to turn the heat on.

"I don't know if this is the right thing or not, but I always find hard liquor helps a shock," he offered, pulling a bottle of scarlettberry rum from under his arm. "Or alternatively, I can go and find some tea?"

His thoughtfulness brought a small smile to my lips, and I reached out of the blankets to accept the rum. "This will do perfectly. I'm already half-drunk, so what's a little more?"

Lee smiled back at me and handed over the alcohol. "I'll grab some candles so we're not just lurking here in the dark."

"Won't that draw attention?" I worried, glancing up at all the glass panels of the section we were in. "Are we even allowed to be here?"

Zan grunted a noise, his fingers pausing a moment on my feet. "It'll be fine; we come here all the time. No one will bat an eyelid."

Lee nodded his agreement and disappeared again, only to return moments later with an armful of candles, which he started setting out around our area and lighting.

"This is an interesting mark," Ty observed, stroking a finger across my birthmark. "Is it a scar?"

I shook my head, twisting the cap off the scarlettberry rum. "I don't think so. I've always had it, so I just figure it's a birthmark." Taking a long sip of the burning alcohol, I moaned my appreciation. It was *really* good scarlettberry rum. Then again, anything found within the palace was going to be better quality than anything I'd had in the Pond.

"Share," Zan instructed, holding out his hand for the rum, which I reluctantly handed over. I was instantly glad I did, though, as he held my gaze and wrapped his lips around the neck of the bottle in what was one of the sexiest non-sexual acts I'd seen in a long time.

Okay, ever.

What the hell was going on with me?

"Shit," I cursed under my breath, tearing my eyes from Zan and burying my face in my hands.

"What's up, Calla?" Lee asked, crouching in front of the couch and peeling my hands off my face. "What did you just think of?"

"Nothing." I shook my head. "I just... this whole thing, the craziness of the situation I'm in, just all sort of hit me. Is this seriously how my life ends? Dressed in expensive finery and sneaking around to see you three until I piss the wrong person off and get poisoned? How the hell did I end up here?"

The three of them were all quiet for a moment, which I sort of appreciated. It showed they were thinking about what I was saying, rather than dismissing my fears on reflex.

"It might be a shock, given everything you've experienced this far," Lee answered me in a careful voice. "But there was a lot more involved in the invitation process than just looks and status. If you got accepted, then it was fate."

"Fate?" I snorted my disbelief. "Lee, you don't honestly think I'm stupid enough to believe in our god of fate anymore? Trust me when I say I was never meant to be here. This whole thing is just one *giant* mistake."

Ty's grip on me tightened a fraction, and I glanced up at him.

"If that were true, then you never would have met us," the lethal combat instructor pointed out with an edge of vulnerability to his voice. "I refuse to believe that's an accident."

I couldn't help the bitter laugh that bubbled out of my chest, but I placed a gentle hand on his stubbled cheek and met his eyes unflinchingly. "Ty, this *friendship* I have with you and Lee... and Zan, I guess... it has no future. There will be no happily ever after for us; we can only make the most of the short time there is left. Even if circumstances were different and the Royal Trials weren't a factor, do you honestly think at some point you wouldn't ask me to choose between you?" I shook my head and hurried to continue before he could make weak protests. "No, this whole mess... it's my own stupid doing. Until I can see a way out that doesn't involve a funeral pyre or a bridal gown..." I trailed off with a shrug. "Well, until then, I can only do my best to have fun. Don't you think?"

Looking around at the three handsome tutors, I saw the predictable frowns on their faces and sighed. It felt like all I could do lately was talk about my impending death, and I still had zero ideas how I could save my own ass. It was starting to feel pathetic and whiny—not at all like me, which was just another example of how I'd changed in less than a week.

"So..." Zan spoke first, glancing at his friends before pinning me with his dark gaze. "It sounds like we need to turn this night around. Unless it'd help for you to talk about what happened tonight, Luna?" I shook my head frantically, shuddering at the memory of the girl dying on the floor mere feet from where I'd stood kissing one of her murderers. "All right then," Zan nodded. "Better grab us another bottle of rum in that case."

He handed the open one back to me, then scooted off the couch to fetch more liquor.

In the soft candlelight, I noticed a few changes to the area we sat in—most noticeably, the large pot overflowing with white flowers on the table.

"Hey, you found more ophelia blooms?" I grinned as I admired the beautiful plant. "So much for dying out, huh? You were just looking in the wrong place."

Lee looked over at the plant with a strange softness to his face. "Yeah, I guess so. It's weird, though. Just in the last few days they've been thriving. The small patch you found has already grown to maybe six times that size."

I smiled, strangely thrilled to hear the rare flowers were doing so well. "Maybe they just needed some love and attention in order to thrive."

"Don't we all," Zan muttered, rejoining us with *two* more bottles of rum. "All right, let's set ground rules. No talking about death."

"Or royals," Ty added, and Lee nodded his agreement.

"Done," I accepted, sipping from the open bottle I held. "And no personal questions. No asking about families or childhoods... or homes. Okay?" Because I struggled at the best of times to maintain my Callaluna disguise when *sober*. Trying to fabricate a luxurious, aristocratic upbringing when all I'd known was the watery, mold-infested, and crumbling buildings of the Pond would be damn near impossible while drunk.

"Agreed," my three new friends responded, and Zan returned to his seat on the couch.

"With all those topics off the table," Ty said, tugging me back into his chest, "shall we play a drinking game?"

Lee dragged over an armchair and got comfy in front of the

heating boxes himself. "What did you have in mind?"

"How about," I suggested with a sly grin, "sword in the sheath?"

Zan spat out the mouthful of liquor he'd just taken and started coughing. "What?" he gasped out, blinking at me in disbelief.

"What?" I shrugged. "As if palace servants don't know sword in the sheath."

"Uh, sure. But why do *you*?"

Pursing my lips, I gave the etiquette teacher a prim look. "What did we say about asking personal questions?" Zan grinned and gave me a nod. "Good, now does anyone have a deck of cards? I'll deal."

CHAPTER 15

Sunlight beat down offensively through the windows, and I groaned, covering my eyes. My head was pounding, and the insides of my eyelids felt like they were crusted with sand... or broken glass.

"Good morning, ladies," Lee greeted us, walking to a desk at the front of the room and dropping a stack of books onto it. They landed with a thump, and I saw Lee echo my own wince of pain at the sound.

Thank Aana, he clearly felt just as shitty as I did.

"Today we're learning about alchemy." He rubbed at his eyes, and I bit back a grin. He might actually feel *worse* than me. For a gardener, he was surprisingly crappy at lewd servant games. Almost as though he was proving my point, a long yawn escaped his mouth before he could continue on his "intro to alchemy" speech.

I didn't blame him, though. It was all I could do to keep my own eyes open, and I had my face propped up on my hands. Jules had given me a stern talking-to when she'd woken me up, which hadn't helped. Something about Ty scaring the shit out of her just before dawn when he'd dropped me off at my room passed out drunk.

As it'd turned out, despite Lee's total incompetence in drinking games, Ty and Zan had more than made up for him and seriously drank me under the table. Bastards.

"Lady Callaluna?" Lee's voice interrupted my half-asleep daze, and I startled. Blinking a couple of times to clear some haze, I took a wild guess that wasn't the first time he'd said my name.

"Huh?" I blurted out with all my natural grace.

"I said," Lee repeated with a small smile. "Can you please help me gather some equipment from the supply cupboard? You look like you could use some fresh air."

Gracelin and her little crew started giggling across the room, and I instinctively flipped them off. It didn't even register that a *lady* would never use crude hand signals until several shocked gasps came from my classmates.

Ah, crap.

Whatever, it was done now.

Gritting my teeth against blurting any Pond scum insults, I pushed off my tall stool and followed Lee out of the light-filled classroom. Our tables had already been set with beakers and a few other bits, but maybe we needed to fetch the actual supplies? Like the bits that we put inside the beakers? Truthfully, I had no freaking idea what was involved in alchemy and was just guessing.

"How do you feel?" Lee murmured as the door to the class closed, leaving us alone in the marble-lined corridor.

I snorted a laugh, rubbing at my tired eyes. "About as good as you, I expect. Whose crappy idea was it to play sword in the sheath again? I suck at that game."

A wide grin spread across Lee's weary, hungover face, and he rolled his eyes. "Clearly, so do I. Come on, this way." He tugged me by the elbow into a small storeroom underneath one of the many staircases.

Once inside, he closed the door behind us and flipped a switch, which lit the room with a dim, magic light.

"So, what supplies do we need?" I asked, scanning my eyes over the shelves filled with all kinds of jars and boxes. The whole room smelled strongly of dried herbs and preserving liquids, which made sense given some of the things floating in jars.

"Uh, none really," Lee admitted, giving me a sheepish smile when I cocked a brow at him. "I just wanted an opportunity to do this." He snaked a hand around my waist, tugging me in close to him and spinning us. My back met the door just moments before his lips met mine.

For a long, indulgent moment, I simply sank into his kiss. It was perfect, divine, and so incredibly taboo. Our late night meetings had been bad enough, but now we were making out in a supply room *during* a class for the trials? Oh yeah, I was utterly screwed if the gods really did still exist.

"Lee," I groaned as his lips left mine and started kissing a fiery path down my neck. "Is this..."

"A really bad idea?" he murmured against my skin. "Probably. Do you want to stop?"

All the air gusted out of me in a rush. "Gods no."

With this admission, I seriously couldn't help myself. My hands went to the collar of Lee's shirt, fumbling at the buttons to expose a bit of that hard, muscled chest I'd gotten a few glimpses of the night before.

He, too, seemed caught in the same fervor, lifting me with strong hands so that my legs could wrap around his waist, and his warm palm slipped under my long skirts. I'd been too damn hungover—or possibly still a bit drunk—this morning when Jules had dressed me in a huff. So I'd ended up in a floor-length, floral-patterned skirt with a closefitting, cream blouse. In fact, it made my tits look great, which I appreciated... especially now as Lee's lips caressed the curve of my breast.

"Calla," he groaned. "These last days have been torture for me. Seeing you and knowing..." He trailed off, but I think I knew what he'd meant.

"Knowing that I'll be dead soon? Forget about it," I ordered him. "Just make the most of now."

He paused, pulling back to stare at me seriously for a long moment. His hand that *wasn't* up my skirt stroked at my cheek as his beautiful blue eyes peered into the depths of my soul. "I'll do whatever it takes to keep you with me, Calla." His words seemed heavy, like they carried the weight of an oath. "With us."

I had never experienced the range of emotions running through me—it was all totally unchartered territory—so I had no idea what the hell to say back. "Thank you" seemed a bit weak and "don't bother" seemed so pessimistic. So instead... I kissed him.

He accepted my kiss without hesitation, and his hand slipped higher under my skirt, finding the thin cotton of my underwear and stroking a light finger underneath the band at my hip.

Mentally, I cursed Jules for remembering to give me panties today and considered whether it was possible for them to disappear through sheer strength of willpower. My hips pressed harder into Lee, encouraging him to take things further as my body tingled and buzzed with anticipation of what was to come. But right as his fingers moved to that heated, needy, cloth-covered area between my legs, he froze.

"Shh," he shushed me when I opened my mouth to protest. "Someone is in the corridor."

His voice was hushed, and I bit my lip to keep quiet as he listened. Moments later, he screwed up his nose in frustration and stepped back to gently return me to my feet. "We need to get back," he whispered to me, looking just as frustrated as I felt. "That was Lady Savannah and some others. The only reason they'd be in this wing is to visit our class."

"Crap," I cursed, tugging my clothes back into place. "Do I look okay?"

Lee ran his eyes over me. Slowly. I had no idea a simple look could be so damn arousing, but I was ready to pounce him again right then when his gaze returned to my face. "Shit, Calla. You look like you've been making out in a supply room, and I'm so turned on it feels like I'm about to explode."

My eyes bugged out. "We can't go back looking like that! Even if I don't care about my own life, I can't let you get in trouble with me."

Lee's lips pursed for a moment, and he frowned. "Okay, I'll grab some of these supplies and head back first. There's a powder room another four doors down, if you want to fix this gorgeous mess and then come back to class?" He snagged one of my white-blond curls that had escaped Jules' fancy, braided crown.

"Shit," I cursed again, imagining what the rest of it looked like after our make-out session against the door. "Okay, good plan."

Lee quickly gathered an armful of clay jars, then paused before exiting the room. His eyes closed, and he took a few long breaths through his nose.

"You okay?" I asked, frowning.

His left eye cracked open, and he gave me a playful scowl. "Shh, give me a sec." His eyes shut tight again, and he took a few more breaths while muttering under his breath, "Grandmama's underwear, moldy fruit, weeds in the gardens, Zan's dirty socks..."

"You good?" I checked when his eyes reopened, and he sighed.

"As good as possible. Don't take too long, okay? I'll worry." He smacked a quick kiss on my swollen lips, then slipped out of the supply room quickly before I could grab him to engage further.

A quick glance in the powder room mirror told me everything I needed to know. There was no fixing this. My cheeks were flushed and my lips red and puffy. The best I could do was to tuck away all the wild curls that had escaped my braided crown and pray that everyone assumed I had just gone a bit heavy on the makeup this morning.

Returning to the alchemy lab, I tried to slip in unnoticed. Of course, luck was not on my side, and I tripped over *something*, which sent me sprawling face first onto the floor. When I turned to see what had sent me flying, though, there was nothing there… Except Gracelin sitting at the nearest table and smirking at me like a demon.

A loud throat-clearing from the front of the room halted what could have turned into a nasty bitch fight, and I dusted myself off as

I stood once more. Lee met my embarrassed gaze with an unreadable look, and I cringed.

"Apologies, Tutor Lee. I must still be half asleep." The lie felt like acid on my tongue, but the guests standing beside him made me rein my anger in.

He gave me a tight smile and nodded to my vacant seat. "That's totally fine, Lady Callaluna. Lady Savannah was just introducing the newest participant in the Royal Trials. Her Highness, Princess Sagen of Asintisch will be filling the space that was vacated early by Lady Hyacinth."

My brows shot up, but I refrained from commenting as I slid back into my seat. Asintisch was one of the seven minor kingdoms that Teich had once ruled over, and if my memory served me correctly, Sagen was the youngest of seven princesses. Was that even allowed? Not that my knowledge of the Royal Trials was all that sound, but I was pretty sure all participants needed to be from Teich. Then again, the royals themselves weren't native to Teich, so maybe allowances had been made.

"Your Highness, please take a seat," Lee offered her with impeccable, courtly manners. "We have a lot to cover in this morning's class, so we really should get started." He turned back to Lady Savannah and the several guards dressed in Asintisch colors in a clear invitation for them to leave.

Savannah gave a sharp nod, her hawklike gaze sweeping over the rest of us in the room. "Your Highness, Ladies, it was lovely to see you all."

It could have been my liquor-damaged imagination, but I could have easily finished the remainder of her sentence, the part she hadn't said aloud. It was lovely to see us all... *alive*.

Sighing heavily, I rubbed my forehead and tried to get my head back into focus. I needed to be learning *alchemy*, not fantasizing about Lee's touch on my skin or speculating on why Asintisch had sent one of their princesses to compete and possibly die in these barbaric trials.

A rustling of fabric beside me alerted me to the fact that the seat Sagen had chosen was the vacant one beside me. Mustering up a friendly smile, I held out my hand to her.

"Hi, I'm Callaluna," I said quietly as Lee started the class. I had intended it as a nice gesture, but Sagen wrinkled her nose and peered at my hand like it was covered in shit. Her almond-shaped eyes flashed with disgust, and she flipped her glossy black locks over her shoulder.

"Don't speak with me," she hissed back. "I am royalty. Treat me as such."

Stunned at her frostiness, I let my hand drop back to the table and returned my focus to Lee. The last thing I needed was to make *another* enemy; Gracelin was annoying enough as it was.

I shifted on my seat slightly, trying to block the new addition out and listen to what Lee was saying. The rough idea, as I understood it, was that we were making potions. This morning we would practice the alchemical fundamentals by creating some harmless potions, then for our test we would be required to step it up a notch by creating a potion that would ignite *any* surface when thrown. Including stone and glass.

"Try not to mess this up," Sagen sneered at me as we began measuring out the required ingredients for the first potion. "I don't want your failures to influence my own class scores."

Despite the fact that her statement made little to no sense whatsoever, I let it slide. I was too damn tired to be arguing with a stuck-up princess over things that really didn't matter.

Biting my lip, I concentrated on *learning*. For once I wasn't even doing it because of the binding oath, I just genuinely wanted to learn what Lee was teaching. These subjects, alchemy and botany, they were clearly where his passions lay. When he was instructing, his eyes lit up with a fire that I'd only seen twice before—once on the couch in my room and once just now in the supply closet.

I blocked out all other distractions and followed his instructions, delivered in that smooth voice that sent tingles running down my spine and my belly fluttering every time he spoke my name.

"Now, if you're confident that you have completed all the steps correctly, please drink your created potions," Lee invited us. "If it you did it correctly, your fingernails will change to the colors you

173

chose with your crystal powder."

"What if we got it wrong?" a girl at the back of the room asked, sounding nervous. "Will it hurt us?"

Lee gave a half smile and shook his head. "No, these are starter potions. It might give you a different outcome, but nothing that will harm you. The effects will only last for a day or so, as well."

Mentally I ran through the whole process again, checking that I'd remembered everything. My instincts were tingling, which suggested I'd forgotten a step, so I scooted off my stool to doublecheck the supply counter on the side of the classroom in the hopes something might jog my memory.

Seeing nothing unusual, a step I might have missed, I shrugged and returned to my table, where Sagen was admiring her new scarlet fingernails.

Of course she'd gone bloodred. It suited her.

I inspected my own vial of clear liquid, then shrugged and swallowed it back in one gulp.

There was no magical poof or sparkles or anything. I could have just drunk water for all the difference it made. Worse yet, my fingernails stayed the same naked natural they'd been all along, rather than the pretty lavender color I'd been aiming for with the purple crystal dust I'd chosen.

"Ah," Lee cringed, coming over to my table. "Looks like you mixed up the keratocila root with kerastansa weed."

"Huh?" I frowned at him. "How do you mean?"

He looked apologetic, but when he reached out to snag one of the curls that had escaped my braid again, I clearly saw what he meant.

My nails hadn't turned purple. My *hair* had.

Snickers and giggles from the other girls in the class had me blushing furiously, and I ground my teeth together hard. There was *no way* I had mixed those herbs up; I had been meticulous in checking every ingredient.

Unless I hadn't been as careful as I'd thought? I *was* crazy tired, after all.

"Don't worry, Lady Callaluna," Lee reassured me, dropping his voice a little quieter. "I think it suits you."

I sighed heavily at my own failure and cleaned up my equipment. "A day, you said?"

"Or two," he admitted. "But it's temporary, I promise." Returning to the front of the class, he wiped all of the notes from the blackboard to start again. "Okay, moving on to the next lesson in alchemy, which involves metals."

The rest of the class went smoothly, which only made me doubt myself further on the hair-nail mix up. I was a hundred times more cautious on the next potions, though, and on more than one occasion I found the wrong ingredient on my table. Had I been grabbing the wrong things? Or was someone messing with me?

My hangover was making me slower than usual. Of *course*

someone was messing with me! The question was: who?

Either way, I managed to pull off the rest of the practice potions without another hitch, so I went into the afternoon test feeling confident in myself.

"Okay, your highness, ladies. We will be doing this test one by one," Lee announced as we returned from an awkward lunch with the queen and some of her friends. On the plus side, the mask I'd been given on entering the dining room had had enough feather embellishments that no one had noticed my hair.

"Each of you will mix the potion while Master Chemy and I observe." Lee indicated to an older man in servant's garb beside him. "Then you'll throw the vial at this board." He tapped a large square of what seemed to be obsidian. It was black stone and so highly polished it had almost a mirror finish.

"This will take a while to get through all eighteen of you, so please be patient until your turn comes," the older man—Master Chemy—told us with a small smile.

He and Lee began moving from table to table, watching each girl as she mixed the highly explosive potion, then threw the vial at the stone board. If it ignited the stone, it was a success. If nothing happened, it was a fail. How they would then score it in a way to provide a clear "loser" was beyond me. Honestly, I didn't envy them the task, either.

My turn came, and I took my sweet time ensuring I had

everything *exact* as per the instructions we'd been provided. When the stone went up in blue flame, I couldn't help letting out a little squeal of delight, and Lee gave me a small, private smile.

"Very nicely done, Lady Callaluna," he murmured, but his eyes were promising all kinds of dirty things that made my stomach flip with excitement.

"She didn't do anything better than anyone else," Princess Sagen muttered in a sour voice, "except make sex-eyes at the teacher all day long." She turned toward me now with a sneer on her beautiful face. "You *are* aware we're here to marry a prince, not a servant, right?"

It took all of my willpower not to explain to her that if she wanted those murdering pieces of shit, she was damn well welcome to them and I wouldn't stand in her way. Instead, I smiled sweetly and batted my lashes at her.

"Jealous, Your Highness?" I purred. "Would you rather I turn these sex-eyes on you?"

Her own eyes widened in shock, and her mouth moved with silent words. Clearly she hadn't expected *that* response, and I snickered under my breath.

Lee and Master Chemy had already moved on to the next table, and now that I'd passed, I could relax. Shoving the lovely Princess Sagen from my mind, I laid my head on my arms and closed my eyes. There were still ten more girls to go, so I may as well have a little nap while I waited.

It couldn't have been that long since I'd closed my eyes when I was jolted back awake by the sound of breaking glass. The sound came just a split second before I was shoved out of my seat and onto the floor with Lee halfway on top of me.

For a stunned moment, I could do nothing but stare wide-eyed at the place where I'd been resting my head just seconds before. The place that was now engulfed in fire.

What the actual fuck...?

"Oh gods, I am *so* sorry," Lady Carissa—one of Gracelin's crew—simpered like an idiot. "I don't even know how that happened! I'm just so very clumsy sometimes."

Master Chemy blasted the desktop with his little handheld extinguisher, which he'd been using on the stone slate between each test, then scowled at the lady who'd thrown the vial. "I think we can call this one a fail, don't you agree Tutor Lee?"

"What?" Carissa squealed in protest. "But I didn't fail; I made the potion right! Look!" She pointed a colored fingernail at the charred evidence that used to be my work station.

"You also almost killed another lady," Lee snapped at her, offering me a hand up from the ground before turning his stormy glare on Carissa. "That will always be a fail. Is that perfectly clear for everyone in the room? I won't accept this sort of behavior, accident or not."

Carissa's mouth flapped a few times in disbelief before she burst out crying and ran from the room. I frowned after her, a bit shaken at what the hell had just happened. Was she really that clumsy? Or had it been deliberate?

I got my answer as we were being dismissed for the day and Gracelin found an opportunity to brush past me.

"You won't always be so lucky, *imposter*," she hissed in my ear as she passed, then tossed her hair and linked arms with Princess Sagen to strut out of the room.

Of course those two would become fast friends. Each was as poisonous as the other.

As if she could hear my thoughts, Sagen cast a venomous glare at me over her shoulder before they disappeared from sight, and I groaned.

"You okay?" Lee murmured, walking slightly behind me as I left the room.

"Other than the purple hair and near-death experience?" I asked in a dry voice. "Yeah, I'm fine. Just thinking how it feels like I've been here a year already and we're not even past the first week."

Lee grunted a noise of agreement. "Pressure-filled environments will have that affect. On the upside, it feels like I've known you for a whole year already too..."

I glanced over my shoulder to catch his flirtatious grin. "Will I see you guys later tonight?" I whispered the words, so no one would accidentally overhear us.

"I'll make sure of it," he whispered back, then leaned past me to hold a door open. "Come to the sanctuary after dinner. No drinking games tonight, though, okay?"

I chuckled, then nodded. "Agreed. I don't think my headache can handle any more liquor just yet, anyway."

"See you later then, Calla," he whispered before we parted ways to our own rooms.

CHAPTER 16

"I need you to come back here right after dinner," Jules informed me as she helped me dress that evening. "So don't get any smart ideas about running off to fuck those teachers of yours, all right?"

My jaw dropped open. "What? Excuse me?"

"What?" she repeated. "I'm not judging. I'm just saying I need you back here, so give your greedy cunt a break just for tonight, okay? Absence makes the heart grow fonder and all that crap."

"Jules!" I screeched. "I'm not *fucking* them!" *Not yet, anyway. And not for lack of trying...*

She frowned at me in confusion. "Why not? The gods gave you perfect tits and a tight vagina for a reason, babe. Use them." I opened my mouth to protest, and she cut me off. "But not tonight.

I'm serious, Ry. Straight after dinner."

Something about the urgency in her voice had me frowning. "Why? What's going on that is so important?"

Pursing her lips, she took her time on the buttons of my bodice before replying. "Bloodeye wants to meet with you."

That information dropped into the air like some sort of explosion, and my jaw almost hit the floor. "What?" I screamed at her. "Here? He's coming *here*?"

Juliana shrugged and looked uncomfortable. "I don't know, Ry. He just said to make sure we were both here after dinner because he needed to discuss your progress."

"My progress?" I frowned, confused and angry all at the same time. "What *progress*? What the hell does he think I'm doing here other than staying alive?"

"I don't know!" Jules snapped back at me, losing her temper. "Do you honestly think he tells me anything? I'm nothing more than a common whore to him, remember?"

I took a long inhale, then released it while swallowing all the ranting and raging I wanted to do. "You're a shitload more than a common whore, babe, and you know it."

Jules gave a bitter laugh and tossed my mask to me. "Not to him, I'm not."

"He's an idiot." I wasn't just placating her; I really meant it. Master Bloodeye was an idiot for not seeing the value in his "common whores." Jules would be the perfect spy if he used her to her full capabilities.

Of course, it didn't help that Juliana had been harboring a not-so-secret crush on the crime lord since she had hit puberty.

"Okay, so come straight back after dinner." I nodded, thinking about how I'd get word to Lee and the guys that I wasn't coming. "Got it. How do I look?" I tied the black lace mask over my face and turned to show her. My dress was a shorter one tonight, barely skimming the tops of my knees, but with cute little lace sweetheart sleeves to cover my wounded shoulder. Not that I'd need to cover it for much longer—whatever cream the medic had given me to keep applying daily was working wonders, and it had almost healed already.

"Like a damn princess, you bitch," Jules joked, pouring herself a glass of wine from the carafe on the table. "I'll try not to get too drunk while you're gone."

"And I'll try not to die. Fun times all around." I gave her a tight, humorless smile and made for the door.

"Oh!" she called after me, "Hold up, I have something for you." She disappeared into the enormous wardrobe and dug around for a bit before reappearing with a folded note in her hand. "Almost forgot to give this to you."

Curious, I took it from her and flipped it open. "Flick?" I asked her with a frown. "You got a note from Flick? How?"

Jules shrugged, dodging my eye contact. "Told you I would sort it out. See, he's doing okay and knows you're going to get him out." She tapped the page in my hand, and I nodded.

It was definitely Flick's writing. I should know; I was the one who had taught him how to read and write the year before. His note was brief but did indeed assure me that he was well and not wallowing in despair that he'd been abandoned.

"Okay, go now," Jules instructed me, taking the note back and giving me a shove toward the door. "I *really* don't want you pissing anyone off any more than you really have to, so try not to be late."

Rolling my eyes at her dramatics, I left her in our rooms and headed to the great hall for dinner. Before pushing the doors open, I crossed my fingers and sent up a silent plea to the gods—any gods—that there wouldn't be any more surprises tonight.

Jules hadn't been totally dramatic when she was hurrying me along, as I really only had a few moments to find my seat before the royal family made their grand entrance decked out in their fine clothes and masks.

Thankfully, I was again spared the torture of sitting next to the princes, but unfortunately, they were only a few seats away and well within earshot, should any of them feel inclined to chat.

Gritting my teeth, I very carefully kept my eyes on my plate and avoided Prince Alexander's burning gaze. I had definitely been too drunk the night before to even have considered kissing a monster like that. So if he could somehow take the hint that I'd rather never

THE ROYAL TRIALS: IMPOSTER

have it mentioned again, that would be ideal.

"Oh, Lady Callaluna." A mocking sort of voice drew my attention from my empty plate, and I looked up to meet Princess Sagen's deep brown eyes across the table, "I almost didn't see you there. But how I could miss you with that horrific hair, I'll never know." She dissolved into peels of cruel laughter, and I sighed inwardly. It was becoming painfully clear just *how* those ingredients had become mixed up on my work station today.

The new addition to our mix was seated between Prince Alexander and Prince Thibault, while Prince Louis was further down the table beside Lady Agatha.

In looking at Sagen, it was unavoidable that I could see two of the princes as well, so I couldn't ignore the curious looks they were giving my lavender locks.

Giving Sagen a tight smile, I twirled one of my loose curls around my middle finger and sighed. "I really was aiming for a dull, inconspicuous brown or black, but it just wasn't meant to be. Tell me, do you often fade into the background with that boring color you have? Because that's what I was hoping to achieve."

Oops, so much for keeping my big mouth shut.

Sagen glowered, her mean smile slipping from her face, even as a few other ladies covered their smiles with napkins. "What a shame you passed today's test, Callaluna," she murmured with eyes narrowed in a death glare. "With such sarcasm, you're hardly fit to be queen. Is she?" This last part was directed to Prince Thibault as she stroked one of his biceps with her red-clawed hand.

To my amusement, he gently peeled her paw off him and laid it on the table. "I wouldn't know," he replied. "Lady Callaluna hasn't graced me with all that much of her time thus far."

"Something we will need to rectify, brother," Prince Alexander added. "But as for that hair..." He paused, and I shivered at the intensity of his gaze. I couldn't even see his eyes that clearly in the dim lighting, but holy gods' balls, I could *feel* it. "I think it's lovely. Really suits you, Lady Callaluna."

"Huh?" I spluttered, choking on a little bit of my own spit like a really classy bitch.

"What?" Sagen snarled almost in unison with Gracelin, who'd been listening in from her place down the table.

Prince Thibault coughed a noise that sounded suspiciously like a laugh. "I have to agree, brother. It's very eye catching; I think I'll have a hard time taking my gaze from Lady Callaluna all night."

My teeth ground together hard, and I swallowed back the insults I wanted to spew. Sagen looked furious, but she had no idea how badly I *didn't* want the prince's attention on me all damn night. It was really starting to look like I'd severely pissed off Aana somewhere along the way.

Any further banter was cut short by the nightly toast. Wine was placed in front of all of us, and by now we knew the drill. Before the soups were served, one of us would die.

It came at just the right time, reminding me exactly what kind of monsters held us captive in their obscene game. Unable to help myself, I cast a look of disgust at both princes, who still stared at me, then picked up my glass and focused on the bubbles.

I'd keep my head down and ignore everyone. I'd get through this night and the next and the next... until I found a way to free myself from the binding magic or won. Either way, I was getting out of this nightmare with my skin intact. I was too stubborn for anything else.

CHAPTER 17

The girl who died that night was Lady Carissa, the one who'd "accidentally" thrown her fire potion at me instead of the stone board. As I dragged my feet back to my room, my stomach churned with the sick feeling that Lee had scored her lowest because of that. But he wouldn't do that. Would he?

"Ry," Jules hissed, swinging the door open before my hand even reached the handle. "What took you so long?" She grabbed my wrist and hauled me inside the room, slamming the door shut again before I could even open my mouth to respond.

"There's my girl," boomed the heavily bearded man who was waiting inside, and I found myself swept up in a massive bear hug.

I let out a squeak of surprise and peeled myself out of the stranger's grip before squinting up at him. "Master Bloodeye?" He grinned back at me mischievously and whistled. "Impressive disguise. I didn't even recognize your voice, and how the fuck have you hidden your eye?"

Considering I'd always known him to wear an eyepatch, he certainly *seemed* to have two fully functioning eyes. Had the patch been a ruse this whole time?

"Ah, nothin' but magic, girlie. Cost me a pretty penny too, don't doubt that." He laughed a throaty chuckle, then stepped aside to let me further into the room, where Mistress Mallard was seated on the chaise lounge.

"Necessary precautions, Anthony," she scolded him, like this was an argument they'd already had. "Rybet, lovely to see you still in one piece. I'm sorry I haven't been able to give you those lessons I promised. Things have been"—she paused, her mouth tightening— "challenging."

I waved her off and smiled. "Don't worry about it; I've been surviving. Turns out most of these ladies are painful bitches in their own right, so no one has really noticed my lack of decorum." There was a tense, somewhat awkward silence for a moment, and my nerves were immediately on edge. "So, what was important enough for one of the kingdom's most wanted criminals to risk sneaking into the palace? Have you found a way to get me out of this insanity?"

"Get you out?" My mentor and father figure roared with laughter, and I frowned at him like he'd just sprung a second head.

"Why would we get you out? You have no idea how long I've wanted a true insider in the palace!"

My jaw dropped in shock. "What do you mean? You're not getting me out?" My gaze ran between Bloodeye and Mallard, finally settling on Jules, who was refusing to make eye contact with me. "Do you not understand what is happening here? They're *killing* us! Ladies aren't being sent home when they fail, they're getting *poisoned*!"

"We understand," the disguised crime lord assured me. "Just as you understand that you must do everything possible *not* to fail."

For a long moment, I remained speechless. Shocked. Surely he hadn't just said what I thought he had.

"You... you want me to *stay*?" I could hardly believe what I was saying, and my stomach churned again with bile.

Master Bloodeye grinned at me, a cruel-looking smile that held no warmth. "I don't just want you to stay, little Rybet. I want you to win. If you don't, well, I don't think I need to waste my breath on threats of punishments. The royals will take care of that for me, won't they?"

All the air gusted from my body as his words hit home. "No, that's not... I can't... This is insanity! I thought you'd help me get out of this!"

"Don't be an idiot, girlie," Bloodeye snapped, his voice like steel. "From the reports I hear, the princes are already taking an interest in you. You stand a good chance of winning, and when you do"—he smirked with greed and ambition— "then you'd be wise to remember who raised you. You owe me your entire life, Rybet. Never forget that."

My lips moved, but no sounds came out. I had no words to express the hurt I was experiencing. Master Bloodeye's words stabbed through me like daggers, and I very quickly came to the harsh reality of my situation. I wasn't his pseudo-daughter, like everyone had accused me of being. I was his employee, an asset to be used however he saw fit, no different from Juliana and the other whores.

"I expect you to start making an effort with those royal pricks, Rybet. Endear yourself to them and make them love you. No more of this disrespectful backchat or combativeness. Flirt, smile, and charm them. Juliana can coach you in this, I'm sure. But if they want to take that sweet little body for a test ride, you'd better damn well lay it out on a platter for them. Am I clear?" His tone was ice cold and completely foreign from the man I knew. "If you don't, I will know."

"How?" I choked out, tasting the acid of my bitterness as I spoke. "You just said you don't have any agents on the inside."

"I said I *didn't*. Thanks to your quick thinking, now I do." He smiled at me smugly, and my heart sank.

My gaze lifted from my former mentor to my best friend. "Jules?" I squeaked out, not wanting to hear her answer. Not that she intended to give me one. Her head was bowed so far I couldn't even see her face any more. That traitorous bitch.

TATE JAMES

"I hope this evens our score, Anthony," Mistress Mallard commented with a prim tilt to her head. "After this, I owe you nothing more. I told you many years ago that I wouldn't be your mole, and I still mean it."

Bloodeye gave her a nod of acceptance, and she rose from her seat, giving me a tight nod. "I apologize that you've ended up in this position, Rybet. But for what it's worth, I wish you all the best."

I didn't bother responding to her; I was still too stunned at the turn of events the night had taken.

"I'll walk out with you, Patricia. I think my message has been received loud and clear here." He, too, stood and peered down at me. "I look forward to glowing reports of your progress with the princes, Rybet. The next time I see you, you'll be a princess, soon to be queen." He paused, his smile dropping. "Or you'll be dead."

With that jewel of a proclamation, he and Mistress Mallard departed my room, and the door slammed with a heavy sound behind them.

For a long time, I just sat there shocked into silence. Until Jules spoke.

"Ry," she croaked out, raising her guilty face to look at me, but it was too much.

"Get out," I ordered her in a deathly quiet voice. "I can't stand to look at you, Juliana. Just get out."

She sucked in a breath to argue, and my temper snapped.

"Get *out!*" I screamed at her, turning the full extent of my fury—at Bloodeye, at her, at *myself*—all squarely on Juliana. My so-called best friend.

She hesitated a moment but gave me a small nod and left the room, closing the door softly behind herself.

Alone, I broke.

CHAPTER 18

The next morning, I woke before the dawn. To be truthful, I hadn't really slept at all. Master Bloodeye's words kept echoing around inside my head, and images of Juliana's guilty fucking face wouldn't leave me alone. She had returned some hours after I'd kicked her out, pausing at the foot of my bed for a moment before slinking into her own bed in the annex.

I didn't wait for her to get dressed, instead just throwing on the most comfortable items I could find in the closet, seeing as it was likely to be another combat class with Ty. Pairing a black, stretchy knit top with supple leather pants and a pair of flat boots, I almost felt like myself again, whoever the hell that was.

Bloodeye had been clear in his threats the night before. Rybet Waise no longer existed. I was Lady Callaluna... or no one. There would be no returning to my former life as a pickpocket. Even if I did find a way to escape the binding oath and defy Bloodeye's orders, I'd be dead before my boots even hit the puddles of the Pond. He'd see to that.

"Hey, why didn't you wake me?" Jules asked in a sleepy whisper as she emerged from her annex. "I could have picked something out for you."

"I've managed without a maid all my life, Juliana; I think I can handle getting dressed alone." I snapped the words at her, still burning at the knowledge that she was spying on me. Our entire friendship was in question, but somehow I couldn't stop worrying about what she might have told our boss regarding my tutors. Were they at risk now, too?

If Bloodeye thought they were a distraction or that they posed any risk in disrupting his plans, he wouldn't hesitate to get rid of them. For a man who'd arranged the deaths of noblemen and politicians, a couple of palace servants would pose little to no trouble at all.

Jules sighed, watching me lace up my boots in silence. "Don't do this, Ry," she implored me. "You know I had no choice."

I scoffed, as I finished tying my boot then stood up to face her. "There is *always* a choice, Jules. Always." Feeling a lump thicken in my throat, I spun and opened the door to leave before pausing. "Just tell me something honestly, Jules," I asked her, not turning to look at her lying face but needing to ask the question. "Was that note really

195

from Flick? Is he okay?"

"Yes," she replied. "But... he's not in the dungeons."

Her admission made me spin to face her, frowning in confusion. "He's not? What do you mean?"

She shrugged uncomfortably. "I mean, he never went to the dungeons. Apparently someone took pity on him the day he was arrested and set him free again before even reaching the palace."

I gaped at her, a little bit speechless. "So, me coming here, ending up in the Royal Trials, this whole goddamn fucked-up thing... it was all for nothing? Flick was never in danger?"

She shrugged again, giving me a pathetic, puppy-dog kind of look. "Not for nothing, Ry. You could become the next queen of Teich. Some would call that fate."

My mouth twisted in disgust, and I yanked the door back open. "Don't call me that anymore. Rybet Waise is dead, or did you not hear what your master said last night?"

She made a noise of protest behind me, but I was in no mood to hear it, instead slamming the door behind myself and stomping down to the dining hall for some breakfast, hopefully before the other ladies arrived.

For once, luck was on my side, and I was able to snag some pastries and a mug of hot tea before anyone, other than the staff, saw me. I didn't bother pushing my luck in hanging around to eat, just took my prizes and set off to the combat training arena. Usually

Jules would tell me in the morning where I needed to be and for what class, but because I hadn't been feeling overly chatty with her, I was just going to take a guess.

"Lo!" Ty exclaimed as I stomped into the arena with my hands full of breakfast. "You're alive!"

Frowning at him in confusion, I continued over to the tiered seating to set down my food and drink before sitting down myself. "Yeah, I'm alive. Why, did you think I might have been offed at dinner last night?"

Ty scowled at my bad-taste joke and towered over me with his huge arms folded across his chest. "I would have known if you were. But when you didn't show up at the sanctuary..."

I cringed. With everything that had happened with Bloodeye and Jules, I'd completely forgotten that I was supposed to meet the guys after dinner. Still, it was probably for the best. I needed to start breaking this little liaison off before it endangered them any more than it already had.

"Sorry," I murmured, sipping my tea. "Something came up."

"No shit," he scoffed, sitting down beside me and snagging one of my pastries. "You look like you didn't sleep a wink last night."

I grunted, narrowing my eyes at the pastry in his hand, then moving the rest of them to my other side for protection. "Is that your way of saying I look like crap?"

"As if you ever could, Lo." He laughed. "You look sexy as sin in all that black, but you also look tired. Do I need to hurt someone for you?"

An image of Ty fighting Bloodeye's men flashed across my mind, and I shuddered. He was good, no question about that. But he was no Pond dweller. Those of us in Bloodeye's employ were trained to fight dirty, without mercy or honor. I simply couldn't picture Ty fighting like that, regardless of the situation he was in.

"No, nothing like that," I lied, taking another sip of my tea. "Just personal problems."

Ty made a noise in his throat but let it go. For a long time, we sat in companionable silence while I finished my breakfast—with his help, of course.

"So, tonight?" he asked as I stood and brushed crumbs from my clothes.

"Tonight, what?" I asked, raising a brow at him. Gods damn him, he was gorgeous halfway reclined on the bench seat, with the sunlight making his green eyes gleam like jewels under black lashes.

"Will we see you tonight after dinner? I know that the whole elimination thing is hard on you, so we just want to make sure you're okay." The look the big soldier gave me as he said this was pure vulnerability, and it cracked my heart to refuse.

But it was for their own damn good, so I shook my head. "Like you said, I'm pretty tired. I think I just need a good night's sleep tonight."

His eyes narrowed at me, and I dodged his gaze. Much better to inspect the few pastry crumbs still on my shirt.

"Fine," he conceded after an awkward pause. "The other girls will be here any minute; you can help me set up for the day."

Nodding vaguely and feeling sick to my stomach, I followed him over to a heavy trunk.

"What are we doing today, oh wise one?" I asked, unable to stop myself from trying to lighten the mood. I barely knew these guys, yet cutting ties with them was going to be a hell of a lot harder than I'd really considered.

Giving me a toothy grin, Ty pushed the trunk open with the toe of his boot and displayed an impressive collection of short daggers.

"Knife work," he told me with a smug smile. "Something tells me you're going to be good at this too."

Shit. As bad as this was going to be for *laying low*, I couldn't stop the flutter of excitement that zapped through me at the sight of all that pretty steel.

He was right. I was *damn* good with a knife.

Maybe this day wouldn't suck so hard after all.

The first half of the day flew by, and before I knew it we were facing our test in knifework. I'd managed to successfully avoid Ty as much as I could, but thanks to the binding oath, I wasn't able to avoid showing off my existing experience with the short blades.

Interestingly, though, I wasn't the only one who knew her pointy end from the dull. Several other ladies—including Gracelin—showed mediocre proficiency, but the biggest surprise was Sagen. The exotic, dark-haired beauty from Asintisch had matched me skill for skill all day, and I was quietly looking forward to this test to really determine who was better with a blade.

Ty had informed us that our assessment would be in throwing. We'd need to aim at three different targets at varying distances, and our scores would be based on which rings of the targets we hit.

Commander Hansel, the same elderly soldier who had assisted with the test on our first combat day, handed out three blades each to all the ladies, then accepted a clipboard and pencil from Ty to score.

"When your name is called," Ty announced, raising his voice to be heard by everyone, "you'll step up to this line." He walked over to the black, painted line on the gravel and tapped it with his boot. "From here, you'll throw your knives at each of the three targets you see assembled. Anyone who steps over the line will be marked down. Understood?"

Several ladies murmured their understanding, and Ty gave a short nod.

"Then let's begin. Commander Hansel, who is up first?"

The older man cleared his throat and consulted his list, calling out the first lady's name. She stepped nervously up to the line and took aim.

One by one, my rivals took their turns. Some had improved noticeably since the morning, which was a testament to Ty's teaching, but still no real threat. Until it was just Sagen and me.

The two of us eyed each other warily, waiting for Commander Hansel to call whoever was up next. Sagen was just as competitive as I was, so the result of this test would be interesting, to say the least. Could a spoiled princess from Asintisch really be better at knife throwing than a Pond criminal?

"Princess Sagen, you're next," the commander announced, and her lips pursed with annoyance. I knew why, too—same reason I gave her a smug smile as she stepped up to the line. By going last, I had the advantage of knowing how she'd scored, while she could only guess at which rings I might hit.

Carefully, Sagen balanced the first blade in her hand and sighted the closest target. It was common practice in a lot of Teich to throw from the hilt, using a hammer grip. It protected the throwers hand from the blade, but it also impacted accuracy. As I had suspected she might, Sagen flipped the blade over and held it in a pinch grip, where only her thumb and forefinger gripped the flat of the blade right at the tip. It was a much more sophisticated throw than what Ty had taught us and was designed to throw with both maximum speed and force.

Coincidentally, it was also the way I'd been taught.

Sagen hit the first two targets with ease, striking the red-dotted bullseyes on both boards dead center. Her third throw, though, was just a fraction less accurate and landed on the thin yellow ring around the bullseye.

Ty let out a low whistle, clapping as he collected her knives and marked down her scores. "Very impressive, Your Highness. Is this a skill that is common among your people?"

The look Sagen gave our sexy trainer was full of contempt and disgust. "No."

Without wasting her breath to elaborate further, she flipped her glossy black hair over her shoulder and brushed past me to join the other ladies in the spectators' stands. They were all cheering excitedly for her, and the superior look on her face spoke volumes about how safe she felt in her score.

"Lady Callaluna," Commander Hansel said. "Lucky last. Please step up."

Blocking Sagen and the other bitches—I mean, competitors— from my mind, I moved into position behind the line and moved my first blade into a pinch grip, same as Sagen had done.

I couldn't help myself and glanced over at Ty before I sighted my target to throw. He was staring at me with an intensity that made me shiver, but his jaw was set tight, and he gave my grip a stern look. Almost like he was warning me not to show off? Or was it that he thought I'd make a fool of myself by "copying" the foreign princess?

Tearing my eyes away from him, I focused on the first target. Just as I had done a thousand times before, I let my peripheral vision fade out so that all I could see was the red dot in the center of the target. I took a long, slow breath, then released it carefully. At the tail end of my exhale, the knife flew from my fingers with a snap of my elbow, landing perfectly dead center of the target.

"Good," Commander Handel said quietly. "Next target."

I gave him a small nod and moved a few steps to the side to be sure I had the second target dead in front of me. It was a mistake that loads of the other girls had made, assuming that they weren't allowed to move from the static spot. But it was a line, not a dot, for a reason, and you'd always get better accuracy from straight on than at an angle.

Again, I released my blade and struck that happy little red mark in the middle of the board. Sagen and I were tied. If I could hit the bullseye on this last throw, I'd beat her.

Not that we won anything for it, but damn, it'd feel good. That prissy bitch had been rubbing me all sorts of wrong ways since she'd arrived, and I was almost totally sure she'd been the one messing with my potions in Lee's class.

The third target was a long way away; only a couple of the other girls had even hit the board, let alone touched the target. But it was no different from the training Master Bloodeye had put me through as a child, so I was confident about scoring well on it. Could I beat

Sagen, though?

Breathing calmly, I found my *zone*, the place that Bloodeye had joked was unique only to me where I could zero in on my target and visualize it a whole lot closer than it really was.

The knife left my fingers with ease, hurtling through the air end over end until it hit the wooden board with a heavy *thunk*.

My heart stuttered, and I squinted to get a better look. Had I done it? It looked damn close, at any rate. Ty strode over to mark the score on his paper, then turned to me with a sly grin.

"Just hit the edge of the bullseye, Lady Callaluna," he announced loud enough to be heard by the spectators too. "That makes you today's top scorer. Congratulations."

Biting back the grin of triumph that wanted to break through, I gave Ty and Commander Hansel a respectful nod, then wiped my now sweating hands off on my shirt.

"Ladies, you're all dismissed for the day. Don't forget, tomorrow you're back in the library with Zan, and then the following day will be the conclusion of the first trial. I implore you all to rest well and take the last test seriously, as the consequences of failure are dire." Ty ran his gaze across everyone, then paused on me. "I hope you are all prepared."

For a brief moment, the Pond dweller in me toyed with the idea of exploiting my friendship with Ty to gain knowledge of the second trial... or even what the final test on Saturday might consist of. But as quickly as the thought came, I brushed it aside. I needed to be distancing myself from the temptingly seductive teachers, not getting closer. If I wanted hints, then I'd damn well better be nice to the royal assholes at dinner.

"Lo," Ty called quietly after me as I followed the other ladies out of the arena. "Can we talk a moment?"

When I made the mistake of turning to look at him, my resolve almost slipped. His emerald green eyes begged me for answers, and it pained me to turn a cold shoulder so soon into our acquaintance.

Still, it was better now than later, when serious feelings might actually get hurt.

"Sorry." I shrugged and shook my head. "I need to wash up. See you at the final test on Saturday, I guess. If I'm still alive." This last part was delivered with a level of bitterness that I'd intended to keep to myself. Not caring to hear his response, I took off out of the arena and made my way back to my room.

CHAPTER 19

had meant what I said to Jules that morning. There was always a choice in any situation, and I despised the saying "there was no other choice" because it was a lie. Simply because the *other* choice might suck goose balls, didn't mean it was any less of a choice.

In light of that, I had a choice.

I had several choices, if I were being honest with myself.

None of them were particularly great, but they were still there.

So, I chose. I chose to live and fight another day.

It may have felt a whole lot like I was rolling over and admitting defeat, playing the part of Bloodeye's perfect little protégé just as I had for my whole life, but that was far from the truth. He thought I could make it to the end, and that gave me a certain level of confidence in my chances. But the idea of me, an imposter, becoming queen of Teich and then just handing over the kingdom to a criminal like him... it was laughable.

If he truly thought I would go through with his plan, he didn't know me at all. And it was this that I banked on.

That night, I remained stoic as Jules dressed me for dinner in a strapless, floor-length gown that glittered like starlight when I moved. My shoulder had healed enough that it no longer needed a bandage, and I rejected the wrap Jules tried to give me to hide the wound.

As I secured the matching mask to my face, looping the ribbons under my pale purple curls, Jules made a pathetic, sobbing sound that snapped my resolve to ignore her.

"What did he threaten you with?" I asked softly, hoping, *praying* she would have a plausible reason to betray me. Or at least a damn good story.

"Nothing," she whispered back. It was the answer I'd both suspected and dreaded, but it in no way shocked me. The lives we'd led, just like the lives of thousands of others who'd lost everything during the Darkness, they didn't make us into altruistic people.

Pond dwellers looked out for themselves and no one else.

"So he bribed you, then?" I felt sick saying the words, hearing how little our years of friendship meant to her. She nodded miserably and didn't offer any more explanation.

Sighing heavily, I left the room and made my way to dinner with the weight of my choices dragging at every step. Juliana had looked out for herself, and now it was my turn to do the same.

When I swept into the great hall, I was no longer an imposter. I was Lady Callaluna of Riverdell, and gods help anyone who stood in my way.

"Oh great," Sagen sneered at me from across the table when I located my place card and stood behind my chair to await the royals' entrance. "I get the pleasure of dining opposite a purple-haired freak of nature. Maybe if I'm lucky, you'll be the one drinking poison tonight."

Determined to ignore her childish jabs, I simply smiled and stroked my pale purple curls, which I'd left out for the night. "It's a shame it's already fading," I sighed. "I feel like it really helped me to stand out."

"It certainly did," a husky man-voice agreed, and Prince Louis took the empty space beside me. "Not that you needed any help in that department, Lady Callaluna."

Sagen spared me a glare, then quickly turned on the charm for the prince who was to be dining with us that evening. She hadn't even bothered with a proper mask, instead sporting one painted on with glittery makeup so her heavy lashes weren't hindered as she batted them in Prince Louis's direction.

"Prince Louis," she cooed. "How lovely to have you join us. I was hoping to get the opportunity to converse with you tonight after your brothers made such excellent dining partners last night."

The prince's mask was almost complete, only showing his face from the lips down, but even so, I could spot a fake smile when I saw one.

"Your Highness," he murmured back. "A pleasure. When my father told me you would be joining the Royal Trials, I was most surprised."

Sagen laughed a throaty, sexual laugh but the tension in her brow made me feel like I'd missed a subtle insult somewhere in Prince Louis greeting. "Surprised in a good way, I should hope?"

"Of course," Prince Louis responded, but the brief hesitation made a liar out of him, and I bit back a laugh as I pulled my chair out to sit. "Allow me," he said, placing his hands on the back of my seat and pushing it in for me as I sat. Like the perfect gentleman. Or a prince.

"Thank you, Your Royal Highness." I forced a polite smile onto my face as I thanked him and met his eyes for the first time without flinching. Surprisingly, they weren't the eyes of the murderous bastard I'd been expecting. Instead, they were... almost kind.

But that made no sense, so I chalked it up to the dim candlelight and shoved it out of my mind. I had a job to do, and the fact that it would piss off Princess Sagen only gave me more incentive to do it well.

"Call me Prince Louis," he said with a small, almost mischievous grin. "Titles can get so impersonal."

I gave a small nod but said nothing more for fear of betraying my real feelings toward him.

Operation Flirt with a Coldhearted Royal Bastard was officially underway. I just needed to get through the death of another rival before the appetizers were served.

As expected, moments later the waitstaff appeared with glasses of sparkling wine, placing them down on the table in front of each dinner guest. A tense silence swept through the room as each lady eyed her own drink with fear and dread. Beside me, though, a petite brunette was starting to hyperventilate.

"Are you okay?" I whispered to her, noticing her chalky, pale face and beads of sweat forming on her forehead.

She shook her head frantically, not taking her eyes from the glass in front of her. "I can't do this," she whispered back in a panic. "I can't. I can't do it. I can't." Her hands trembled so hard on the edge of the table that her cutlery began shaking, so I placed a hand over one of hers to try and calm her. "It's me," she insisted, still staring at the wine. "I know it's me. I can't do it, though. I can't die like this; I'm too young and-and-and—"

"Shhhhh," I attempted to sooth her as her breathing came in faster gasps. "You can't know that for sure. There was no clear loser today, and Ty never announced anyone's scores except mine and Her Highness's."

"True," Sagen chimed in from across the table. "But you did fail pretty hard, so it could totally be you tonight." She shrugged with a callous disregard for the other girl's feelings, then turned her fluttering lashes back on Prince Louis.

This only served to panic the girl even further, and she began making a high-pitched whining noise that could only be a whole new level of freak out.

"Hey, listen to me." I tried to get her attention in a soothing voice. "You don't know it's you. Not for sure. Just take a few deep breaths and find your center of calm. You'll feel so much better for it."

It sounded like a whole bunch of bullshit, and it was. Find your calm? What the fuck use would that be if her wine really *was* poisoned? Still, my conscience wouldn't allow me to simply sit there and ignore her panic attack.

"Look, I bet I can smell if it is or not," I suggested, peeling my hand from hers where it gripped the table. "They wouldn't poison more than one of us, so if they smell the same..." I trailed off with a shrug and picked up the flute of wine in front of her.

Bringing it to my nose, I hesitated just the briefest moment. What if it was the type of poison that started working when inhaled? What if it didn't even need to be ingested?

"It should be safe to smell," Prince Louis murmured under his breath so quietly that I was sure no one else heard him. "Concentrated cyano algae need to be consumed to do any real damage."

His words made me glare sharply in his direction, suddenly remembering he was there and at least partially responsible for whoever died in a matter of minutes. "Cyano algae?" I repeated, frowning. "You mean this poison is made from red-tide?"

Prince Louis's lips tightened as he stared at me. "You know it?"

"I know it's incurable," I responded in a voice dripping with venom. "And a horrifically painful way to die. You royals really are a bunch of sick fucks."

Fuck the plan to flirt with this asshole; it was all I could do not to throttle him right there at the dinner table. Cyano algae were a type of algae that only grew in the Pond, to the best of my knowledge. Locals called it red-tide because of the painful, spreading rash it caused when it came into contact with skin. Everyone knew how dangerous it was, and I was shocked to hear that someone had distilled it down into a poison to kill off ladies in the Royal Trials.

I'd come into contact with it a time or two myself, so I could vouch for how painful the rash was. I could only *imagine* how excruciating it would be to feel that from the inside.

Unfortunately, it emitted almost no odor, so it'd be impossible to smell it when mixed with wine. Not that I was going to let on about that; my poor dining companion was in enough of a state as it was. So I took a quick sniff of her glass, then picked up my own and did the same.

"Totally identical," I reassured her. "Not even a hint of poison to be smelled." I replaced the glass in front of her and was relieved to see her breathing slow back down a little.

"If you're so sure," Princess Sagen commented with a cruel twist to her mouth. "Why don't you swap glasses?"

"Excuse me?" I blinked at her in shock. Surely she wasn't serious.

She grinned like a razor-toothed *drachen*. "You heard me, Callaluna. If you are so confident that her glass isn't poisoned, why don't *you* drink it? Or were you just lying to make her feel better about impending death?"

"Were you?" the panicked girl whimpered on the edge of another meltdown.

There was no time to argue, though, as the king stood and tapped his glass with a metal teaspoon, calling for everyone's attention. His speech was the same as every night, full of bullshit and thinly veiled threats, so I felt no need to listen.

All the while, Sagen glared her challenge at me.

"Fine," I growled, when the king raised his glass in a silent command to *drink up*. Quickly, before I could change my mind, I switched glasses with the girl beside me—whose name I still couldn't remember—and took a long sip.

Several of the ladies who'd been watching in fascination gasped in horror, and even Sagen's brows rose in surprise. Guess she'd really underestimated the size of my ovaries.

Well, that and the fact that I'd had no sparks from my natural intuition when I'd handled the glass to smell it. It was the one thing that had kept me alive this long, so it seemed stupid not to continue trusting it now.

Everyone else drank as they were commanded to, and it turned out to be another girl further down the table who drew the short straw that night.

"I can't believe you did that," the trembling girl from beside me breathed as she watched the unlucky victim being carried out of the dining hall.

"Neither can I," Prince Louis snapped from my other side. "Of all the stupid, reckless, arrogant things—"

"Arrogant?" I spluttered, cutting him off and pinning him with a death glare. "Oh, you're a fine one to go throwing that word around, *Your Royal Highness.*"

"I would save the venom if I were you, Lady Callaluna," Prince Louis warned me, leaning in close so that only I could hear his words. "You're already walking thin ice after running from the dance the other night."

I snorted my severe lack of care for what *he* thought was best and opened my mouth to tell him as much.

"Please, My Lady," he cut me off, placing a firm hand on my knee under the table. "Just let's suffer through this dinner without any more deaths. Things are depressing enough without you getting dragged to the dungeons for disrespecting your monarchs."

As badly as I wanted to tell him exactly where to shove his concerns, I really did need to bite back my temper. My new objective was to endear myself to the princes, no matter how palatable I found the task, and my current attitude was far from endearing.

"Of course," I replied in a falsely calm voice, offering him a tight smile. "Please excuse me, Prince Louis. I think the sight of ladies dying night after night must be affecting my temper."

The young royal pulled back a fraction, removing his hand from my leg and staring at me intently, like he was frowning under his mask. "Yes, I imagine that's to be expected," he murmured.

Anything else he might have said was—thankfully—interrupted by Sagen once more. She really was determined to make an impression, and for once, I was happy to let her command attention. I needed the reprieve to pull my shit together, anyway.

Little did I realize just how accomplished she was at keeping that attention once she had it. I found myself not needing to say a single word until halfway through the main course, and even then it was only because Prince Louis turned to me very deliberately and asked my opinion on the subject of discussion.

"My apologies," I simpered, swallowing the piece of bread I'd just bitten into. "I wasn't listening to a word Her Highness was saying. Can you repeat the question?"

The corners of the prince's lips twitched, like he was fighting a smile, but he politely obliged. "Her Highness was just commenting on the state of some of the outlying townships of Teich and those that border with our neighboring kingdoms. Apparently some have become completely deserted in recent months."

I blinked at him, feeling like I was missing something. We'd been hearing about these mysterious disappearances for some time in the Pond, where gossip seemed to run more rampant than the palace. Entire towns full of people were just disappearing like they'd never existed, leaving no trace of where they might have gone.

"So, what was the question, Your Highness?" I repeated, failing to see what he was actually asking me.

"Her Highness suggested someone may be forming a people's militia. It's common knowledge that our rule over Teich is not universally supported, so what do you think?" Prince Louis pinned me with the full weight of his attention, and I ate another piece of bread while I considered a diplomatic response.

"I think it is possible some people may do that, sure. But whole townships? Women, children, elderly... *animals*? I think that is implausible for this specific discussion." I shrugged and used the rest of my bread to soak up meat juices from my plate.

The prince made a humming noise, like he wasn't too sure what his own opinion was on the matter.

"Oh, okay. I didn't realize you were an expert in this area, Callaluna." Sagen snorted an ugly sound and rolled her eyes. "So what is your explanation for it all?"

I frowned at her, considering just how dumb she really was under all that bravado. "Magic, obviously."

There was a confused silence, as everyone who'd been partaking in the discussion stared at me.

"How so?" Prince Louis prompted me, and I sighed. Conspiracy theories about the balance of magic were *not* lighthearted dinnertime conversation.

Dabbing at my mouth with my napkin, I collected my thoughts and condensed them. "It's the same as what's happened to the Wilds. The same as the Darkness and the Plague. Our land's magic is still not satisfied with the balance, and it's punishing us."

"That's insanity," the girl beside Sagen chuckled. "That stuff is all in the past; the princes fixed it all when they cured the Plague."

"Are you sure?" I challenged her, and her smile faltered.

"Yes?" she replied, sounding less sure of herself. "Nothing bad has happened in the ten years since then. Isn't that proof enough?"

I scoffed a laugh. "No, nothing has happened *here*. In Lakehaven. Can you say for sure that nothing strange or unfortunate has happened in other cities? Or other kingdoms?" I raised a brow at Sagen. "Has Asintisch been the picture of health in the past ten years?"

Sagen's mouth tightened so much I worried it might disappear, but she didn't deny my implications.

"Interesting theory," Prince Louis commented, sipping his glass of claret. "What do you suppose would be the way to fix it?"

Smiling sweetly at him, I took a sip of my own wine. "I haven't the slightest clue, Your Highness. None but the royals possess magic anymore, so how could a mere aristocrat hope to find answers to what may be the death of our entire world?"

Louis narrowed his eyes at me, and I stared back with an innocently neutral expression. It was hard to tell in the candlelight, but his eyes seemed lighter than his brothers. Maybe green or blue?

"Ladies!" a herald boomed, standing beside the king's seat. "We have a special surprise for you tonight. All the way from Her Highness the lovely Princess Sagen's home kingdom of Asintisch, the talented Tanzer and Kunst."

Everyone applauded politely, and Sagen beamed like they were applauding *her* and not the two lithe young acrobats who were descending from the ceiling on strips of silk.

Seductive music accompanied their performance, played by two men with cellos in the corner of the room, and the two acrobats held everyone's full attention. They were utterly mesmerizing as they defied gravity, twisting and spinning, climbing and dropping.

It was when their performance was drawing to a close—evident by the increasing tempo of the tune and dramatic way the young girl paused in her partner's grip like she was checking to make sure everyone was paying attention—that my scar tingled and my gut clenched with foreboding.

Something bad was about to happen.

All of a sudden, the female performer tumbled from her partner's embrace. The gathered audience of diners gasped as one, their horrified eyes glued to the girl's fall, so no one was watching when a dagger whispered through the dimly lit room and flew directly toward Prince Louis's heart.

No one except me.

With no time to think, I simply reacted.

My hand shot out as quick as lightning, and I hissed in pain as my fingers closed around the moving blade. It had been a reckless choice, for sure, but my hand could heal a few slices from a flying dagger. I doubted Louis could heal from four inches of steel through his heart.

Time seemed to slow, and I blinked at my blood dripping onto Louis's dinner plate, scarcely believing it had worked. I'd stopped the blade.

Louis sucked in a sharp breath, staring at the bloody blade in my grip just an inch from his chest. His lips parted to say something, but Princess Sagen's scream drowned out whatever it was he said. All I caught was "...Calla..." before the entire room flew into motion.

In hindsight, it probably didn't look great. Everyone had been focused on the death-defying tricks above the banquet table until the girl landed her fall safely. Clapping and applauding, they'd all looked around the table once more to gush over the performance and found me with a dagger poised over Prince Louis's heart.

Shit.

"Lady Callaluna tried to murder the prince!" Sagen screeched like a banshee, shoving back from the table and pointing an accusing finger at me. "She's a murderer!"

Other ladies joined in, shrieking and babbling with all the
intelligence of a pillow full of feathers, and I really needed to fight
an eyeroll that could strain my eyeballs. The whole thing was utterly
absurd. For one, I could hardly be a murderer if no one was dead,
and for two, I wasn't stupid enough to attempt an assassination in
such a public arena.

"She did not," Prince Louis snapped, scowling at Princess Sagen
even as he placed a gentle hand on my wrist to lower it to the table.
"Any idiot can see she just *saved* me. Look." With strong fingers, he
opened my hand and revealed the mess inside.

Until I saw it, it'd been just a dull, burning sort of pain. But the
second I saw it, the pain seemed to increase by roughly six thousand
times. The throwing dagger had been sharpened to a paper-thin
edge and had sliced through my palm and fingers like they were
made of warm butter. In some patches, gleaming white bone and
cartilage showed through, but for the most part it was just a bloody,
shredded mess.

"You need medical attention," Louis muttered, and I refrained
from pointing out how painfully obvious that statement was. Around
us, the commotion was only getting worse with the king storming
toward us and guards hovering all around, unsure who the hell they
should be dragging to the dungeons.

"I'm taking Lady Callaluna to the medical wing," Louis

announced to his father, who had just arrived beside us and was glaring down on me with a face like thunder.

"You're going nowhere until we work out just what in Zryn's name happened here, son!" the king bellowed, and I found myself tensing against the sheer volume he projected.

Prince Louis shoved his chair back and stood toe-to-toe with his king and father. "If she doesn't receive help now, she will lose the use of that hand. I won't reward her good deed like that, sire, nor should you ask me to."

There was a tense pause before the king grunted and moved back a fraction of a step to allow Louis to help me from my seat. "This isn't over, son. No one brings weapons to my dinner table and gets away with it. Am I perfectly clear?" This question was aimed at me, but I was too dizzy with pain to do much more than nod meekly.

Prince Louis plucked the blade from my bleeding mess of a hand, then wrapped a handkerchief around my palm before leading me from the dining hall.

"You saved my life," he murmured as we hurried through the silent corridors toward the medical wing. "I didn't think you'd care much if someone tried to assassinate us royals. After all, we're not the rightful ruling family, are we?"

I made a noise in my throat, clutching my hand to my chest. "Like I care who is *rightful* or not. There was a power vacuum, and your parents stepped in to fill it. Nothing to be ashamed of there."

"Huh," he grunted. "So why do you dislike us all so much?"

I gritted my teeth together hard, fighting through waves of agony to keep on my feet and not pass the hell out. "Can we discuss this another time?" I asked him, feeling sweat roll down the back of my neck. "Like when all my fingers are firmly reattached to my body?"

He snorted a laugh, which I found highly inappropriate given the circumstances. "They haven't come *off*, Lady Callaluna. They're just... less attached than they were."

I rolled my eyes but said nothing. If that was meant to be a joke, he had a crappy sense of humor.

"I am just curious why you'd take such a grievous injury when you could have just as easily let me die. I didn't even see that blade coming, so no one could have accused you of failing to stop it." He turned his head slightly, watching me from the corner of his eye as we walked.

Sighing heavily, I answered as honestly as I dared. "Because unlike you and your royal family, I don't casually discard human life like that. If I *can* prevent it, I will." I paused, and he said nothing. "Now please, shut the hell up? I'm really in pain here."

CHAPTER 20

When I woke, I was alone.

Soon after arriving in the medical wing, I had been given a bitter-tasting tea, which saw me lose consciousness mere moments after sitting on the edge of the bed, so I had no idea what had been done to my wounds or what the diagnosis was.

Sitting up, I rubbed my eyes with my good hand, then peered down at the massive ball of bandages around the other.

"Fuck a duck," I murmured, holding it up to my face to peer at. The gauze was wadded so thickly that I had no idea if I even had a hand left at all, let alone functioning fingers. At least I wasn't in pain anymore, even if the whole room was spinning dangerously.

"Calla!" Lee exclaimed as he entered the medical wing and

spotted me sitting up. "Lie down! Damn it woman, you're on some heavy-duty painkillers right now."

Blinking up at him, it took me a couple of tries to pin down which Lee was the real Lee. "No shit," I agreed, and it came out slurred like I was drunk. "What happened?"

Lee scowled down at me, his clear blue eyes scolding. "You stopped a thrown dagger from killing Prince Louis by grabbing it out of thin air. With your *bare hand*."

I giggled at the horrified way he said it but shook my head. "I know that. I mean, what happened after." I waved my bandage-ball hand at him. "With this?"

"Oh," he huffed. "Prince Louis dropped you off here and made sure you were knocked out, then came to get me. I assisted the medic on duty to stitch up the gashes on your palm and across your fingers, while making sure you stayed unconscious through it all."

Nodding slowly, I tried to get my head to stop spinning but had no luck. "Will my fingers still work?"

Lee raised his brows at me, looking slightly insulted. "Calla, love. I'm the alchemy tutor for a *reason*. Of course they will work. They might even be fully healed by tomorrow morning, if you're lucky."

"That's incredible," I breathed in awe. "You're so talented." I let my head drop back to the pillows and admired all three of Lee's fuzzy forms. "And so damn sexy. Why are you all so damn sexy? And *nice*. I wish these trials were to marry one of you guys." My mouth was just spilling words like vomit, and I couldn't muster the energy to stop it. Hell, I wasn't even embarrassed by what I was saying. After all, it was the truth.

Lee choked back a laugh and sat on the edge of the bed to take my good hand in his. "I think that daffodil-puff tea is hitting you a bit hard, beautiful."

"Mmm," I hummed, agreeing with him.

"Besides, the princes aren't all that bad. You must have seen some redeeming quality in them for you to save Prince Louis last night." Lee's strong fingers stroked down the palm of my hand in a way that made me groan. Who knew hands could be such a damn turn-on?

"No," I disagreed, still sounding slurred. "Just following orders."

Lee's fingers stilled, and he frowned slightly. "How so?"

"Win the Royal Trials or die trying, that's what he said. But never go back; there is nothing left for me there." I was babbling now, on the verge of drifting back to sleep.

"Who, Calla?" Lee demanded, giving my arm a little shake. "Who said that? Was it the king?"

I snorted an unattractive laugh. "He wishes. Another bastard who has shown his true soul, and it is *black*, Lee. Black as tar. People with souls that dark don't deserve power."

"I agree, Calla. But who are you talking about?" He reached up and brushed some hair off my face. "Who threatened you, love?"

"It doesn't matter," I told him, dropping my voice to a whisper as I confided, "He underestimates me, Lee. I'll do what he asks, but only as long as it works for *my* plan. He'll never get what he wants, not from me." I shook my head firmly, then felt my stomach clench and roll as the room set off spinning again. "I think I might be sick."

Lee sighed, smoothing his hand over my hair, then stroking my cheek. "You'll be okay, love. Just sleep it off."

"Sleep," I murmured, already closing my eyes. "That's a good idea. You're so smart, Lee. Smart and handsome and... nice..." I yawned heavily, and whatever else I was saying trailed off into unintelligible mumbles that even I couldn't understand. But sleep sounded so good.

"Luna," Zan's velvety-smooth voice cracked through my deep and dreamless sleep. "Luna, wake up."

His hand was on my shoulder shaking me gently, and I wanted to tell him to fuck off and burn in the fiery pits of hell so I could keep sleeping.

"Such language for a lady," he chuckled, and I dimly realized I'd voiced my thoughts aloud.

"Like you didn't already know that," I muttered, not bothering to open my eyes. Our night of drinking and games had seen me fly my true colors pretty proudly when it came to my less-than-ladylike language. Something the three teachers had found hilarious at the time.

Zan grunted and shook my shoulder again. "Well, now isn't the time, lovely Luna. You need to get up. Now. I left you to sleep as long as I possibly could."

"Why?" I groaned, still not wanting to open my eyes.

"Because it's already lunchtime and the royals won't allow you to miss this afternoon's test," he informed me. "It was hard enough convincing them to let you rest all morning, but they wouldn't budge on the test. All competing ladies must participate, or it goes against the binding oath."

This little gem of information made me snap my lids open and glare at Zan.

"Are they fucking serious?" I seethed. "I saved their son's life and can't get a pass for one freaking test?"

Zan looked just as mad as me, but realistically, what could he do about it? The king and queen had proved themselves right royal assholes, so it was doubtful that the words of a tutor would make any impact on them.

"I'm so sorry, Luna. If there was anything I could do…" Zan grimaced, looking more apologetic than he needed to be, so I gave him a small smile.

"It's fine, Zan. I just…" I pushed myself awkwardly up to sitting and blinked a few times to clear the fuzz from my brain. "I just need a moment to wake up."

A sly grin twitched his lips, and he raised a brow at me. "And find some clothes, perhaps?"

It took me a second to understand what he meant before I scrambled to cover myself with the sheet. Apparently someone had thought it reasonable to strip me out of my starlight evening gown, and I only wore a strapless, sheer lace corset. On the upside, it lifted my boobs up into some seriously awesome cleavage. On the downside, it did little to nothing to disguise my nipples, thanks to the translucent fabric.

Dammit all to Zryn!

"No need to be embarrassed, Luna," Zan teased. "I know you're harboring a secret crush on me. I would have seen those sooner or later." He delivered a wink that did nothing but embarrass me further, and I felt my cheeks flame.

"Pig," I scowled. "Can you find me some clothes, please?"

He grinned at my half-assed insult and presented a pile of fabric from behind where he'd been sitting. "I stopped by your room on my way here and grabbed these. Figured you might need them."

Suspicious, I checked through what he had selected from my closet and immediately guessed that Jules hadn't been there to help him. "Pants, huh?" I looked at him with curiosity, and he shrugged.

"You seem more comfortable in pants than dresses." He paused, then ruined the nice sentiment by adding, "Besides, I'm dying to see your ass in those." He flicked the heavy blue fabric of the pants in my hand, then needed to duck my bandage ball as I tried to swat at him. "I might leave you to get changed. Yell if you need help."

"I'm sure you'll be more than happy to lend a hand," I muttered under my breath as Zan left the small, curtained cubical. Truthfully, I probably did need help dressing. I'd only worn this type of fabric once before—as it was a relic from before the Darkness and therefore insanely expensive—but from memory, it wasn't the easiest thing to dress in with two fully functioning hands, let alone one.

Still, I was too damn stubborn to actually accept Zan's offer of help, so I spent the next few minutes struggling into all kinds of complex poses as I wriggled, struggled, and forced myself into the tight blue garment.

"You okay in there?" Zan called out, sounding like he was fighting back a bit of laughter, which just made me more determined to do it myself.

"Fine!" I snapped back, then gave the waistband one more, heavy yank that saw it move into place. "Ah-hah! Success!" I thought I'd crowed my victory quietly, but the snickering outside my cubicle said otherwise. Whatever. Now I needed a shirt... and to attack the zipper and button fly. "Come on, Ry," I breathed to myself so silently I knew Zan wouldn't hear me. "You can do this. Strong, independent women don't need help from a man to dress themselves."

It took a little while longer, but eventually I threw back the curtains feeling rather damn proud of myself. That feeling was quickly doused by Zan cracking up laughing at me.

"What?" I snarled, glowering at him.

"Nothing," he snickered, coming closer and placing his fingers on the top button of my lilac-purple silk shirt. "You just mismatched the buttons a little." With deft motions, he unbuttoned my entire shirt, then rebuttoned me in the correct holes. He even went so far as to roll my sleeves neatly for me, seeing as I couldn't button the cuff over the thick bandage on my wrist. "There, much more presentable."

"Um, thanks," I muttered, feeling a bit like a child who'd put her shoes on the wrong feet. "Oh, shoes? I don't know how much people will appreciate me wandering around the palace barefoot."

"Here." He held up the pair of black leather boots I'd worn the day before to Ty's knife class. "Will these work?"

Nodding, I took them from him and dropped them to the floor to push my feet inside. Unwilling to look like a total child who couldn't tie her own shoes, I bent over to lace them up myself. Zan made a sort of strangled noise in his throat, then crouched in front of me and swatted my useless hands away.

"It wouldn't kill you to accept my help, Luna," he commented as he laced my boots, then offered me a hand up again. "Come on, we need to get to the library before lunch break ends. I did my best to alter the test in the time I had, but..." He sighed. "I just really hope you were paying attention during school."

Wait. *School?*

"Uh, in what way?" I asked him, probing for more information. I was an orphan raised by a crime lord in Lakehaven's slums. School hadn't really been an option. Hell, I was lucky I could even read and write; lots of kids my age in the Pond couldn't.

Zan opened his mouth to reply, but was interrupted by the elderly, sternfaced medic who had stitched my shoulder earlier in the week.

"Heard you were leaving," she muttered, scowling at me. "Against my better advice, but who am I to deny the process of the Royal Trials?" She rolled her eyes, and I saw a hint of sympathy there for me. "Here, you need to drink this. The healing creams that Lee used are incredibly effective, but they hurt like hellfire while your flesh mends. Your pain medication is due to wear off in less than half an hour, so drink up unless you want to end up passed out on the library floor."

Taking the small bottle from her, I offered a small smile. "Thanks, that definitely doesn't sound fun."

The medic gave me a stern nod, then gave Zan what looked like a silent warning before leaving us to continue out of the room.

"You'd better drink that now," Zan advised me. "It can make you a bit woozy, but it's a million times better than the pain you'll be in if it wears off. Trust me, I've been there firsthand."

"That bad?" I uncapped the bottle and gave it a cautionary sniff.

It didn't smell too appalling, but just in case, I downed it all in one mouthful. "Blergh. Okay, what were you saying about the test this afternoon? And school?"

"Oh, yes," Zan replied as we walked through the palace hallways. "Today's lesson was just on the general history of Teich and Lakehaven. All about Queen Ophelia's reign and her tragic death, which led to the Darkness, then the Plague. There were a few more in-depth discussions, but I did a quick edit of the test to take out anything that's not taught in the Lakehaven general curriculum. So, you *should* be fine, provided you paid attention in class, which I am just now realizing is possible you didn't."

"Excuse me?" I spluttered. "What makes you think that? I could have been the perfect student for all you know!" *And I really could have... if I'd ever had the opportunity to attend a school.*

He snorted a laugh, glancing at me from the corner of his eye. "Yeah right, Luna. You practically have 'delinquent' written across your forehead. I find it incredibly hard to picture you in a ladies' finishing school."

He had a fair point. Still, that didn't help me now...

"So this test is all just... uh... common knowledge? Maybe you can give me a few examples of questions?" It was worth a try.

Zan grimaced and shook his head. "I wish I could, lovely Luna. Rules are rules, and you know what happens when we try to break them. Editing the test was as good as I could come up with on short notice, seeing as I really thought Prince Louis could talk the king and queen into letting you skip this one."

"Unsurprising that he didn't," I murmured, shrugging and feeling the pain meds spread through my body like honey. "Doubt he even gave me a second thought after dumping me with Lee and that... uh... that medic whose name I can't remember."

Zan sighed, looking like he was holding back secrets. But it was too late to pressure him for more info as we had arrived at the library and some ladies had already returned from their lunch break.

"Just... stay calm and try your best," he said quietly as I made my way over to a vacant desk and chair. "You'll be fine, Luna. I have faith in you."

Despite his encouraging words, the tightness to his lips and eyes spoke a different story. He was worried, and rightfully so. If only he knew just how worried he *should* be.

Stay calm, he'd said. Sounded easy enough... if this test wasn't about to totally expose me for the imposter I was.

Groaning, I dropped my head onto the desk and tried to wish myself out of this mess I'd wound up in. What were my options? I could pretend to pass out and end up back in medical wing, but it was doubtful the binding oath would let me get away with that one.

Come to think of it, the binding oath was likely to zap me no matter how I tried to get out of the test. So, my best bet was to take it and pray to Aana that the "history" we learned in the Pond was cohesive with what they taught the good little ladies of Lakehaven.

Maybe Zan could be creative in his marking, if he felt inclined to save me from death by poison tonight at dinner. Maybe I should have let him "help me dress" after all, considering I might be dead by morning. Hell, I was practically dying a virgin, considering how awful my few experiences with actual sex had been.

Booklets of paper were handed out among the sixteen of us who remained in the Royal Trials, and Zan slipped an ink pen onto my desk to use. It was a sweet gesture, considering I didn't have one myself, but unless it was magically loaded with the correct answers, then I was royally screwed.

My heart sunk even further when I flipped the first page open and found it wasn't multiple-choice. In the back of my mind, I'd been banking on my intuition to guide me to the correct answers, but that could have only worked if there were both correct and incorrect options on the page, not just the infuriating space for me to write my own answer, which I stared down at like it had personally offended me.

Shit.

Sucking in a deep breath, I tucked my hair behind my ear and picked up my pen awkwardly in my left, undamaged hand.

My eyes scanned over the first question, and a little bit of anxiety lifted. Maybe it wouldn't be all that bad, after all. I knew the answer to that first one, and I couldn't imagine it being any different based on where the information was learned—Pond or finishing school.

Carefully, I scribbled my answer in almost illegible handwriting, and cursed Prince Louis again inside my head. Of course I had to save his life with my dominant hand. It would have been far too convenient to have sliced up my left hand.

Biting back yet another self-pitying sigh, I focused on the test booklet. The new pain meds were starting to kick in, and Zan hadn't been lying about feeling woozy.

"Focus, Calla," I hissed to myself, then almost burst out laughing. Even I was getting confused with who the hell I was these days. Maybe I needed to give myself a whole new name...

Realizing I was daydreaming, I shook my head sharply to try and clear it before peering down at the paper again.

I can do this. I can. These questions aren't too hard, if I just... focus.

CHAPTER 21

The knock on my door as I dressed for dinner was not a total shock. I'd suspected I might hear something more before walking into that gilded death trap.

"Well, hello gorgeous," Jules purred as she answered the door. "How can I help you?"

"I'm here to see Lady Callaluna," Zan replied in a gruff voice. "It's urgent."

There was a short pause within which I knew my former best friend was swallowing her own jealousy. She was so used to having men fall all over her and barely glance twice at me that this had to be an uncomfortable shift for her.

Not that Zan was *falling all over* me. Not by a long shot. But she didn't know that.

"She's busy," Juliana replied in a snippy tone.

"I'll be brief," Zan insisted, his voice full of steel that said he wasn't taking no for an answer. Jules must have noticed the same thing because moments later there were footsteps in the sitting area, and then Zan appeared in the doorway to my bedroom.

"Hey," he greeted me with a frown touching his forehead.

I groaned, sagging to sit on the edge of my bed and not caring this time that I was in nothing but my underwear. "That bad?" I asked him, and he grimaced. "Okay, so... That's that, then?"

He shook his head. "Not necessarily. Someone else was equally as low, and they won't eliminate both of you. But..." He trailed off, leaning his shoulder against the doorframe and reminding me just how tall he was.

"But what?" I prompted, just wanting him to deliver the bad news like ripping off hot wax.

He scratched the back of his head and sighed. "But her answers were just wrong. Like... she's just not a smart girl. Yours were, well, insulting."

I blinked at him a few times, trying to work out what the fuck he'd just said. "Excuse me?"

"For the question, 'Who was most likely to be behind Queen Ophelia's murder and the subsequent loss of baby Princess Zarina?' You answered, 'King Titus, or at least his belly-crawling scumbag of an advisor. If I ever saw someone willing to kill a queen, it's that asshole.' And then you drew a snake with a moustache like Lord Taipanus." Zan glared his accusation at me, and I squirmed.

"Okay, so... maybe that wasn't the most socially acceptable answer, but it's speculation, so how can it be *wrong*?" I defended my answer with a weak argument, and Zan shook his head, looking disappointed.

"I couldn't even suppress the tests. Lord Taipanus sent someone to collect them the second I finished scoring everyone." He pursed his lips. "I think you need to... run or something. I don't know. I just... I'm really worried what's going to happen tonight, Luna."

"She can't!" Juliana interrupted us, barging past Zan and into the bedroom to glare at me. "Not only would the binding oath kill her, she has made a commitment to see this through."

Seething at her reminder of the rock and hard place I was jammed between, I glared back at her.

"So what?" Zan snapped. "She runs a risk of dying with the binding magic versus dying of red-tide poison at dinner? There is no guarantee the magic would kill her, but the poison *will*."

"Running away is *not* an option," Jules declared, scowling at both Zan and myself. "You don't know for sure that it will be you tonight, Ry—ah, Lady Callaluna. The servants have all been talking about how enamored Prince Louis is after you saved his life last night, so I hardly think that he'll let his psychotic parents kill you tonight. It'd be bad form, don't you think?"

I glanced between Jules and Zan, chewing my lip. She had a

point that there was no *certainty* it would be me with poisoned wine tonight, but even if it was...

"Zan, has Lee ever worked on an antidote for red-tide?" I asked in a small voice, and the brunette tutor cursed under his breath.

"Luna, you can't run this risk," he implored me, but I just gave him a small shrug.

"Look," I said, trying to keep my own panic at bay. "I know that there is no *known* cure for it, but we also both know how great Lee is with botany and alchemy. You can't really expect me to believe that these girls have been dying of the same poison all week and he *hasn't* tried to create an antidote."

Zan's jaw was clenched tight, but I knew I was right by the way he dodged my eye contact. "He's been trying, yes," he finally admitted. "But I don't know if anything has worked so far or if he is just too hesitant to try it out on anyone."

I nodded a couple of times. "Okay, so here's what we do. If it's me tonight, then as soon as you can, you get me to Lee. If his antidote works, great. If not... Well, I'm really no worse off than trying to run, am I?"

Zan ground his teeth together so hard I could hear them from where I sat. "You don't get it, Luna. That poison, it's—"

"I know," I promised him. "Trust me, I know full well what that poison can do." I shuddered at the memory of my last brush with red-tide. Interestingly enough, it had been after my first time having sex. It had been inside one of the many crumbling, abandoned mansions that made up the Pond, and seconds after *he'd* finished, his girlfriend had shown up with a pipe wrench. I'd found myself climbing down the outside of the building totally naked, and the red-tide had just barely brushed my thigh.

Even so, it had kept me bedridden for over a week feeling like my skin was melting off and begging for someone to kill me.

"Look, it is what it is. I have no doubt I'll make it through tonight, regardless of how it pans out." I gave both Jules and Zan a confident smile. "I'm harder to kill than you might think."

Jules coughed a laugh. "That, I believe. I'll get your dress."

She bustled out of the room to fetch that evening's dress from where she'd been steaming it in the sitting room, and Zan arched a brow at me.

"She seems like an odd choice for a maid. Very outspoken."

I shrugged. "Unfortunately, I'm stuck with her. My... family... they insisted she stay with me, and I just found out she has been reporting back to them on my 'progress' here."

Zan's dark brows dropped into a scowl. "That's not okay, Luna. She's spying on you?"

"Like I said, I'm stuck with her." I changed the subject to avoid any more probing questions into me and Juliana's relationship. "Now, am I allowed to take this bandage off yet? No one has given me any more of those painkiller potions, so I'm guessing the worst of it should be over."

He grunted, then pushed off the doorframe to come and sit beside me. "Yeah, Lee told me I could take it off while I'm here." Taking my bandage-ball hand, he placed it in his lap and started unravelling the gauze.

"Huh," I murmured. "He didn't want to come and do it himself? What if I never see him again? Or Ty for that matter?"

"Seriously?" Zan barked, pinching my leg just on this side of painfully.

Rubbing my leg and fighting a grin, I shook my head. "No, but sort of. I kind of thought we were, you know, close? If I had thought one of you might die, I'd probably want to pop by and say, you know, good luck. Or something?"

"Good luck?" Zan repeated, squinting at me. "What happened to being 'harder to kill than everyone thinks'?"

I gave him a small smile. "That's still true. But they don't know it, do they?"

He huffed like I was being deliberately difficult and focused on unwrapping the bandage. "I didn't tell them about the test," he finally admitted. "But you're more than 'close,' and you know it. You're all they can talk about this week, which is... worrying."

I wrinkled my nose. "How is that worrying?"

"Well," he started, discarding the wad of bandages before starting to pick at the sticky pad across my whole palm. "Because despite how Ty looks and acts, he isn't as tough as people think. Deep down he is a romantic, looking for his one true love. If you were to die in these stupid, *stupid* trials, he'd be heartbroken. And don't even get me started on what a mess Lee would be."

His words gave me pause, and I was silent for a moment as he peeled the sticky fabric back from my hand and exposed the tender, pink skin underneath, dotted with black knots of stitching yarn.

"But... you wouldn't be all that upset?" I whispered, totally unable to stop the words from spilling out of my mouth. Why I had to pick at this scab, I had no idea. Maybe it was the whole life-or-death moment I was stuck in.

Zan's mouth tightened, but he didn't reply or even look up at me until he'd finished cutting and removing all the little stitches from my *almost* fully healed palm. When it was all done, he gathered up the little pile of rags and then looked up at me with a carefully neutral expression.

"I can't afford to be, Luna. There is a lot more going on in these trials than you realize, and not just for the 'competitors.'" His voice was cold, almost closed off, and it made me want to pry him open with a damn nutcracker.

But I still had a certain level of dignity, despite the fact that I'd grown up on the streets. So I nodded sharply and said nothing as he left my room and Jules returned with my gown.

Inside, though, my heart was cracking. Had I been an idiot reading too much into the flirtatious banter with Zan?

CHAPTER 22

Walking into dinner that night, my whole body was numb. I'd talked a brave game in front of Zan and Jules, but I had nothing to back it up. I possessed no magic of my own, nor did I have any sneaky tricks up my sleeve to wriggle out of certain death. At the end of it all, I still had a choice. It was just a shame that all my available options led to death... all except that slim chance that maybe, just maybe, it might not be me drinking poison at tonight's toast.

"You again," I groaned as Prince Thibault pulled out the chair beside me. A smile touched his lips at my less than polite greeting, but he said nothing in response.

Indeed, no response was needed as Prince Louis took the seat on my other side and Prince Alexander directly opposite, staring at me with the intensity of a hawk with its prey.

"Gosh, I must have done something right to be graced with your company again," I murmured and buttered myself a piece of bread. Screw dying on an empty stomach, and the palace cooks made incredible bread.

"You did," Prince Louis responded, placing his hand gently over mine, then turning my palm over to inspect the remaining scars. "You saved my life last night, Lady Callaluna. I needed to formally thank you for that."

"Oh yeah?" I turned to him with a sarcastic brow raise, which he couldn't see, thanks to my heavy, peacock-feathered mask. "How about thanking me by granting a pardon to leave the Royal Trials?"

Prince Louis's mouth opened, but only a surprised sound came out. It was Prince Alexander who responded to me.

"We couldn't, even if we wanted to," he snapped in an almost angry way. What he had to be angry at *me* about, I had no idea. Still, I was in no mood for royal prickishness, and that small bit of attitude flared my temper.

Narrowing my eyes at him from behind my mask, I seethed. "Of course not, Sal and Aana forbid the royal princes of Teich have any say over their own Royal Trials. That would be insanity. Guess that explains why you haven't lifted a finger to help your citizens since the Plague ended. It's not because you're self-involved, coldhearted assholes; it's just because Daddy won't let you."

My caustic, contemptuous manner must have rubbed the oldest prince the wrong way because his fist balled around his napkin, and his jaw clenched hard. I could see a great comeback building, but it would sadly have to go unheard. The king had just stood and was tapping his glass to call the dreaded death toast.

Offering Prince Alexander a sarcastic smile, I picked up the glass of wine, which had just been placed in front of me, and held it lightly between my fingers. The three white marks on my back that I'd had since birth burned with warning, and my stomach sank to my feet. A spike of intuition at the same time as I touched my glass? Couldn't be a coincidence.

Hopefully... *hopefully*, my bravado with Zan earlier had held a kernel of truth and I might still get through it. If I only took the smallest of sips, then the magic could be appeased but I could ingest minimal poison.

King Titus prattled off his usual meaningless speech, then raised his glass with a sick smile on his face. This was it.

My birthmark continued to burn its warning as I lifted the glass to my lips with a shaking hand. Could I really go through with it?

My gaze was totally glued to my wine; everyone around me faded away into nothingness as my tunnel vision filled with nothing but golden, bubbling liquid. Was this how all the other girls had felt? Surely I could just... not drink?

Testing the theory, I paused my glass an inch from my lips.

Instantly, it became like my hand was no longer my own, being forced closer and closer to my mouth as though attached to a puppeteer's strings. Before I could even gasp at the uncomfortable sensation, the glass was against my lips and tipping up.

Thankfully, the second the wine touched my tongue, the horrific feeling of possession left my hand, and I slammed my glass back down on the table in disgust.

All three princes and several of the ladies seated near us stared at me in confusion, like it was really such a shocking thing that someone might be impolite at a time like this. Or, I guess, I assumed it was confusion. The masks really did make it hard to read facial expressions at the best of times, let alone when one was anticipating convulsing and dying in a matter of moments.

"Are you okay, Lady Callaluna?" Prince Louis asked in a quiet voice, touching his gloved fingers lightly to my forearm.

Was I? How long did the poison usually take to do its damage?

My silent question was quickly answered—but not in the way I'd expected. Further down the table, a woman with dirty blond hair and a magenta satin gown collapsed out of her seat in a clatter of dishes and cutlery before convulsing on the floor.

The sight of another lady—instead of *me*—suffering the effects of red-tide had me speechless. I'd been so sure it was my turn. I'd failed Zan's history test, and all my senses had been going haywire like they were warning me not to drink the wine.

Unless... unless it really was just superstitious coincidence that my birthmark tingled when bad things were about to happen. I'd always denied that it was magic, but I *had* believed there was something to it. Some sort of inbuilt danger radar or something.

Maybe not.

All the air gushed from my body, and I sagged in my seat as the waiters lifted the half-dead girl and carried her out of the dining hall.

"Yeah," I whispered, answering Prince Louis's question. "Yeah, I'm fine."

Reaching for my *untainted* glass with trembling fingers, I raised it back to my lips and took a proper sip this time. If ever there was a time for alcohol, this was it. My birthmark continued to burn, but this time I just shifted and scratched at it through my dress.

"I take it you thought it might be you tonight?" Prince Thibault murmured, keeping his voice low but sadly not low enough not to be heard by the lady opposite him, who snorted a laugh.

"I'm shocked it wasn't," she commented in such a callous way that it actually gave me pause. Who was this chick, anyway? And what the fuck had I done to her?

Prince Thibault cleared his throat and gave the woman a small smile. "Why do you say that, Lady Felicia?"

Felicia, that was her name. It rang absolutely no bells in my head though.

"Because there was no *way* she passed the test today. Not only did she miss the entire morning class, she fell asleep no less than three times during the test. If the tutor hadn't kept waking her up, she would have turned in a blank booklet." Lady Felicia sniffed in my direction, like she'd actually been hoping that's what I would do.

"What a bitch," I exclaimed, then quickly realized I'd said it aloud and not inside my head like I'd really intended it to be. Whoops.

Prince Thibault covered his mouth to cough, but I was at least seventy percent sure he was trying not to laugh. Thankfully, we were spared any more uncomfortable conversation about my scholarly failures as the ladies sitting to the other sides of the princes all excitedly engaged them in conversation.

Apparently as the week had progressed, the sight of a competitor dying at the dinner table had become less and less of an event, and each woman was making the most of her opportunity to make an impression on the royal morons.

Not that I was complaining. After the stress of thinking I was tonight's sacrificial lamb, I just needed a damn break. I'd return to my plan of *endearing myself* to them... tomorrow. Tonight, I just wanted to get through the meal and get the hell out of there.

It was roughly halfway through the main course that I noticed something was wrong. Something was *really* wrong. Pausing, I carefully placed my cutlery back on my plate and dabbed at my mouth with my heavy linen napkin. Glancing down at the starched, white fabric, I saw my fears confirmed.

Blood stained the whiteness, and I could taste more pooling within my mouth. Combined with the feeling that my stomach was slowly disintegrating and the heavy ache in my limbs... it was pretty obvious what was going on.

I was fucked.

"Excuse me, Your Highnesses," I whispered, just loud enough to be heard but trying to keep my mouth shut. If I wanted to make it to Lee before I died, I needed to not alert *anyone* to the fact that I, too, had been poisoned. "I'm afraid I am feeling a bit faint," I told them, folding my napkin to place it on the table. "Must be lady business. May I be excused? I would so hate to stain these lovely chairs."

It was the most stupid, upper class problem I could think of, but I was confident it would have the same effect on men of all classes. The only difference being, in the Pond we just got on and dealt with it. Here, though, it wouldn't be considered all that unusual for a lady to act like she had an incurable disease at that time of the month.

"Of course," Prince Thibault replied, placing a huge hand under my wrist and helping me out of my seat. Honestly, at any other time I would shy away from such a gesture, but in that moment it was a blessing. My knees were so weak I wasn't totally sure I could have stood up on my own. "I hope you will be feeling better by morning, Lady Callaluna."

I offered him a tight smile but didn't bother forcing any more words out. As it was, I could taste so much blood in my mouth that my teeth would no doubt be coated if I tried to speak. Instead I just bobbed a quick curtsey—thank you, Zan—and hurried out of the dining hall before anyone could stop me.

Once I'd reached the corridor and made it out of sight of the guards, who stood on either side of the dining room door, I collapsed against the wall and spat out the mouthful of crimson, metallic fluid.

Staring down at it staining the gray slate tiles, I shuddered violently. This was so damn bad.

Just get to Lee. If anyone can help you, it's Lee.

Over and over in my head I repeated this lifeline as I staggered through the palace. My best bet was to check the sanctuary; that seemed to be where the three of them hung out whenever they weren't teaching.

Please, Aana. Please let Lee be in the sanctuary.

Tears streamed down my face as I gritted my teeth against the pain, but logically I knew I couldn't keep ignoring it much longer. My whole body was engulfed in flames from the inside, and I now knew how tame the red-tide skin-contact poison was in comparison to this distilled, ingested version. It was the same unmistakable burning pain, but a thousand times worse. If I had wanted to die then, this time it was a foregone conclusion. I *would* die from this if Lee had nothing to help me. It was only a question of how long I'd suffer first.

"Lee?" I croaked out, and I collapsed against the front door of the sanctuary and used my weight to push it open. There were no candles lit, that I could see, and no one responded to my pathetic cries for help. Still... I had no other ideas of where to find him, so I continued inside further.

Empty. Not a person in sight, and certainly no flirtatious, sunshine-haired gardener.

I was well and truly screwed.

Unable to fight through the pain enough to think of another idea, I dropped onto the velvet chaise couch beside the plant full of ophelia blooms and closed my eyes. If this was how it all ended, at least I could die with the sweet, nostalgic scent of those beautiful flowers surrounding me.

Time passed; I had no idea how much. Minutes or hours? It felt like eons as my body shook and convulsed through waves upon waves of agony while the red-tide ate through all my vital organs. But it was raised voices that brought me back to the present.

Cracking my lead-like eyelids open, I tried to look around. Everything was still and silent. Had I imagined it?

But no, there it was again, two men arguing somewhere nearby, but not inside the sanctuary.

Squinting, I tried to work out where the sound was coming from as the voices grew louder and clearer. I was in the glass-paneled former sunroom, so it was possible that one of the windows was open and the arguing men were outside.

"You promised me two eliminations tonight, Taipanus," the first man snapped, and my eyes widened further at the familiar voice. *King Titus?* "What in Zryn's name happened? I gave you free rein with your little poison bottle; how bloody hard is it?"

"Sire," the slippery spymaster replied. "I did have two glasses poisoned. Both of the girls that failed today's history test were to be given them."

"Oh? Well the mouthy blonde still looked pretty damn alive when she *walked herself* out of the dining hall tonight. How do you explain that, Taipanus?" The king sounded like a serious piece of work, and if I'd had even half my usual strength, I would have been sorely tempted to march out there and confront him, royalty or not.

"Your servers must have messed up somehow"—Taipanus sniffed— "because my poison is infallible. No one can survive its touch."

"Yes, well. We have bigger issues to deal with, and I'm growing concerned that we left these infernal trials until too late. What is the news from the border towns?" The two of them moved somewhat, and suddenly I could make them out through one of the windows. I assumed they'd chosen this location to speak because of what Lee had told me when he first brought me to the sanctuary—people thought it was haunted, so everyone steered clear. What better place to discuss confidential information?

Taipanus shifted, looking uncomfortable in a way that I hadn't realized the Snake was capable of. "News is not good, sire. We have been restricting the flow of information to the people, but some things slip through. So far, all the common folk know is that people have been disappearing from towns. They think that it's an act of war, that one of our neighboring kingdoms is plotting an attack and thinning our lines of defense."

King Titus grunted and scratched his beard. "So, no one knows what is really happening?"

"No, sire." Taipanus shook his head. "Only a select few know that the people haven't been disappearing, they've been *changing*. Such information would cause widespread hysteria that we can't afford."

"Agreed." King Titus sighed heavily. "Tell your men to do their best to eradicate these creatures. Burn entire towns to the ground if that's what it takes. We need to get through these trials. By the end, either we will have killed the little princess, or we will have her completely under our control." He paused, and if I could have spoken, I would have been yelling obscenities and exclamations. "How is that potion going, by the way?"

Taipanus stroked his moustache like some sort of fictional villain. "Ah yes, it's coming along beautifully. Are you still quite certain you wish to make your son a vacant shell, too? We could just use it on his wife after the coronation and use her as our puppet."

"I'm sure," King Titus snapped. "I didn't go to all the effort of stealing this throne only to let my foolish, bleeding-heart children reap the benefits."

Taipanus laughed then, a horrid, hacking noise that made me want to plug my ears. "As you wish, my king."

They moved away from the window then, and the rest of their conversation was lost to me. Not that I could have listened any longer if I'd tried. The sticky, warm trickle of liquid down my neck combined with the sudden absence of noise suggested my ears were now bleeding too.

At least I would die knowing the truth, for all the good it would do. King Titus and his Snake had been responsible for Queen Ophelia's murder, and what was more shocking still... they believed the Princess Zarina was alive.

Not just alive, but *here in the trials*? It was an insane idea. But then, was it really so implausible? The land's magic was making it damn clear that it wasn't happy with the current rulers. Why do that if Ophelia's bloodline was extinct?

Finally—and surprisingly, the most shocking revelation—was that the king's evil and twisted plans didn't even spare his own sons. Whichever prince ascended to the throne would be little more than a meat puppet, existing only as a figurehead for Titus to continue ruling behind the scenes. It made me furious, dizzyingly so, and for once I wished I could see those royal twats once more to warn them.

As the world faded away and I gave myself over to the pain of death, I cursed myself for a great many things, not the least of which was my attitude toward the royal princes of Teich. Perhaps I'd been going about things all the wrong way... If I had wanted them to change, to *help* the citizens of Lakehaven rather than ignoring them, it might have been better to try a more persuasive approach.

So it was then—as I lay on the chaise lounge in a spreading pool of my own blood as my skin swelled and split—that I made myself a promise. If by some miracle I survived the poison, I would change tactics. The princes were in the same doomed ship as me, so we might as well get some good done while we could.

CHAPTER 23

Death smelled so much worse than I had ever really thought it would, like potent herbs and wet soil mixed with a harsh sanitizer and blood. So much coppery blood. In short, death smelled *bad*.

And it was bright. Wasn't death meant to be all dark and shadowy? Not that I was any expert, but that's sort of what the broadly accepted idea of death was.

Cringing against the brightness that seemed to be right in my damn eyes, I raised an arm to cover my face—and ended up smearing a toxic-smelling concoction all over myself.

"What the—" I mumbled, peeling my glop-covered eyelids open and frowning. "Where the fuck am I?"

"Calla?" Lee's panicked voice met my ears seconds before his face loomed into my blurry field of vision. "Holy shit. Guys! Ty, Zan! She's awake!"

"Lee?" I croaked, blinking to try and clear my vision. I was in my bedroom, with Lee. Was he dead too? No wait, that was stupid. Which meant, "I'm still alive?"

The handsome blond gardener laughed, but it had an edge of hysteria to it. "Yeah, beautiful. You're still alive. Holy gods, you're still alive."

"Lo!" Ty exclaimed, shoving Lee aside and launching his huge form at me in a huge bear hug that made me hiss with pain. My whole body felt as though it'd been through a meat grinder, and my skin was so raw that it was agony to have him touching me.

Lee growled a curse and peeled Ty off me. "Can't you see you're hurting her, you giant oaf? Look, you made her cry!"

Sweet Aana, even my tears rolling down my cheeks stung like acid. Perhaps Lee was wrong, and this was some form of afterlife punishment.

"Shit," Ty cursed. "I'm so sorry, Lo. I just... We thought you wouldn't make it."

I tried to force a reassuring smile, but it all hurt too much. "I probably wouldn't have. By the fact that I'm here now, I take it Lee's cure works?"

Ty glanced at Lee, who shook his head while still staring at me.

"No?" I squinted at him, trying to make sense of what was going on. "But I'm not dead, and I'm all covered in this... goop." I lifted a lead-like arm again to demonstrate, and Lee pursed his lips, frowning.

The bed sagged on my other side, and I glanced over to find Zan perched on the mattress, staring down at the quilt. "The *goop* is just healing all the splits in your skin," he explained. "Lee's antidote for the red-tide did nothing. In fact, it almost seemed to make you worse."

I gaped at Zan, then turned to stare in shock at Lee, who was flushed and frowning.

"Seriously?" I asked the botanist, and he shrugged awkwardly.

"It certainly seemed to," he admitted. "After that, we let you vomit it all back up and then just did whatever we could to treat the symptoms. The actual poison itself, though, your body seemed to just metabolize it naturally. It's actually pretty incredible; I hadn't even known it was possible."

Stunned, all I could say was, "Huh." I'd been so sure I was dying. "Maybe because I've been in contact with red-tide before? Is it possible to build a tolerance?"

Lee's brows shot up. "Maybe? That could explain why you were able to fight it off when no one else has."

"Lo," Ty said quietly, frowning down at me. "Why would you have ever been in contact with red-tide before? It's not a common algae, and as far as I'm aware, it only grows in swamps and places like the Pond."

Shifting uncomfortably under three sets of curious eyes, I

searched for a change of subject. "How long have I been... out?"

"Not long, which is equally as shocking as the fact that you've processed the poison naturally." Lee glanced at his simple, leather-strapped wristwatch. "It's just after dawn now. We found you last night in the sanctuary around half an hour after you'd left dinner. What made you go there, anyway?"

I'd thought that was fairly obvious, but maybe not? "I was looking for you."

"Oh." Lee blinked at me a couple of times, then looked away like he was uncomfortable.

"Today is the final test, right?" I turned to Zan, and he nodded. "Do you think I'll be okay? I don't want..." *Lord Taipanus or the king* "... anyone knowing I was poisoned last night too. That would lead to way too many questions, don't you think?"

Zan gave a short nod, his mouth tight. "I don't know, Luna. You're still in bad shape. Lee?"

Lee had just picked up a soft, damp cloth and began ever so gently wiping some goop off my forearm. "Maybe?" he replied. "I sort of don't see any way around it, given the king wouldn't let you skip a simple history test."

I grunted a disgusted noise, agreeing with him. Fuzzy, fractured memories of the night before flittered across my mind, but I couldn't quite grab onto any details. Something about the king and his Snake and the unmistakable feeling that they were people to fear, now more so than ever before... But if only I could remember why.

"You're right." I sucked in a deep breath as Lee's cloth pressed just a little hard, but I was relieved to see unblemished skin being revealed from under the goop. "How long do I have?"

"Testing starts in just a little over four hours," Ty told me. "But if we can get your name moved down the list, you'll get more time. There's no rule that says you have to sit there and wait with the other ladies."

"Let's do that then," Zan agreed. "If we can get you last on the list, you'll have around eight hours from now."

I nodded. "Okay. Eight hours. What should I do in the meantime?" This question was directed at Lee, who was turning into my personal physician.

"Sleep," he ordered me in a firm voice. "That's the only thing you can do, and it's ultimately going to give your body the best chance of recovery. Zan and Ty can come and grab us if anything changes or if they can't get your name moved."

"Us?" I echoed, focusing on totally the wrong aspect of the situation.

Lee gave a short nod, rinsed his cloth, and started on my other arm. "Yes, I'll stay to monitor you."

I bit back a smile but couldn't deny the fact that him staying made me feel stupidly girly inside. "Okay, sure. To monitor me."

Zan and Ty looked less than impressed at being dismissed but didn't argue the sense of the plan. Lee was tending my wounds, and there was no point in all three of them hovering over me while I slept.

"I'll be fine," I reassured them. "It's amazing what a little rest can do."

Ty leaned over, being much more careful this time, and placed a gentle kiss against my hair—probably the only place on me not covered in Lee's herbal concoction. "Sleep well, little one. We will be thinking of you every minute until we see you again."

It was such a sweet thing to say, but the big soldier was gone before I could reciprocate with words of my own.

Zan stood from his perch on the edge of my bed and started for the door before pausing and turning back to scowl at me. "Just... don't die again, okay Luna?"

A bit stunned and confused, I just nodded, and he left the room.

"Again?" I asked Lee. "What does he mean?"

"Exactly what he said," Lee muttered, shifting to sit further on the bed so he could reach my upper arms. "Technically, you died a couple of times last night."

"What?" I exclaimed, trying to push myself up to sit but groaning as my body protested.

Lee sighed. "Your heart kept stopping. I couldn't even do anything to help you. We just had to sit here and pray that it would restart. Which, obviously, it did. Zan was right about you being harder to kill than you look."

Despite the seriousness of the situation, a small smile crept across my lips. Turned out I hadn't just been talking shit after all. "I'm tougher than I look, Lee. But..." I bit the side of my lip and looked at him through lowered lashes. "I'm sorry you had to see that. It can't have been fun, for any of you."

Lee huffed a noise, rinsing his cloth again and moving to my shoulder. "It was one of the most horrific things I've ever lived through, Calla, and that includes seeing people die during the Plague. But I'm glad I was here. You seemed to know we were with you. Your crying eased when one of us was holding your hand."

I had no idea what to even say to that, so I said nothing for a long time.

"What did you guys do with Jules?" I asked finally, noticing my fake-maid was nowhere to be seen. "Please tell me Zan locked her in a cupboard somewhere."

Lee cracked a smile and shook his head. "Not that he wasn't tempted, but we simply convinced her that she wasn't needed here."

I frowned, hardly believing that a girl who'd claimed to be my best friend since we were eight years old would just leave me to die with a bunch of virtual strangers. Then the phrasing Lee had used clicked in my head. "You paid her to stay away."

"We did." He nodded, totally unapologetic.

My lips tightened, and I swallowed the lump of disappointment in my throat. Of course Jules had chosen money over my welfare. Chances were, she thought I was already dead by now. If I was lucky, she might report this back to Bloodeye and give me a break from their spying.

"Good," I muttered, then yawned heavily.

"Go to sleep, Calla," Lee whispered in a soft, caring voice. "I'll stay with you. Just rest up and get through this test, okay? For us."

I murmured my agreement, letting my heavy lids fall closed as Lee continued his slow, gentle strokes to clean my skin of his herbal formula. The motion was hypnotizing, and it wasn't hard to follow instructions and sleep soundly.

CHAPTER 24

"Okay, I can do this," I whispered to myself, staring at the heavy, wooden door that would lead me into the final test of the week. This was the conclusion of the first Royal Trial, and if I survived this... well, then I would be a third of the way there.

When I'd woken again in my room, Lee had been curled around me protectively, and I'd wanted nothing more than to stay there in his arms forever.

I felt rested and refreshed, if still a bit weak. Most of all, my thoughts were clear. Memories of the night before had begun floating back to me, and I shivered as I thought of the King and Taipanus' revolting plan. Whether that conversation had really happened or was a figment of my poison-corrupted mind, I wasn't totally sure.

But it was enough to make me cautious.

My resolve had returned. If we only had two weeks left, then I intended to make a difference. I'd do everything in my power to force the princes to see sense—to see what their father was doing to our home. And if it turned out that I'd imagined the whole thing... well, there was still no harm done, and the people of Lakehaven and Teich might be better off for it.

I needed to make it through this final test first, though.

Lee had given me a brief rundown of what I was to expect as he'd walked with me to the testing hall. As detailed as he *could* be was still rather vague, but I appreciated all the help I could get.

"Room one, botany and alchemy," I murmured under my breath as I paused with my hand on the doorknob. "Room two, combat and knife skills. Room three, politics, history, and etiquette."

All of our classes for the week were combined in this test that could make or break our participation in the Royal Trials. Each stage held very real possibilities of death, and despite what we'd been led to believe—that only the lowest scoring lady would die—it could be a whole lot more of us than that. As in... anyone who failed.

The winner was determined on how fast the stages were completed, and that *oh so lucky* lady would get the privilege of alone time with a prince. Despite the fact that the sheer misogyny of this "prize" turned my stomach, it could be the perfect opportunity to start working on my plan.

"Botany and alchemy." I muttered again, turning the huge doorknob and opening the door. "I can do this."

Inside the dim room, all I saw was a large table set up with all manner of alchemical ingredients and three doors at the end of the room. That was all. But Lee had definitely said that this stage was alchemy *and* botany, so there had to be more to this than I could see.

Stepping carefully into the room, I tried not to flinch when the door slammed shut behind me, starting my timer.

As quickly as I could, I searched the whole room for any hints of the botany aspect. At first glance, I found nothing. But when I took a deep breath to calm my nerves, something familiar pricked at my nostrils.

Silvered axeroot.

An herb that we had learned about in our first class of the week, it was capable of soothing rashes when applied as a whole leaf. Its secondary use was by smugglers, as it could be ground up and boiled down to create an ink that only became visible when set alight.

"Which means..." I hurried back to the table of supplies and quickly located all of the ingredients, which confirmed my theory. "Fire potion. Perfect."

Relying on my memory and instinct, I quickly mixed up the fire potion, which Lee had taught us during his second class. Pouring it into a small glass bottle, I popped the cap in and then went in search of the space that contained a secret message.

My initial guess had been the doors. Perhaps two might say "don't enter" and one would say, "you're cool to come through here." But to my disappointment, none of them carried the distinctive, muddy scent of silvered axeroot.

Feeling a bit like a bloodhound, I made my way around all of the walls and then checked the floor. Nothing. So where was it? Every now and then, I caught a hint of it, which confirmed my initial guess... but where the hell was it?

There was only one option left. Craning my neck, I peered up at the dark ceiling of the room and considered the possibility that the message was written up there.

It really was the only place left, and I'd already spent too long in this room; I needed to move on. So I sucked in a deep breath and held it as I hurled my potion bottle at the stones above my head. Fingers crossed, I crouched and cowered as my potion exploded with shards of glass and the whole room lit up with flames.

As the flames faded, a series of glittering words and symbols were revealed, and I hurried to read through them all. Half of the message had been substituted by alchemical symbols, just to make things harder, but it was clearly a formula for another potion. But a potion for what?

My question was answered moments later, as a thick, green gas began seeping into the room from the air vents.

"*Shit*," I cursed, instantly recognizing the gas as the sister herb to silvered axeroot. Obsidian deathweed was exactly as pleasant as the name suggested, and I had been poisoned quite enough for one week, thank you.

Running back to the table of supplies, I gathered the ingredients listed on the glittering recipe above my head. I had no idea what it would do, but it had to be something to escape the gas.

Thankfully, obsidian deathweed was a heavy gas, and it gathered across the floor first before slowly beginning to fill the room. By my guess, it would only be a couple of minutes until it reached face height, but that was more than enough time for me. I'd finished mixing the potion by the time the gas reached my waist, then lost precious seconds chewing my lip and working out what the fuck I did next.

Was it something I drank? It couldn't be, as some of the ingredients would be lethal if consumed. So it must need to be dispersed to counter the gas.

I hesitated another second, but when the thick green gas touched my shoulder, I made my decision and hurled the potion at the floor.

For a moment, nothing happened, and I squeaked in panic. Then all of a sudden, the green gas began whipping around me in a tornado as it was *consumed* by the potion I'd released on the floor. That clear liquid I'd splattered the tiles with quickly sucked up every last drop of the deadly gas until the room was free and clear of threats once more.

"Cool trick," I murmured to myself as I eyed the remains of the potion on the floor. "Now what?"

As though answering me, the door in the middle of the three clicked open, making me realize the other two were just decoys, probably to trick people into throwing their fire at the wrong place.

Conscious of the fact that I was being timed, I wiped my sweaty hands off on my pants and wrapped my fingers around the edge of the door to pull it open.

"Room two. Combat and knife work. This should be easy." I whispered the encouragements aloud, hoping they would feel more real. "Should be."

Gritting my teeth against whatever surprises were still in store, I stepped through into phase two.

The second room was even more bare than the first, but I'd learned my lesson on how deceptive that could be. Near the door, which slammed shut behind me, was a small podium containing a short sword and three throwing knives.

Clear enough, but who was I supposed to fight and where should the knives be thrown?

Keeping my eyes on the empty room, I slipped the throwing knives into my pockets, then picked up the sword and tested its weight in my hand.

Sure enough, the second I had the weapon in my grip, my opponent appeared seemingly out of nowhere. His blade whipped up, aiming to take my head off, and it was only through my years of practice that I dodged and rolled out of the way.

As I rolled to a stop around halfway across the room, two things made me gasp. Firstly, the entire section of floor I'd just rolled over cracked and crumbled, dropping away into a seemingly bottomless pit below the room.

Secondly, was my opponent.

"Lord Taipanus?" I spluttered, crab crawling back a few more steps and seeing the floor crumble away as I moved. Worse still, Taipanus seemed totally unconcerned by the lack of solid ground beneath his feet as he advanced on me with his sword raised.

Yelping a curse, I dodged another swing and scrambled to my feet. Fuck chitchatting, I needed to beat this sucker.

Our blades met with a nerve-grating clash of steel, and I gritted my teeth hard. I was still weak from my night of poison, and Taipanus's strike reverberated through my arms painfully. It only took a few more blows exchanged to notice a key aspect to his style.

It *wasn't* his style.

Or at least, if it was, then it was a pretty damn huge coincidence that it was also *my* style. Confirming my theory, I noticed every one of his attacks, parries, and defenses were textbook moves I'd learned from Master Bloodeye. So how did one beat themselves?

By being unpredictable, I guessed.

Throwing my less than considerable weight into my next few moves, I went as erratic as possible. Totally throwing my experience out of the window, I fought on pure instinct. For the most part, it worked. But one small slip up saw Taipanus's blade nick my upper arm, and it was very real blood that trickled down my skin.

Well crap. That ruined my vague idea that he had been nothing more than an illusion. Illusions couldn't make you bleed... but this version of the King's Snake certainly could.

With renewed urgency, I pressed my attack harder. Not dumb enough to forget the sheer drop into darkness that chased my heels, I needed to duck past Taipanus rather than retreat. This movement would see me gain even more ground toward the end of the room... and the door that hopefully led to the last room.

It was after one such duck that I spotted my opening. Funny enough, it was an error I'd made often while training with boys in the Pond, and one that left Taipanus' whole left side unguarded just long enough for my blade to slide between his ribs and end the fight.

"Yes!" I exclaimed, bouncing with glee as the disgusting older man crumpled to the stone floor, and I yanked my bloodied sword from his body. "Kind of makes me wish you were the real Taipanus," I panted as I stood over the moustached man in his death throes. "Somehow I doubt he'd go down so easily, though."

Fake Taipanus met my eyes, and there was something familiar there. Something pleading. His lips moved, and I crouched closer to hear what he was trying to say. When I did, my blood ran cold.

"Lo," he whispered. "How could you?"

Startled, I sat up, and my gaze flew back to his face. A face that no longer sported the curled, greasy moustache and heavy lines of Lord Taipanus. Instead it was a pair of piercing green eyes that met mine, full of betrayal. It was a strong, chiseled jaw dusted with black stubble that blood trickled down, running from lush lips, which I knew kissed like I was the only woman in Teich.

"Ty?" I whimpered, hardly believing what I was seeing. "What? How?"

The gorgeous combat trainer coughed then, a wet, rattling sound full of blood and pain, and I covered my mouth to choke back a sob. How could this have happened? How had I not known it'd been Ty behind that illusion? Of course it had been! He'd been going easy on me *deliberately*. That stupid, fool man!

"Lo," he breathed when his rattling cough stopped. "I love you, Lo. I know it's only been a week, but I felt it in my soul. Didn't you?"

Frantically, I shook my head back and forth. Not to disagree, but to try and deny what I was seeing. Ty couldn't be dying, it wasn't possible. It wasn't *fair*.

"Ty, this can't be happening," I sobbed, my hands pressing to the ugly wound in his side to staunch the bleeding. A wound that *I* was responsible for. Surely they wouldn't leave one of the trainers to die in this *stupid* game? Then again, they'd been actively killing ladies of highborn families all week, so what would the royals care about a soldier? A servant, no less.

Still, it didn't stop me yelling for help. Begging. But the room remained silent... Not even the sound of Ty's ragged breathing filled it anymore as he slipped into death.

"No," I whispered, feeling the tears stream down my face and my nose run with snot. My heart was breaking in half, and I could scarcely believe the utter cruelty of these Royal Trials. Surely this wasn't the way Queen Ophelia and her ancestors had conducted them. This was *wrong*. So completely *wrong*.

I knelt there sobbing, my hands slick with sticky blood for what seemed like an eternity until the gut twisting realization hit me that I'd been tricked. Again.

"Ty's" body faded before my eyes, leaving behind nothing. Nothing. Not even the blood on my hands had been real, despite the fact that I could still feel its wet stickiness and smell that sharp coppery tang.

Now I was *really* pissed off.

Pushing myself off the ground with weak, shaking knees, I approached the door, then ran my hands over the smooth wood and found no handle. No way to open it, which meant there had to be more to this test.

Taking one of the throwing knives from my pocket, I slapped it against my palm as I looked all around me. Most of the room was gone, and I stood on a short ledge less than three feet wide in front of the door, which narrowed things down somewhat.

"Of course," I muttered, then laughed bitterly. My face was still stuffed up from crying over a fake death, and I was in a foul mood. But sure enough, right beside the door I'd entered through was a push button with a red circle painted around it.

What was the betting that button unlocked the door to the third room?

Shaking my head at my own stupidity for not seeing it sooner, I flipped the knife over into an easy pinch grip and hurled it at the button. As expected, the second my blade depressed the square, the door behind me clicked and swung open.

"Just like that, on to room three," I sighed. "Politics, history, and etiquette. Great."

For the third time, the door slammed behind me, and I shivered. Watching Ty die at my own hands had shaken me more than I cared to admit, fake or not. It only served to reinforce how close I'd let myself get to them. It wasn't safe, for them or for me. The only saving grace so far was my suspicion that the Trials chamber was an entity of its own, pulling images from my own mind rather than someone actually *knowing* about my affection for Ty.

"Okay, so here I am. What do you have for me this time?" I shouted my challenge into the empty room, but really didn't expect an answer. I didn't get one either, which was probably the best thing for my already frayed nerves.

The floor of the room was laid out in squares, each painted with a colorful crest representing each of the eight kingdoms, including ours. I dimly recognized it as a gameboard from a game that had been popular pre-Darkness. It was one that required pieces be moved onto correct squares according to trivia question answers, so I could only assume that in this case, I was the game piece.

In the pit of my stomach, I just knew this would have been a game discussed during the history lesson I had missed. That, combined with my apparent lack of knowledge in the aristocratic history of Teich, didn't bode well for this room.

Shit.

Standing at the edge of the gameboard, I studied the squares and wracked my brain for how the game was supposed to start. I'd played it once with Master Bloodeye when I was very young, so the details were more than a little fuzzy. Something about paying respect to the kingdom of our allegiance? I only recalled that detail because Bloodeye had made a joke about how he owed his allegiance to no kingdom.

So if that was correct, I needed to begin on the symbol for Teich.

Stepping forward, I placed both feet onto our kingdom's crest and waited.

Nothing happened.

I had to be missing something. This was a human-sized version, rather than a board with inch-high figurines, so the rules were probably more literal. If the game opened by paying respects, then perhaps that needed to be a more literal show.

Feeling just a fraction stupid, I tucked one foot behind the other and bent my knees into a deep, traditional curtsey, as befitting royalty in Teich. When I straightened back to standing and found my first game question hanging in the air with glittering letters, I sent up a silent thanks to Zan for teaching me how to curtsey.

"Okay," I breathed, reading the question. "Which kingdom was first to offer its assistance when the Time of Darkness struck Teich?"

I chewed my lip and considered the *correct* answer. It had already been proven that the facts and history I'd learned in the Pond differed greatly from what the upper class taught their children. So I knew the answer *wasn't* Woustenland, even though they technically had been the first. The new King Titus had shunned their offer and waited for Asintisch to step up. So, I stepped cautiously across to the closest Asintisch crest.

Again, nothing happened until I *paid my respects* to that kingdom, after which my new question appeared in hovering letters above the gameboard.

"Who is the major trade partner of Asintisch?" I chewed my lip as I considered this one. I knew little to nothing of our neighboring kingdoms, but had a *feeling* they traded in silks. Or was it dyes? So which kingdom would have the most need for those items? Surely not Isenmedin—they were known as a warrior kingdom and specialized in creating the finest bladed weapons in our world. They'd have no need for silks or dyes, anyway.

I ran through the remaining options in my head until I'd narrowed it to just two. Us—Teich—or the Schon Islands. What would happen if I got the answer wrong?

Not willing to test the theory with my own body, I pulled one of the spare throwing knives from my pocket and tossed it onto the crest for the Schon Islands. Nothing happened... but did that mean it was correct? Or just that the game wasn't fooled by my test?

To be sure, I tossed the other knife onto the nearest symbol for Teich. The knife hit the square and bounced. It never made the decent back to the floor as the whole tile shot up in a white-blue column of flame and disintegrated the cheap weapon in midair.

"Schon Islands it is," I muttered to myself, still feeling the heat of that fire even as it disappeared as quickly as it had appeared. Careful not to touch any other squares, I hopped onto the crest for the Schon Islands and collected my last remaining knife.

Wobbling slightly, I executed the traditional curtsey for that kingdom, and my new question appeared. It was a political marriage question, and one I already knew the answer to. Six generations ago, the Schon Islands had formed an alliance with Isenmedin by marrying their youngest princess to the Isenmedin crown prince.

There was an Isenmedin crest directly in front of me, but there were still a *lot* of squares to get through before I reached the other side. Was it against the rules to take a farther away tile?

Only one way to find out.

Lining up my throwing knife to the Isenmedin crest four more tiles away, I tossed it with precision, and it struck the tile dead center.

When nothing happened, I grinned. Maybe this game wouldn't take so long after all. I just needed to get *myself* over there now.

Sucking in a deep breath, I coiled my muscles and pushed from the tile I was on with all the power I still possessed. It wasn't much, certainly nothing compared to my ability had I been full strength, but it was enough. Just.

The heel of my boot clipped the tile beside my targeted one, and I just barely yanked my foot out of the way before foot-long, deadly sharp spikes shot up from the tile.

"Holy freaking gods," I breathed, feeling my heart pounding. "That was close."

Still, my sneaky plan had worked, and I was now five squares closer to the end.

For the next three questions, I repeated the same method, and I quickly found myself within one square of the end of the gameboard. Assuming it was probably against the rules to just skip the last question and jump off the board, I needed to answer this one correctly.

"Which kingdom is responsible for the Darkness?"

It was a trick question; it had to be. No one *knew* who had killed Queen Ophelia, no one except the killers themselves... and me, if my poison delusions were to be trusted. King Titus had originally come from Verrater, where he'd been the ruling king's cousin. His link to royalty was weak, but it had been enough to satisfy the balance of magic at the time. Not so much anymore, it seemed. But that was a train of thought for another day.

There was no way the royals would admit their guilt in this game, so Verrater's tile was clearly not the correct answer. Each of the other kingdom had weak enough reasons that they could be called responsible, but nothing stood out as a clear answer. None except one.

Gritting my teeth against the sheer hypocrisy of the answer, I stepped forward onto the crest of Teich.

So, we were responsible for the Darkness, were we?

My blood boiled in anger and indignation on behalf of our former queen. Someone needed to expose the usurper who'd stolen her throne, and it was starting to look like that someone was me.

CHAPTER 25

I emerged from the last room with a renewed clarity in my purpose within the Royal Trials. I wasn't here to win myself a royal husband or a throne or even to gain a foothold within the court for my former mentor to make a grab for power.

Our kingdom deserved better than a greedy, murderous piece of shit for a king. Hell, our whole world did, considering what was currently happening with the balance of magic.

"Callaluna!" Agatha exclaimed as I entered what seemed to be a waiting room of sorts. "You made it! I knew you would."

"Uh, yeah." I frowned, looking around and only counting six other ladies—eight, including Agatha and myself. "I thought I was last?"

Her eyes widened at this, and another girl gasped. "You could have been," Agatha replied. "I was sixth to enter and only the third to arrive here. I get the feeling that failing that test was a little more permanent than we were led to believe."

I nodded, remembering what Lee had warned me before I started. "Yeah, I think it was. So, shit. Eight of us left."

"What a shame," Princess Sagen sneered, strutting over to strike a pose in front of me. "I had really hoped the ranks might have been thinned out a little more."

Giving her a tight, sarcastic smile, I resisted the urge to punch her in the face. "Your Highness, I'm so glad *you* made it."

Holy Aana, she was like a cockroach. No money to be won for guessing who my biggest competition was.

"I'm pretty confident I had the fastest time too," she bragged, flipping that glossy hair in her uniquely infuriating way. "Which means I will get my choice of the princes for the whole night. Hmm, I wonder which I'll pick. Prince Thibault has such broad shoulders and strong arms I bet he could really throw a girl around the bedroom. Then again, Prince Alexander has that angry, brooding thing that is just so damn sexy." She gave an exaggerated sigh and pretended to fan herself. It was almost pathetic how obviously she was trying to make us jealous. Especially given she didn't actually *know* who had won.

Come to think of it, Lee had mentioned on day one that our scores across the whole week would contribute to our overall test score. So, considering Sagen had missed the first few days, there was probably a good chance she wouldn't be winning shit today.

"What about Prince Louis?" Agatha asked in a small voice. "You don't like him?"

Sagen rolled her eyes dismissively. "Youngest prince, barely ever speaks in public? No. He won't be getting the throne, so why waste my time?"

Agatha and I exchanged a look, and I was sure she thought Sagen was just as stupid as I did. But each to their own.

"Fascinating," I murmured. "If you'll excuse me, I need some water."

Without waiting on her response, I brushed past her and headed for the refreshment table at the far side of the room.

"She's threatened by you," another lady informed me as I filled my crystal tumbler with citrus water. "You came through that test *fast*."

Raising my brows at her, I tried to place her name. *Hazel... I think.* "How do you know?"

"Because Gracelin came through before you, so we had a reasonable indication of how long it took you." Lady Hazel—I was pretty sure that was her name—smiled at me, and I found myself smiling back.

Agatha sidled up beside us and poured her own glass of water. "Not to mention you're the clear favorite with the princes."

"Huh?" I blurted. "How so?"

Both girls looked at me like I was insane. "Seriously?" Agatha asked. "They've sat near you at dinner how many times this week?

Plus, they seem to go out of their way to make conversation, even when you clearly aren't interested."

"And then there was that kiss at the dance," Hazel added with a teasing smile. "You don't think that slipped past anyone's radar, do you?"

My stomach flipped at the reminder, and it was like I could feel Prince Alexander's strong, confident grip on me all over again.

"Ladies, please gather around," Lady Savannah called out, entering the room and clapping her hands sharply. "You have completed the first trial. Congratulations. There will be a ball tonight in your honor, where the week's winner will be announced. Please take the rest of the afternoon to rest and prepare yourselves. Lots of important people will be in attendance tonight, so keep your senses sharp and your etiquette flawless."

She turned sharply to leave the room without taking questions from us, but the paleness of her face and the trembling in her hands suggested she'd been just as blindsided by the *eight* deaths as we'd been.

Making my way to the great hall that evening, I found myself battling a severe case of nervousness for what was to come. I wasn't as dense as I had been making myself out to be; I knew full well I stood a good chance of being the first trial winner. But if that was the case... what would I do?

Regardless of how Lady Savannah wanted to phrase it, the so-called *prize* was the opportunity to spread my legs for some royal cock. Like I said, I wasn't dense; I knew that would be expected. So, could I really go through with it? Especially knowing my heart lay elsewhere... several elsewheres, if I wanted to be totally honest.

Not that it was realistic or, truly, very smart to be involved with my sexy teachers. The illusion of killing Ty and all the gut-wrenching sorrow that had accompanied it proved that once and for all.

Perhaps this would be good for me. If there was one surefire way to end things with the tutors, I had a feeling that letting a prince up my skirt would be it. So why did I feel like such an asshole for even considering it?

"Suck it up, Calla," I muttered under my breath, smoothing my hands over the delicate fabric of my gown. I'd given up calling myself Rybet. That was a name given to me by Master Bloodeye, and he'd taken it back. Calla, Luna, Lo... those were names uniquely mine now, despite the fact that I was still an imposter.

Jules had still been nowhere to be seen when I'd returned to my room, but another maid had been there in her place to help me dress for the ball. She'd actually done a better job than Juliana had managed all week, too. My gown was an elegant, sapphire blue with a full skirt and short train. She'd pinned my long curls up delicately in the back, leaving the shorter pieces loose around my face to give the effect that I'd just cut a good foot or so from the length. As for a mask, I currently wore a barely-there scrap of metal filigree pushed up into my hair. I would put it in place before being announced, but the whole mask tradition was making me horribly claustrophobic, so I was putting it off as long as possible.

"Can you believe that eight ladies died today?" Agatha murmured, falling into step beside me in her own ethereal ballgown. It was a girly shade of pink and covered in little fabric butterflies, but it suited her somehow. "At this rate there won't *be* anyone left to win."

I grunted a noise of agreement. "Do you have any idea what the second trial will be?"

She tilted her head side to side, like she was saying both yes and no at the same time. "Sort of," she eventually admitted. "Or rather, I know what it *would* have been in Queen Ophelia's time. These trials seem a lot more... literal, though."

"Bloodthirsty, more like." My stomach clenched and rolled again. Perhaps I was still suffering some ill effects from my poisoning. "So, what is it *supposed* to be, then?"

Agatha sucked in a breath and glanced around us, probably making sure no one else was likely to benefit from her knowledge. "Traditionally the second trial would be a quest of sorts, usually to recover a magical artifact. The winner of the second trial would be named the kingdom's Seeker and awarded a place of honor in the royal household, regardless of who won the final trial."

"Huh," I sighed. "Well, I don't see that happening this time."

Agatha shook her head in agreement. "So, a quest?"

"Traditionally." She nodded. "If we are leaving the palace, do you think the princes will be joining us?"

Giving her a sidelong look, I grinned. "Princes? Or one in particular?"

It didn't take a genius to see Agatha had a huge crush on Prince Louis. She turned almost the color of scarlettberry rum whenever he was within touching distance, and I wasn't totally sure if she had actually plucked up the courage to speak with him yet.

"Maybe you can ask him to dance tonight," I suggested, waggling my brows at her and smiling at the embarrassed flush rising in her cheeks. "For what it's worth, he seems like the least abhorrent of the three of them."

Agatha rolled her eyes and lowered her voice as we drew closer to where the other remaining contestants waited outside the great hall. "I think it's an act," she whispered. "I think they're not as bad as they seem."

I gave her a faint smile and sighed. "Perhaps."

It was the best I could offer. If she'd said this to me even three days ago, I would have laughed in her face for being so gullible. But now, I wasn't so sure she was wrong.

"Good, you're all here," a smartly dressed man snapped, and I recognized him as Harry, the herald from day one when we'd all been presented and inspected. "I will announce each of you, one by one.

The order you are announced is the order you ranked in this week's trial, starting with the lowest score and ending with the highest. Understood? Good, let's begin." He barely even glanced at us, let alone waited for a response, as he opened the door and stood inside to project his voice. "Lady Hazel of Redbark."

"Shit," Hazel groaned, then adjusted her mask and straightened her shoulders to sweep into the ball with a level of refined dignity that I knew I could never fake.

One by one, names were called, and ladies entered the ball "in our honor." Surprisingly, Gracelin was announced before Agatha, and I shared a small smile of victory with her.

Soon, though, it was just me... and Sagen.

"Congratulations on scoring so high," I said to her with a polite smile as the last lady left us to make her dramatic entrance.

"Shut up, *Callaluna*," she sneered back at me, spitting my name like a curse word. "The sheer fact that you even think you're in my league is a joke. I'm a princess, for Zryn's sake. You're *nobody*, and you'll die as *nobody*."

The situation would have been funny, if only she'd known how right she was in that statement. I was nobody. But that didn't mean I couldn't make a difference.

Sagen opened her perfectly painted mouth to insult me again—I assume—but was cut short by Harry the Herald clearing his throat and throwing us a pointed look.

"Her Highness Princess Sagen of Asintisch," he announced to the room, and Sagen glared venom at me.

"You rigged this somehow," she hissed at me. "You and those tutors you've been sneaking around with all week. Just wait, I'll see you pay for this."

Whatever other threats she wanted to throw at me had to wait, though, as Harry was clearing his throat again and she needed to make her entrance. With one last death glare in my direction, Sagen flipped her hair and tilted her nose in the air to enter with all the regal grace befitting her princess status.

"Looks like you had quite the week, Lady Callaluna," Harry murmured as we waited for Sagen to take her time on the steps leading down into the ballroom. "I'm glad you beat that entitled little shit out. It'll do her good to have her pride knocked down a bit."

I glanced at him with raised brows, and he gave a small smirk.

"I never said that," he chuckled. "Ready?"

Giving him a short nod, I tucked my mask into place and waited while he announced me to the room.

"Lady Callaluna of Riverdell," he boomed. "Winner of the First Trial."

I snorted as I passed him, noticing how he felt the need to rub Sagen's loss in her face just that little more. While I lacked that aristocratic grace that all the other contestants carried, I hopefully made up for it in sheer confidence.

My chin tilted up and my shoulders set back, I held my head high as I made my way down the steps. My gaze didn't falter or flinch once as various nobles and highborn ladies nodded to me. Not even when the king raised his wine glass to me in greeting did I look away.

These people were nothing to fear. They were *just* people. The fear they instilled in us poor folk was entirely of our own doing. We let them treat us like lesser creatures, so they did.

"Lady Callaluna," Prince Thibault greeted me as I reached the podium upon which the royals were situated. I swept possibly my best curtsey to date, then straightened to nod at the musclebound prince.

"Your Highness," I responded, accepting a glass of wine from his hand as he stepped down to my level.

A small smile played at his lips, and he opened his palm, extending something in my direction. "I wanted to get in first and say I would be honored if you chose to spend some time with me after the ball tonight. I think we would have a great many things to converse on."

Startled, I stared down at the key in his hand, then back up at him. Despite his claims of wanting to "converse," there was a wicked hunger in his gaze that made me shiver. Somehow, I doubted that would be all he had in mind... and I wasn't so confident in my own strength of will to resist him.

"That's, um," I started, licking my lips and clearing my throat. "That's a flattering offer. May I consider it?"

His sexy smile spread wider, and he gave a small head dip. "Of course, but take the key anyway. Just in case."

Unsure what the hell to say, I took the delicate key from his gloved hand and held it up to inspect it. There was an intricate "T" carved into the handle, and a circle stamped with the royal crest dangled from a green silk cord.

"Uh, thanks?" I offered, hesitating a moment before tucking the key into the inbuilt bra of my ballgown. The middle prince watched where his key disappeared, and I swear his breathing hitched a little. I found myself blushing. "Ballgowns don't tend to include pockets, Your Highness," I informed him in a tart voice. "Where *else* was I supposed to put it?"

The tall man tossed his head back and barked a laugh. "You'll see no complaints from me, Lady Callaluna," he chuckled, taking my hand and pressing a lingering kiss to my knuckles. "I hope you'll save a dance for me later."

Before I could accept or decline, an older couple decked out in shimmering fabrics interrupted us and began chattering to the prince about trade routes or something. Whatever it was, I took the opportunity to fade into the crowd and gather my wits.

Of course, I'd known that as the winner of the first trial, I would need to make a choice tonight... But first, I needed food. And probably a healthy dose of liquor.

This was going to be a long night, and I was already secretly

hoping that Lee or Ty... or hell, even Zan, might be here somewhere—
if only to offer me a moment of normalcy amid the madness.

But it was for the best that they weren't. Seeing them would only
make my inevitable choice even harder, and that was far from what
I needed.

To my disappointment, I only managed to snag a few paltry bites
of food before bending to the social pressure of dancing, thanks to
the many offers I received after leaving Prince Thibault. It became
quickly apparent that I'd made an impression as one-to-watch, and I
was already being fawned over.

Was that what life was like for the princes? Constantly dealing
with fake, pandering idiots who were sucking up for some unknown
future favor? No wonder they never wanted their faces seen. They'd
never get a moment's peace to do normal things, like... Well, I really
had no idea what they'd do if no one recognized them.

It did make me curious, though. Would they pretend to be
someone else, knowing no one would recognize them?

"Lady Callaluna?" Someone interrupted my thoughts, and I
spun around to see who it was as I shoved the last of the delicious
dessert in my mouth. It was a new food to me, something that
apparently came from one of our neighboring kingdoms and

consisted of sponge cake rolled in chocolate sauce and coconut, then filled with cream. It was utterly heavenly, and I hadn't eaten anywhere near enough of them as I'd only *just* been released from the sweaty grip of an elderly, overweight duke.

"Oh!" I startled. "Prince Louis." To my horror, little flakes of coconut and half-chewed sponge cake flew out of my mouth with these words and splattered on the front of his crisp white shirt. Throwing caution to the wind, I planted my hands on my hips and glared as I frantically chewed and swallowed to clear my mouth. "Technically, that was your own fault," I informed the youngest royal. "For starters, you're standing awfully close right now. And another thing, you should never startle a woman who is eating desserts. It's bad for your health."

A wide, almost genuine sort of smile curved his lips, and against my better judgement, I found myself wondering what it'd be like to kiss him.

"Noted. I wanted to see if you might like to dance with me." He held out his gloved hand, and I hesitated. I'd faked it well enough with the men I'd accepted dances from, but Prince Louis was bound to notice my less-than-satisfactory dance experience.

"It's an easy one, I promise," he assured me, seeming to sense my reluctance. "I won't let you fall, Calla...luna."

It was probably my imagination, or all the wine I'd already consumed, but I could have sworn he paused halfway through my name. Weird.

"Sure," I reluctantly agreed. "But don't be surprised if I step on your toes." This last part was muttered under my breath, but he chuckled anyway. Damn sharp hearing.

Thankfully, he hadn't been lying. The music was soft and slow... dare I say, romantic? Prince Louis led the dance with enviable expertise, and I did my best to remember Prince Alexander's instructions from our first dance. *Follow.*

Almost before I was ready, the song ended and Prince Louis was offering me a polite bow, which I needed to quickly reciprocate with a curtsey.

"Thank you, Lady Callaluna," Louis murmured as I rose from my curtsey, which, I might note, I was becoming pretty damn good at. "I wanted to offer you this." He held out a key almost identical to the one his older brother had given me. "Contrary to what you might think, I have no ulterior motives. If you choose to use this key, I swear I will not take advantage of the situation, nor will I pressure you into anything you aren't comfortable with."

Startled, I blinked at him a couple of times. "You mean to say you *wouldn't* fuck me tonight?" The second the crude words left my lips, I cringed. Hardly ladylike.

A naughty smile crossed Louis's lips. "I wouldn't say no, if that's what you're asking," he admitted honestly. "But I won't force you into anything you don't want to do."

There was a tense silence between us while I searched for the appropriate words. Eventually, I just settled on, "I'll bear that in mind."

Accepting the key from his hand, I tucked it into my dress alongside Prince Thibault's somewhat less innocent offer.

"That's all I can ask," Prince Louis accepted and gave me a tight smile. "Congratulations on your win, Lady Callaluna. You deserved it."

With that odd statement, he left me to dance with another lady, and I made my way back to the dessert table, feeling significantly off balance. Maybe I'd been wrong about them? Remembering the cold, arrogant men who'd taunted me on day one when I'd stood before them blindfolded and angry, I found it hard to reconcile them with the polite, almost *respectful* men I'd interacted with tonight. It was baffling, to say the least.

"Lady Winner," another deep, husky voice announced from beside me, and I glanced up to see the third, and oldest, prince. "I'm somewhat impressed. For a moment there, I was worried it might be *Her Highness* dragging me off to her chambers tonight." He gave an exaggerated shiver, and I bit back the urge to laugh.

"Your Highness," I replied, sneaking another bite of the spongy, cream-filled goodness. "Let me guess, you're here to offer me a key to your rooms with the promise that you'll be an utter gentleman and not lay a hand on me?"

He snorted a rather un-princely sound and narrowed his dark eyes at me from behind his mask. "Is that what my brothers did? How insulting. No, Lady Callaluna, that's not what I'm here for."

He fished in his pocket and pulled out a key to match the other two resting inside my dress. "I'll give you this because I'm required to do so. But I urge you not to use it."

I choked on a flake of coconut and coughed for a moment before I was able to speak again. The prick just stood there and watched me suffering, too. Didn't even offer me a damn glass of water.

"Excuse me?" I finally blurted out. "You urge me *not* to use it?"

"That is what I said," he confirmed with a condescending tilt to his mouth. "I hadn't realized you were hard of hearing."

"My hearing is fine, you royal asshole," I snapped back. "But I wanted to check that *you* knew what you'd said."

The oldest prince turned his full attention on me then, blocking my view of the rest of the room and stepping into my personal space with all of his imposing presence.

"Let me spell it out for you, Lady Callaluna," he spoke softly, but it was with an undertone of aggression and threat. "If you use this key tonight, you'll be doing it at your own peril. I'm not my brothers, and I won't offer you sweet nothings and *conversation*. If you come to my rooms, you'd better be stripped of that lovely blue dress and waiting naked by the time I get there because I will accept nothing less than *all of you*. I won't hold back, and I won't woo you with pretty lies. You're an attractive lady, much more so than anyone else on offer right now, and if you were to come to my rooms I would *use* you in every way I have fantasized since first laying eyes on you."

He paused then, and I fought to keep my breathing even. His words should have horrified me, made me want to throw a drink in his face and accept Louis's sweet offer. Or even Thibault's naughty but sincere one. And yet... my heart pounded and my cunt clenched with desire. What was it about this royal prick that turned me on so damn hard?

"So please, Lady Callaluna," Alexander continued, "accept one of my brother's keys because I will *ruin* you."

I stood there speechless as he tucked his key into the bodice of my dress, his gloved fingers brushing not-so-accidentally across my hardened nipple. Without another word, he turned and stalked back into the crowd of partygoers like we'd just been discussing the weather or something equally mundane.

What. The. Fuck?

With trembling hands, I poured myself a large glass of water and took a long drink in a vain effort to cool my flaming lady-parts. One thing was for damn sure—Prince Alexander scared the crap out of me. But his harsh *threat* had decided things.

There was only one logical choice for where I would spend the night. Only one prince offered me the destruction I needed, the utter, irreversible severing of any relationships I'd formed with my tutors.

Reaching into my dress, I withdrew a key and rubbed my thumb over the engraved "A" on the shaft.

Aana have mercy on me. I was stepping into the dark side and couldn't even pretend I wasn't excited by it.

CHAPTER 26

Ice-cold air teased my sensitive skin as I laid my gorgeous gown over the back of the chair, then picked up the blindfold from the bed. It wasn't hard to work out what I was supposed to do, so I sucked a deep breath and tied it over my eyes.

Alexander had given no further instructions, so I'd left my sapphire silk shoes on but released my hair from the countless pins that had been giving me a headache. Now, my long, blond curls offered the only protection from the breeze as I stood in the center of the room and shivered.

Maybe I should have closed the window. But the cool air was helping to keep my head clear. I was about to trash my chances at love, so I wanted to be sharply aware the whole time. This was my choice, and I would need to live with myself in the morning.

For an eternity, I stood there. Waiting. Naked and blindfolded.

"This is stupid," I sighed. "Yet another power game."

Swallowing past the burning sting of disappointment, I decided enough was enough. If Alexander wanted to play games, I'd show him who he was messing with.

Kicking off my shoes, I felt my way over to the bed and yanked back the plush covers. It had been a really long day, and I was still recovering from dying multiple times the night before. If his royal prickishness wasn't going to make the most of his bed, then I would.

Not bothering to remove my blindfold—because it did a fantastic job of blocking the moonlight streaming through the windows—I made myself comfortable in the middle of the big bed and tucked the blankets back around me.

Maybe if I was lucky, Alexander would stay gone all night and give me a good sleep. As laughable as it was, the idea of a good sleep was *almost* as desirable as being "ruined" by whatever Prince Alexander had in mind.

Almost.

Stifling a yawn on the back of my hand, I shifted a little more until I was comfortable, then let myself drift into deep, dreamless sleep.

That fucking cool breeze was what woke me again, and I reached for the blankets that I must have kicked off at some stage. Or I tried to.

My eyes snapped open, and I was met with the startling sight of nothing. Total blackness. Fucking blindfold.

"Oh, I see you're awake," a deep, husky voice commented with an edge of sarcasm, and the mattress dipped beside me. "Sorry about the restraints, but what else was I supposed to do? I came back to my room and found you splayed out across my bed like an offering at Frog's Feast. It would have been rude *not* to take advantage of the situation."

Gritting my teeth in anger, I yanked at one of my wrist restraints, and it only tightened further. That fucker.

"Untie me," I growled, no longer in the mood for games. Not only had he kept me waiting forever and a day, but now he'd interrupted my sleep. We were not off to a good start.

"No," he replied, shifting on the bed until his weight straddled my naked thighs. Leaning down until I could feel his warmth just inches from my body, he whispered in my ear, "You came here of your own free will, Callaluna—against my more sensible advice, I might point out. What did I tell you would happen if you used my key?"

Licking my lips, I sucked in a sharp breath—mentally building my sassy courage back up. "You said you'd ruin me," I breathed out, feeling my hard nipples brush his bare chest and I just barely swallowed a moan.

"That I did," he agreed, but still made no move to touch me

other than where he sat across my legs.

I waited a beat, but he said nothing more. "So?" I prompted him. "What are you waiting for? *Ruin me*. Or was that all just bluster and bravado to try and scare me off?"

There was a pause, and then the bed started shaking. For a second, I thought maybe we were experiencing an earthquake. But no, it was just Prince Alexander dissolving into a fit of laughter.

At least he thought I was funny?

"Oh wow," he chuckled as his laughter died off. "You just really don't know when to keep your mouth shut, do you Callaluna? Perhaps I can remedy that." That was all the warning I got before his mouth slammed into mine, claiming my lips in a dominating, possessive kiss that set all my nerves alight and sucked the breath from my lungs.

He didn't kiss me in the sweet, calm way that Lee had, or even, really, the frenzied, hungry way that Ty kissed me. Prince Alexander kissed me like he *owned* me.

In that moment... he did.

Gasping against his assault, my lips parted and allowed his tongue to meet mine as his hands laid claim to my breasts. His fingers found my taut nipples and rolled them in a delicious way that left me squirming and moaning beneath him.

I needed more. So much more.

In the back of my mind, I was conscious of the soul-burning

pain of betrayal as I let Alexander brand my body with his touch in a way that I could never come back from. There would be no forgiveness for this, and my heart wept for the destruction I willingly entered into.

But I was resolute, so when the prince lifted his lips from mine, I drove another nail into my coffin. "Is that it?" I taunted. "I don't feel *ruined* yet."

Alexander chuckled a dark sound, and his weight shifted off me for a moment. "Silly Callaluna," he scolded, clicking his tongue at me, "I've barely begun."

As he said this, he grasped my legs and spread them apart, settling his weight back on the bed between them. I'd never been so exposed and vulnerable, not ever. For a girl from the Pond, that was saying a lot. But my skills in thievery had kept me safe from whoring, and I was woefully inexperienced when it came to bedroom games. In that sense, it was probably a blessing that Alexander held me bound and blindfolded.

When he touched me again, I gasped a sharp breath of surprise. Instead of the rough, clumsy insertion of his cock inside me—as was my only experience with sex—I was shocked to feel the warmth of his lips and breath against my aching cunt.

"What—?" I panted in a strangled voice as I pulled on my bonds. "What are you doing?"

"Exactly what you asked me to do, sunshine," he chuckled, and the vibration of his laugh made me squeak. "Ruining you." His strong hands pinned my legs open, and his mouth began to work my sensitive core with the same intensity that he'd kissed my mouth.

"Oh shit," I exclaimed, then yelped as his tongue pressed inside me with the most exquisite intrusion. Helpless in his grip, I thrashed and whimpered as he played me like a damn fiddle until I was positive my whole body was about to shatter into a million pieces.

Was this what I'd been missing out on? When Jules and her friends had spoken about enjoying sex, I'd sort of assumed they were just in denial—accepting their lot in life, so to speak. But this... this was a game changer.

"Wait," I gasped as Prince Alexander pulled back and shifted away. "Why are you stopping? Don't stop!"

He laughed a wicked sound, and the mattress shifted as he moved. Never had I been more frustrated not to be able to see anything because the anticipation was driving me to the edge of insanity. "I think I might have created a monster," he commented from somewhere... beside me? No, in front. Maybe at the foot of the bed? Fucking blindfold!

"Tell me, lovely Callaluna, are you feeling ruined yet?"

"Not even close," I retorted, lying my ass off. Prince Alexander had ruined me, that was for sure. But in more ways than one. He didn't know that as his strong fingers stroked down the damp heat of my core, he was sealing my fate. Lee and Ty... even Zan, for all his denial, they wouldn't forgive this. Not *this*. Nor could I forgive myself for loving every damn second of it.

"Give me more," I begged. "Please, make me scream until I forget."

Alexander's fingers stroked me again, then he slipped one deep inside, making me gasp and press down harder onto his hand.

"Forget what, lovely Callaluna?" he murmured, withdrawing that finger, then plunging it back in with a second one. "Tell me what you want to forget, and I'll gladly make it happen."

I moaned as he pumped those two fingers in and out of me, but it was when his thumb found my clit that I cried out. "Nothing," I lied. "Everything. Just... make me forget. Please."

To my horror, wetness gathered in my eyes, and I thanked Aana and her sister gods that the blindfold would hide the tears from Prince Alexander as they trickled down the sides of my face.

He grunted a noise, but didn't push me to answer him again as his fingers plunged into me with an increasing intensity that made me crave his cock. Something told me sex with Prince Alexander would be a hell of a lot more satisfying than anything I'd previously experienced.

It was mere moments later, as his lips closed over one of my nipples, that I shattered. Screams echoed through the room as I rode the prince's hand like a woman possessed, wringing every last drop of pleasure from those fingers while my cunt clenched and pulsed with my climax.

Alexander was in no rush to move off me, almost like he was

reluctant to stop. Truthfully, so was I. What else might he have in store for the rest of our night?

"Satisfied, Callaluna?" he asked in a gruff tone, and his finger lightly traced the path of my tears down the side of my face.

Suddenly unable to speak, I bit my lip and nodded. I *was* satisfied. But I also felt like the most despicable human in our lands. How could I do this? How could I have let one of the royal pricks of Teich use me like one of his playthings? How could I do this, knowing full fucking well how much it would hurt my new friends...?

A long-suffering sigh gusted from the prince, and he shifted to lie beside me but made no move to untie my wrists from the headboard. "Why don't you tell me what has you so upset? I'm generally unaccustomed to this reaction from women after an orgasm."

I snorted a bitter laugh and would have rolled my eyes if they hadn't been covered in cloth. "I'm sure you're not. Just forget it; I'm only suffering the consequences of my own decisions."

He grunted a noise, and I got the impression he had run his hand through his hair in a vexed gesture. How I got that mental image, I had no idea. But it was so clear I could almost picture it.

"You mourned someone during the second room of the test today," he commented, and the rapid change of subject startled me out of my self-pity.

"You were watching?" I retorted, and he clicked his tongue.

"Of course I was. That stage of the test is designed as a

mindfuck. You fight a person you fear, then kill someone you care for. So, who did you kill today, Callaluna?" His fingertip traced a gentle line down my side, and my skin tingled in response.

I pursed my lips and considered not replying. But that would have been pointless. Prince Alexander struck me as the type who got the answers he wanted, no matter what.

"Just a friend," I hedged. "A new friend. I thought I'd stabbed him and..." I paused to swallow the lump of sorrow in my throat. "I hadn't really considered how much they meant to me until that moment."

"They?" Alexander repeated, and I noticed my slip.

Too late to backtrack, I gave a short nod. "They. But that is irrelevant now. They'll never speak to me again when they hear what I did with you tonight."

"Who says *they* will ever find out?" Alexander suggested. "This could just be our little secret. What they don't know can't hurt them, after all."

For a split second, I entertained the idea. But no. "I couldn't do that," I replied firmly, shaking my head. "They deserve better than lies and deception from me."

"Hmm," he responded, continuing to draw patterns on my bare skin with his fingertips for some time. Strangely, the silence between us wasn't... awkward. Considering I was naked, my wrists bound, and my eyes covered in cloth, for it not to be awkward was saying a lot.

"So, there are two men you care for?" he finally asked, and I tensed myself for judgement. There was none present in his voice, though, and without being able to see his face, I could only trust vocal inflection.

I nodded. "Yeah, or... I guess, maybe, three? The third one is, ah, confusing. Complicated or maybe just really stubborn. There's something there though. Or there was."

"Right," Prince Alexander murmured. "Because when you tell them about tonight..."

"They'll hate me. How could they not? I would." The words tasted bitter on my tongue, and my heart clenched painfully.

Alexander hummed a noise as his fingers continued their pattern across my belly. "So why do it? You could have used Louis's key. He's honorable and wouldn't have laid a hand on you unless you'd pleaded."

My jaw clenched, and I forced myself to own my decision aloud. "Because I'm not here to fall in love. I want what little time I have left to count for something more, to affect positive change in some small way, and if that means giving you free access to my body, then that's a price I'm prepared to pay."

"Your body, but not your heart?" he pressed. "You're not here to win a husband and become Queen of Teich?"

I snorted a crude laugh. "Trust me, your royal assholeishness, if you only knew the real me, you'd know that was never, *ever* my intention."

"You really do need to stop insulting me, lady. It's starting to effect my self-confidence." He muttered the words with an edge of amusement in his voice. "But it sounds like pretending to be someone you're not is a common theme around here these days."

I frowned, not that he could see it, but his phrasing was odd. "How so?"

Prince Alexander heaved another sigh, his breath flickering across my still naked breasts. "Holy Zryn, I hope this doesn't kill me," he muttered under his breath. Before I could question him further, his warm hands reached up to my face and pushed the heavy, cloth blindfold off my eyes.

For a second, I needed to blink a couple of times to adjust my fuzzy vision, but when it cleared, I sucked in a harsh gasp. "*Zan?*" I exclaimed, feeling like my brain was exploding.

"Surprise, lovely Luna." He gave me a weak, guilt-ridden smile just seconds before yelling a bloodcurdling sound of pain and collapsing on top of me.

I screamed as he trembled and convulsed, but it was when the blood began seeping from his sultry dark eyes that I really began panicking. At the top of my lungs, I howled for help, over and over until I was hoarse.

My hands still bound, there was nothing I could do for him except watch and scream.

TO BE CONTINUED IN...
The Royal Trials: Seeker

Authors Note

Diving into this new project so soon after finishing Kit's series had me shitting myself. Just… totally crapping my daks. What if I was a one hit wonder? What if I had typecast myself into only ever writing KD and no one would ever want to read anything else from me? What if this crashed and burned and that was the end of my writing career and I had to get a job at the local servo selling pies and pluggers to tourists?! If you understood any of that, you're possibly an Aussie too. Anyway, a few cups of coffee later I verbalized all of these concerns to my author bestie, CM Stunich, who gave me the "really?" emoji face. You know, the one that's squinting? We use it a lot. In chat and real life. Anyway, my point here is that she told me to quit being a little bitch and write the damn book. Who cares if no one else liked it, so long as I was happy with the story/characters/journey I was producing?

So with those words of wisdom under my belt, I dove back into the Pond and started creating Rybet's journey. What started as a standalone retelling of the Frog Prince evolved into something much more exciting, which hopefully you agree with if you made it this far in the book!

Most encouragingly of all, though, was the fact that my mum stayed up til 3am reading it and then yelled at me for that ending.

Lol woops, sorry!

What I'm trying to say here, is thank you to Goldie the Goldfish for giving me daily reminders that we write for ourselves first and foremost, and my awesome Mum for being my biggest fan—even when she doesn't always say it out loud.

Also by Tate James

KIT DAVENPORT SERIES

The Vixen's Lead

The Dragon's Wing

The Tiger's Ambush

The Viper's Nest

The Crow's Murder

The Alpha's Pack

THE ROYAL TRIALS

Imposter

Seeker (coming soon)

Heir (2019)

STANDALONE CONTEMPORARY

Slopes of Sin (Winter 2018)

Co-Authored by Tate James & CM Stunich

HIJINKS HAREM

Elements of Mischief

Elements of Ruin

Elements of Desire

THE WILD HUNT MOTORCYCLE CLUB

Dark Glitter

Cruel Glamour (2018)

Torn Gossamer (2019)

FOXFIRE BURNING

The Nine

The Tail Game (TBD)

Turn page for chapter one of THE VIXEN'S LEAD…

ONE

In the background, the shadowy outline of a naked woman haunted a painting of lilies. The rich imagery held me captive. Reportedly the work was worth a few hundred thousand dollars, but I couldn't decide if it was because of the image or the person who painted it. Maybe both. Whatever the reason, the Beverly Hills gallery had it on its walls, which meant it was without a doubt expensive.

"Nine minutes and thirty-four seconds until security systems are back online. Stop gawking at the paintings and hurry the fuck up!"

How the hell had Lucy known what I was doing? Our comms were audio only. Still, Lucy had a point. I left the painting and crept down the corridor on silent feet. At the end a large, open room held several ostentatious pieces of jewelry displayed in glass cases on pedestals.

They were part of a colored diamond showcase in which the wealthy allowed their prized possessions to be displayed for the common folk to drool over. It was a clear night, and the full moon streamed light through the windows. The moonlight refracted against the jewels and created a rainbow of Christmas lights in the darkness.

Pausing at the entrance to the room, I fished my phone out of the pocket in my black jeans and ran an application labeled "You Never Know," which Lucy had designed to scan areas for hidden security features we might have missed in our mission planning. It took a minute to fully probe the room, and while waiting, I snaked a finger under the short, black wig I wore and scratched at my scalp. Using a disguise was just sensible thieving, but seriously, wigs itched something awful! Maybe next time I would try a hat. The image of myself pulling a job while wearing a top hat or a Stetson made me chuckle.

Seconds later, my screen flashed red with an alert and surprised the hell out of me. It was the first time the app had actually caught something.

"Are you seeing this?" It was a pointless question. She had a mirror image on her computer screen.

"Huh. That definitely wasn't there a week ago when I did a walk through," she muttered, and her furious tapping at her keyboard echoed over the comms. "Okay, it's a laser beam grid linked to a silent alarm that will trigger the security shutters on all external access points. I don't have time to hack into it and shut it down, so…"

I could picture her shrug and sighed. "So, don't trip the lasers, yes? Got it. Send me the map." An intricate web of red lines appeared on my phone, overlaying the camera's view of the room. If I watched the screen and not my feet, it would be possible to avoid the beams.

Conscious of the ticking clock, I carefully started stepping across the floor. All seemed to go well until I got within ten feet of my intended loot. Suddenly my nose started twitching with a sneeze. "Dammit," I hissed, then fought to hold my breath.

"What's going on in there, Kit?" Lucy asked, worry tight in her tone.

I wriggled my nose a few times to shake off the itch before replying, "You know how I often get pretty awesome hay fever in Autumn...?"

Lucy groaned like I was doing this to deliberately test her nerves, but I wasn't trying to tease her. I might actually sneeze.

"I think it's gone," I said, relaxing minutely, and raised my foot for the next step. Of course, Murphy's Law prevailed, and the second I shifted my weight, the urge to sneeze returned full force. I clamped my mouth and nose shut, but I lost my balance even as I tried to swallow my sneeze. My leg rocked into one of the laser beams.

"Shit!"

"Fucking hell, Kit! You have thirty seconds until you are trapped. Get the hell out, now!" Lucy yelled in my earpiece.

Already screwed, I lunged the remaining distance to the display case. The current tenant was a ring with an obnoxiously large, canary yellow diamond surrounded by smaller chartreuse colored diamonds, all inset in a band with pink sapphires. The overall effect was a bit sickening, but who was I to tell the wealthy how bad their tastes were? I often wondered how many of them deliberately wasted their money on tasteless items with obscene price tags simply because they could.

Aware of the ticking clock, I whipped my arm back and smashed my gloved fist straight through the toughened glass. It shattered under the force I exerted. After snatching up the ugly bauble, I dropped a little plastic fox—my signature calling card—in its place.

"Kit, quit dicking around and get out!" Lucy screeched over the line at me. "Twenty-two seconds remaining, don't you dare get caught, or I swear to God I won't let you live this down!"

Satisfied at having grabbed my target, I raced out of the room and down the corridor, not hesitating before crashing straight through a tall picture window and plummeting thirty-odd feet onto the rooftop of the next building. I tried to break my fall by rolling as I hit. Instead, landed awkwardly on my left shoulder. It popped out of its socket. Hissing with pain, I glanced up at the gallery just in time to see the steel shutters slam closed on all the windows simultaneously.

"Kit," Lucy snapped, barely masking the tension in her voice. "Give me an update; are you clear?"

The evil little devil on my shoulder wanted me to mess with her, but my conscience prevailed. "All clear," I said, then added with a laugh. "Plenty of time to spare; not sure why you were so worried!"

"Any injuries?" A growl underscored her words.

"Nope, I'm totally fine. I mean, if you don't include my shoulder, which is for sure dislocated, then all I have are a few scratches from the glass and a tiny bit of swelling in my knuckles. I got the God-awful ring, though!" I was rather proud of completing the job we had come there for.

"That was too close this time, Kit," Lucy admonished me. "You're bloody lucky you heal so fast, but it's still going to hurt like a bitch getting that shoulder back into place. Get sorted then drop the ring to the courier, and call me if anything goes wrong. Otherwise, I'll see you when you get back. Stay out of trouble."

My best friend occasionally cursed like an Australian ever since she developed a Heath Ledger movie crush. "You know, most people would say 'good luck.' You say, 'stay out of trouble.' Should I be offended?" Teasing her was fun, even if my track record wasn't the cleanest. In my defense, I always got myself out of trouble without too much hassle. Lucy didn't dignify me with a verbal response and left the dial tone as she hung up to serve as her answer.

Tucking my earpiece into a zippered pocket of my leather jacket, I headed over to the A/C unit on the far side of the roof. Using it to leverage my shoulder back into place, I kept my cursing to a minimum. It slid back in with a sickening pop, and the relief had me wavering on my feet. After catching my breath, I brushed some glass out of my wig then swung over the fire escape and descended to the street below. Stripping off my gloves, I blended into the crowd. Even though it was autumn, it was still nowhere near cold enough to be wearing gloves unless committing a crime. I nervously checked the time on my watch. I had a *very* long drive ahead of me to get back to school and still needed to drop the stolen ring off with our middleman.

28317708R00196

Printed in Great Britain
by Amazon